THE
SHIFTER

FERRY DOCK

PRODUCTION DISTRICT

DANELLO'S

MARKET

DOCKS

TANNIFF'S

AYLIN'S

TRADESMEN'S CORNER

SHOWHOUSE

TRIVENT'S LEATHERS

MARKET

HEALERS' LEA

MILLIE'S BOARDING HOUSE

CHICKEN RANCHES

FARMING ISLES

DORSTA PRISON

GEVEG ISLES

COFFEE ISLE

THE THREE TERRITORIES

BASEER

SORILLE

GEVEG

VERLATTA

GEVEG ISLES

...NCTUARY

PAIN MERCHANT'S

ARISTOCRATS' ISLES

GARDENS

THE TERRACES

GOVERNOR-GENERAL'S ISLE

THE HEALING WARS: BOOK I

THE SHIFTER

JANICE HARDY

Balzer + Bray
An Imprint of HarperCollins*Publishers*

Balzer & Bray is an imprint of HarperCollins Publishers.

The Healing Wars: The Shifter
Copyright © 2009 by Janice Hardy
Children's Books, a division of HarperCollins Publishers,
10 East 53rd Street, New York, NY 10022.
www.harpercollinschildrens.com

Library of Congress Cataloging-in-Publication Data
Hardy, Janice.
   The healing wars, book one: the shifter / by Janice Hardy.—1st ed.
     p.   cm.
   Summary: Nya, a fifteen-year-old war orphan, becomes a pawn in a
bigger political game when her uncanny—and dangerous—ability to shift pain
between people turns out to be the only weapon she has to save her sister.
   ISBN 978-0-06-174704-5 (trade bdg.)
   ISBN 978-0-06-176177-5 (lib. bdg.)
   [1. Fantasy. 2. Healers—Fiction. 3. Sisters—Fiction. 4. Orphans—
Fiction. 5. War—Fiction.] I. Title. II. Title: The shifter.
PZ7.H22142He 2009   2008047673
[Fic]—dc22   CIP
                                                            AC

Typography by Carla Weise
09 10 11 12 13 CG/RRDB 10 9 8 7 6 5 4 3 2 1

First Edition

For Thomas Hardy and Harlan Ellison.
Only one knows why.

THE
SHIFTER

ONE

Stealing eggs is a lot harder than stealing the whole chicken. With chickens, you just grab a hen, stuff her in a sack, and make your escape. But for eggs, you have to stick your hand under a sleeping chicken. Chickens don't like this. They wake all spooked and start pecking holes in your arm, or your face, if it's close. And they squawk something terrible.

The trick is to wake the chicken *first*, then go for the eggs. I'm embarrassed to say how long it took me to figure this out.

"Good morning, little hen," I sang softly. The chicken blinked awake and cocked her head at me. She didn't get to squawking, just flapped her wings a bit as I lifted her off the nest, and she'd settle down once I tucked her under my arm. I'd overheard *that* trick from a couple of boys I'd unloaded fish with last week.

A voice came from beside me. "Don't move."

Two words I didn't want to hear with someone else's chicken under my arm.

I froze. The chicken didn't. Her scaly feet flailed toward the eggs that should have been my breakfast. I looked up at a cute night guard not much older than me, perhaps sixteen. The night was more humid than usual, but a slight breeze blew his sand-pale hair. A soldier's cut, but a month or two grown out.

Stay calm, stay alert. As Grannyma used to say, if you're caught with the cake, you might as well offer them a piece. Not sure how that applied to chickens, though.

"Join me for breakfast when your shift ends?" I asked. Sunrise was two hours away.

He smiled but aimed his rapier at my chest anyway. It was nice to have a handsome boy smile at me in the moonlight, but his was a sad, sorry-only-doing-my-job smile. I'd learned to tell the difference between smiles a lot faster than I'd figured out the egg thing.

"So, Heclar," he said over his shoulder, "you *do* have a thief. Guess I was wrong."

Rancher Heclar strutted into view, bearing an uncanny resemblance to the chicken trying to peck me—ruffled, sharp beaked, and beady eyed. He harrumphed and set his fists against his hips. "I told you crocodiles weren't getting them."

"I'm no chicken thief," I said quickly.

"Then what's that?" The night guard flicked his rapier tip toward the chicken and smiled again. Friendlier this time, but his deep brown eyes had twitched when he bent his wrist.

"A chicken." I blew a stray feather off my chin and peered closer. His knuckles were white from too tight a grip on so light a weapon. That had to mean joint pain, maybe even knuckleburn, though he wasn't old enough for it. The painful joint infection usually hit older dockworkers. I guess that's why he had a crummy job guarding chickens instead of aristocrats. My luck hadn't been that great either.

"Look," I said, "I wasn't going to steal her. She was blocking the eggs."

The night guard nodded like he understood and turned to Heclar. "She's just hungry. Maybe you could let her go with a warning?"

"Arrest her, you idiot! She'll get fed in Dorsta."

3

Dorsta? I gulped. "Listen, two eggs for breakfast is hardly worth prison—"

"Thieves belong in prison!"

I jerked back and my foot squished into chicken crap. Lots of it. It dripped out from every coop in the row. There had to be at least sixty filthy coops along the lakeside half of the isle alone. "I'll work off the eggs. What about two eggs for every row of coops I clean?"

"You'll only steal three."

"Not if he watches me." I tipped my head at the night guard. I could handle the smell if I had cute company while I worked. He might even get extra pay out of it, which could earn me some goodwill if we ever bumped into each other in the early-morning moonlight again. "How about one egg per row?"

The night guard pursed his lips and nodded. "Pretty good deal there."

"Arrest her already!"

I heaved the chicken. She squawked, flapping and scratching in a panic. The night guard yelped and dropped the rapier. I ran like hell.

"Stop! Thief!"

Self-righteous ranchers I could outrun, even on their own property, but the night guard? His hands might be bad, but his feet—and reflexes—worked just fine.

I rounded a stack of broken coops an arm-swipe faster than he did. Without slowing, I dodged left, cutting up a corn-littered row of coops running parallel to Farm-Market Canal. It gained me a few paces, but he had the reach on my short legs. No chance of outrunning him on a straightaway.

Swerving right, I yanked an empty market crate off one of the coops. It clattered to the ground between me and the night guard.

"Aah!" A thud and a crack, followed by impressive swearing.

I risked a glance behind. Broken crate pieces lay scattered across the row. The night guard limped a little, but it hadn't slowed him much. I'd gained only another few paces.

The row split ahead, cutting through the waist-high coops like the canals that crisscrossed Geveg. I veered left toward Farm-Market Bridge, my side throbbing hard. Forget making it off the isle. I wasn't going to make it off the *ranch*.

More market crates blocked the row a dozen paces from the bridge. The crates were knee high and a pace wide, with tendrils of loose, twisted wire sticking up like lakeweed. Didn't Heclar ever clean his property? I cleared the crates a step before the night guard. His fingers raked the back of my shirt and snagged the hem. I stumbled, arms flailing, reaching for anything to stop my fall.

The ground did it for me.

I sucked back the breath I'd lost and inhaled a lungful of dust and feathers. The night guard crashed over the crates a choking gasp later and hit the ground beside me. Dried corn flew out of the crate and speckled the ground.

I hacked up grime while he swore and grabbed his leg. He'd left a pretty good chunk of his shin on one of the crates, and his bent ankle looked sprained for sure, maybe broken.

He glanced at me and chuckled wryly. "Just go."

I dragged myself upright but didn't run. He'd lose his job over me, and I'd guess he didn't have many options left if he was working for a cheap like Heclar. I knelt and grabbed his hands, my thumbs tight against his knuckles, and *drew*.

For an instant, our hands flared tingly hot from the healing. He gasped, I groaned, then his pain was in my hands. I left the bad leg. It was a good excuse for letting me go, and Saints willing, he'd keep his job. If he didn't, then at least I'd healed his hands. It was hard enough for native Gevegians to find work these days, and bad hands sure wouldn't help.

Knuckles aching, I turned away before he realized what I'd done. It wasn't the first time I'd healed someone out of pity, but I tried not to do it often. Folks tended to ask questions I didn't want to answer.

I took a step forward, but something large blocked my escape. Heclar! He swung at my head and I ducked, but not fast enough.

Pain dug into my temple and I thudded back to the ground. Heclar floated in the silver flecks dancing around my eyes, a blue-black pynvium club in his hand.

That cleared me straight. I was lucky he was so cheap that he'd only hit me with it instead of flashing it at me. The weapon was too black to be pure pynvium, but blue enough to hold a lot of pain. I didn't want it flashed in my direction any more than I wanted to go to prison.

He sneered and pointed the club at me. "Stinking thieves, both of ya."

Without thinking, I grabbed the night guard's shin and *drew*, knitting bone and yanking every hurt, every sting from his ankle. His pain ran down my arm, seared my leg, and chewed around my own ankle. Yep. Definitely broken. My stomach rolled, but there was nothing in it to toss up.

I seized Heclar's leg with my free hand and *pushed*. The agony the night guard hadn't revealed raced up my other side and poured out my tingling fingers into Heclar. I caught myself before I gave him the knuckleburn. That would make his hands clench, and a hard, sudden grip on the pynvium club might be the enchantment's trigger. Be just my luck to accidentally set it off.

Heclar screamed loud enough to wake the Saints. To be truthful, it was worse than he deserved, but sending me to prison for eggs I hadn't yet stolen was worse than I deserved too. The Saints are funny that way.

It still didn't justify what I'd done. What I'd promised to never do again. But life was easy when I'd made that promise—not the constant struggle it was now. And it got harder every day.

I left both men lying in chicken feed and feathers and sprinted for safety. Just five paces to the exit, then another five to Farm-Market Bridge. Once I crossed the bridge, I'd be off the isle and in the market district on Geveg's main island, where it was easier to hide. If I didn't pass out first.

At the foot of the bridge, two boys in Healers' League green were staring at me in wonder. I skidded to a stop and glanced over my shoulder. I had a clear view of the night guard and the blubbering rancher. The boys had seen me shift for sure.

"How did you *do* that?" one boy asked. He was tall and skinny, but with hard eyes for a boy so young. Too young to be an apprentice. A ward, then. The war had left Geveg with plenty of us orphans about.

"I didn't . . . do anything." Breathing took more effort than I had. I held my side as I edged past them, checking for mentors or the cloying escorts who stuck to wards like reed sap. If either had seen me shift pain—I shuddered.

"Yes, you did!" The other boy nodded his head, and his red hair fell into his eyes. He shoved it back with a freckled hand. "You shifted pain. We saw you!"

"No, I didn't . . . I stabbed him in the foot . . . with a nail." I leaned forward, hands on my knees. The silver flecks were back at the edge of my vision, sneaking up on me from the sides. "If you look close . . . you can still see the blood."

"Elder Len said shifting pain was just a myth, but you really did it, didn't you?"

I wasn't sure which Saint covered luck, but I must've snubbed her big at some point in my fifteen years. "You boys better get back to the League . . . before the Luminary finds out you sneaked free to go wandering."

Both paled when I mentioned the Luminary. We got a new one every three years, like some rite of passage the Duke's Healers had to go through to prove their worth. The new Luminary was Baseeri, of course, and like all Baseeri who held positions that *should* have been held by Gevegians, no one liked him. He'd been here only a few months, but already everyone feared him. He ran the League without compassion, and if you crossed him, you didn't stand a chance at getting healed if you needed it. You *or* your family.

"You don't want to get into trouble, do you?"

"No!"

I placed a finger to my lips. "I won't tell if you don't."

They nodded hard enough to bounce their eyeballs out of their heads, but boys that age can't keep a secret. By morning, the whole League would know about this.

Tali was going to kill me.

"Oh, Nya, how could you?"

Tali used Mama's disappointed face. Chin tucked in, her wide brown eyes all puppylike, lips pursed, and frowning at the same time. Mama had done it better.

"Would you rather I'd gone to prison?"

"Of course not."

"Then sink it. What's done is done and—"

"—I can't change it none," she finished for me.

I had three years on her, which usually gave me implied authority, but since joining the League, she'd been forgetting who the big sister was. Hard to do with only the two of us left, but she managed.

"Be grateful I got away." I flopped backward into green floor pillows. Tali sat on the edge of her bed dressed in her Healer's apprentice uniform, her white underdress neatly pressed and her short green vest buttoned. A sunbeam from the small window above poured over her, making the braided silver loop on her shoulder sparkle.

The door to Tali's dorm room was shut, but not sound-tight. Shuffling feet and excited giggles drifted in as the other apprentices readied for class. Morning rounds were about to start, and I had work to find if I wanted to eat today. Tali sneaked some food out for me when she could, but the League rationed it and they watched the wards and apprentices real careful at mealtimes—especially if they were Gevegian. Hungry or not, I wasn't about to let her risk her apprenticeship for me any more than I had to, and I needed a bigger favor than breakfast.

"Are you on this morning?" I asked, wiggling my toes in the sunbeam.

Tali nodded but didn't look at me. I think stealing the heals scared her more than stealing food, though getting caught in the dining hall was a lot more likely.

"Could you?" I lifted my aching hands. The pain from the night guard's knuckleburn made me useless for all but hauling, and I couldn't carry enough on my back to be worth the money.

"Sure, come here."

I scooted over and she took my hands. Heat blossomed and the ache vanished, tucked safely in Tali's knuckles. She'd keep it there until some aristocrat paid the League to get rid of his own pain, then dump both into the Slab. It was risky sneaking the pain past the League Seniors, but I couldn't dump my pain into the Slab even if I could get to it.

The Slab wasn't its real name, but that's what all the apprentices and low cords called it. Its real name was something like Healing Quality High-Enchanted Pynvium, which didn't have the same flair at all. I'd never actually seen it, not even when Mama was alive, but Tali said it was pure pynvium, ocean blue and the size of a bale of hay. I could eat for the rest of my life with what the Luminary must've paid the enchanters for it.

Tali flexed her fingers and winced. "You could have sold that to the pain merchants, you know."

I huffed. The pain merchants weren't quite thieves, but they paid so little for pain, it was practically stealing it. Before I was born, they used to charge folks for healing just like the League did, but they'd discovered they got more pain if they offered to pay for it. They made their money now from using that pain to enchant their trinkets and weapons, which they then sold to Baseeri aristocrats for a *lot* more than they'd gotten by healing folks.

Of course, there were drawbacks to this.

Since they didn't hire trained healers anymore, you could never be sure you'd actually *get* healed if you went to them. Some of their Takers just took your pain and left what was wrong if they didn't know how to heal it. Only folks with no other choice went to them now, and I'd seen my share of "mysterious deaths" among the poor and desperate. You saw just as many limps and crippled limbs from bad merchant healing as you did from war wounds.

I was almost desperate enough to go to them, but I had other reasons to keep my distance. "Too risky. What if they'd sensed I was a Taker and wondered why I didn't dump it myself?"

"Not that many can sense. You're one of the few I know who isn't an Elder."

That talent still didn't buy me breakfast. I'd trade it fast as fright to sense pynvium like she could; to feel the "call and draw of the metal," as Tali had pounded into my head over the summer, trying to get my skill to work right. She'd just turned twelve, and we'd thought to join the League together. Turn us both from untrained Takers into real Healers and live a good life. The League was one of the few Baseeri-run places that accepted Gevegians. Both sides had lost so many healers in the war, and there just weren't enough trained ones to go around these days.

But no matter how hard we tried, I couldn't sense pynvium, couldn't dump pain into it. I'd made Tali go alone, and they'd accepted her as fast as they would've turned me away. I hated her for it at first, then felt guilty as soon as I realized it was easier worrying about just me. But it sure would have been nice to have a soft bed and regular meals like she did.

I rose. "I'd better go. I might find work cutting bait or washing down the docks if I hurry."

"Maybe we could risk you applying to the League now?" she whispered. "Several apprentices are missing, so we're shorthanded. The Luminary's been awful worried about it too."

"What do you mean, *missing?*" I dropped back into the pillows. The war had ended five years ago, but I still remembered how it started. Healers disappearing in the night, stolen from their homes to heal in the Duke of Baseer's war. We didn't know what war. We barely knew who the Duke was back then. That changed pretty fast when his troops invaded, though, occupying Geveg and stealing our pynvium when our Takers started hiding.

"Not like *that*," she said, eyes wide. "At least I don't think so. The Elders said they left because the training was too hard. People even heard the Luminary complaining about it."

"Do you believe them?"

She shrugged. "It happens, but people usually say good-bye when they go."

Unless they didn't leave on their own. I shook the concern away. I was worrying over nothing. Tali was safe at the League. Three meals a day, a soft bed, training from the best Healers in Geveg. All the things I couldn't get for myself, let alone give her.

"Anyway," she continued, "I thought maybe we could convince them to let you heal, and when your shift ended I could do the transfer for you."

My heart flipped like a beached fish. "You didn't tell them about me, did you?"

"Of course not! But you can heal. We'd work as a team is all."

Pointless—and dangerous—to even ask. "No, Tali, you know what they'd do to me if they found out I could shift."

Experiments, prison, maybe even death. A few years ago, the Duke starting claiming that abnormal Takers were abominations and were to be brought to the League if discovered. He'd put up posters all over Geveg, covered every block on the island, even the smaller farming isles.

She shrugged. "I heard they might lower the entrance requirements for apprenticeship down to those just strong enough to heal minor cuts and bruises, so I thought maybe the Luminary wouldn't care. You can heal a lot higher than *that*."

But it wasn't *real* healing, not like what Tali did. "He would care. Besides, it would wear you out, and the League wouldn't risk your health. They need you." Even if they didn't ship me off to Baseer, I was useless to them. I'd keep drawing pain until I was so twisted up in agony I couldn't move.

"Well," Tali said after a brutally long silence, "if you don't want to work here, then next time steal a whole chicken. That way you'd have eggs every morning."

I grinned, even though I *did* want to work for the League and be a real Healer. I just knew it would never happen. "A chicken loose at the boarding-house? Millie would love that."

"So steal a coop as well. And some corn. Maybe a little bit of reed straw for a nest."

I tried to keep a straight face, but the idea of a coop in my room was too much. The giggles came on fast. Tali and I rocked back and forth like children, clutching our sides, tears in our eyes, until the rounds bell rang.

Tali stood, her shoulders quaking. She pushed a blond braid of her Healer's ponytail off her shoulder, jingling the tiny jade and gold beads woven through it. Her hair looked pretty all smooth and straight like that. I couldn't afford the irons to flatten my curls. Neither could Tali really, but League apprentices had to look smart, and they got to share luxuries like hair irons and face powders. Aristocrats didn't want healing from a bunch of scruffy children, and after the war, those were the only Takers Geveg had left. They had to bring in Elders and teachers from Baseer just to train us, and the first crop of Gevegian fourth cords were training now. Next year, they'd be full Healers, allowed to go out and seek their fortunes, though most would probably stay at the League.

"Will you be all right?" she asked. "When did you eat last? I might be able to sneak some food from lunch."

"I'll be fine." My stomach rumbled and she sucked in her bottom lip, once again the worried little sister.

She nodded quickly, then threw her arms around my neck. "You be careful."

"You too. Don't go anywhere alone, okay?" I hugged her back. She smelled like lake violets and white ginger.

"Promise."

"Go forth and heal the sick, young one." It earned me a giggle.

"Go forth and mutilate fish." She smiled but still looked worried. Maybe she was thinking about the missing apprentices, or maybe it was the knuckle-burn she'd taken from me.

We left her room. Tali went left, toward the hospital wing, while I hurried right, toward the exit on the other side of the main entrance hall. It was the closest exit to the docks, and the north gate League guards always let me pass. I was pretty sure the skinny one was sweet on me, but I'd sooner kiss a croc than a Baseeri.

I crossed into the front antechamber and wove among the dozen or so people waiting for heals. Bits of green, white, and silver flashed as apprentices late for class took the shortcut up the back staircase.

"That's her!"

I jerked around before my wits could stop me. Two wards were pointing at me, as wide-eyed and amazed as they'd been last night. Saints and sinners! I couldn't find good luck in an empty pail.

"She's the one who shifted pain," the ward said, loud enough to turn heads. More than a few folks stopped and stared. "She drew it right out of one man and pushed it into another. We saw it, didn't we, Sinnote?"

My empty stomach tightened. Standing between the wards was a League Elder in full gold cords. Eight braids coiled on his shoulders like vipers, the ends dangling down to the edge of his vest-robe. Thick arms strained his crisp sleeves, and his beaded black hair was tied rope-thick at the nape of his neck. A husky man, Mama would have said.

He hooked a finger toward me and pointed at a tile in front of him. "Come here."

Running would make me look suspicious.

19

Disobeying would make me equally suspicious. I'd never make it past the guards anyway, no matter how much that fellow liked me.

"Now, girl."

Nothing good ever followed just two words.

I stepped forward, wondering what time they served lunch in Dorsta Prison.

TWO

The Elder stared down at me, looking as solid as the thick columns that supported the entrance-hall balcony behind him. He folded his arms across his broad chest and tapped a single finger against a biceps. Men in robes shouldn't look that intimidating. That's what armor was for. "Your name?" he asked.

"Merlaina Oskov." Tali would give me Mama's stern face again for lying, but having an Elder know your name was trouble in a box. They paid heed to none but the Luminary, and *he* paid heed to none but the Duke, just like all of Geveg's military-appointed leaders. Wasn't safe to get noticed by any of them.

"Do you know these wards?"

"No, sir."

The chatty one's brown eyes went wide and his mouth dropped open. "But—"

"I work the sundown to sunup shift at the taproom," I said fast. "Don't see how boys would be crossing my path at those hours."

Sinnote pinch-twisted his friend's arm. "I *don't* think that's *her*."

"It *is* her. She's even wearing the same dirty clothes."

"You're *wrong*."

League Elders weren't fools, much as I needed this one to be. "What time did you see her?" he asked.

"Three," the boy said.

"Five," Sinnote said at the same time. He grimaced.

The Elder grinned at his mouth's corners; then he reached for my arm. "Come with me."

I jerked away. If someone was kidnapping apprentices again, getting trapped in a League treatment room was the last thing I needed. "Pardon, but I can't. I have to get home."

"Your family will understand. Now come!" The Elder grabbed my forearm mongoose-quick. His eyes popped wide, then narrowed. "You *are* a Taker."

"Let me go!" My shout echoed in the domed antechamber. Beaded heads turned, and everyone stopped and stared. Green vests shimmered against gray slate and stone as more lingered to watch. A man passing behind the Elder stopped and watched me with an uncertain frown on his face.

"Stop struggling, girl—I'm not going to hurt you."

But he was. My skin burned where his fingers dug into my arm. Saints, he was strong.

The wards gaped. The crowd stared. No one moved to help. Why would they? I was just some river rat and nobody questioned an Elder, though I'd bet a week's lunches that if my hair was Baseeri black, someone would have stepped forward.

"I said let *go*." I kicked him in the knee, smearing grime on his white pants. He let go, sucking breath in a wet hiss.

I ran for the north gate, crossing the rest of the entrance hall and ducking into the side foyer. Apprentices and wards parted as I barreled into them. Gasps and jingles drowned out the Elder's raspy orders, but I could guess what they were. *Guards, get that girl. Lock her up, poke her, prod her, find out if she's the abomination they claim.*

I shoved my way past a knot of first cords by the exit and slammed open the door. Sunshine felt like freedom, but I wasn't off League property yet. The north gate glinted ahead. Copper clanged against stone as I burst through.

Heart racing, I slipped into the crowd coming in for healing. They filled the circular limestone courtyard outside, more than I usually saw this early in the morning, but it didn't look like many were getting inside. Children in velvet played tag between grandmothers in patched cotton. A farmer in muddied coveralls hugged a bleeding hand to his chest. Dozens of fishermen, soldiers, merchants, and servants mixed together like beggar's stew. I elbowed my way through and learned two new swears from one of the soldiers posted at the main bridge.

At the edge of League Circle, bridges and canals fanned out like wheel spokes to the rest of Geveg. Pairs of soldiers stood on every corner, some mast-straight at attention, others leaning against lampposts. A few pole boats bobbed at the end of the floating docks as Baseeri aristocrats stepped out, their military aides and bodyguards close at their heels. On the left, the lake sparkled as far as you could see, already dotted with fishing boats.

I slowed, trying to avoid notice from the closest pair of soldiers. Thankfully, they were bored types, and neither looked my way. I jumped over a low stone wall and dropped under the closest bridge, stomping down a pad of water hyacinths as I landed. Cool water splashed up my legs. I hid knee-deep in lake and flowers and tried not to think about crocodiles.

Considering I'd just kicked a League Elder, that wasn't hard. A croc'll snap you and spin you down underwater, but an Elder mad at me might throw Tali out of the League. He might make her repay the healing we'd stolen. He might . . .

Why weren't the League guards chasing me?

I stood on tiptoe and tilted my ear toward shore. Footsteps, coughs, the nervous babble that always followed crowds, but no shouts. No thudding boots.

He let me kick him and run?

Slowly I climbed up the lake wall and hopped back over. Still no guards. Not even a fuss in the crowd, just the usual small groups of twos and threes, scurrying along with heads down. Maybe the Elder thought he could find me at one of the tap-rooms. I grinned. He'd find no Melana anywhere. Or was it Meletta? Didn't matter. She was gone as goose grease.

There might be guards looking for me, but bright green League uniforms were easy to spot. Folks tended to give way when they saw armed men coming.

My stomach rumbled again. A painful rumble that twisted up my guts and said it was way past breakfast. And lunch. And supper. I headed for the docks, but my guts also said I was too late to cut bait.

"The boats are out, Nya. I've got nothing for you."

"Sorry, Nya, I already had some boys wash the docks. Did it for cheap, too."

"If you'd been here earlier, I had carts to load, but that's all done now."

Every berth foreman had the same answer, though a few looked sorry to turn me away. Especially Barnikoff, who usually found *something* for me to do. He'd lost three daughters and he liked having me around to tell stories to while he scraped barnacles off the hulls, but there were no boats in dry dock today.

Nor was there any work at the bakery, and the butcher had enough people to yank the feathers off chickens and guinea fowl. The glassblower had two girls running sand and didn't need me. A line of strapping boys my age waited outside the blacksmith's, scowling at a girl I knew. Aylin was dancing by a river-rock garden wall outside the show house, a peek at what you'd see inside if you paid the outrageous prices for their food, drink, and entertainment. She gleamed, her pale shoulders stark against the deep red and gold of her dress. Yellow beads traced her neckline and glittered at the ends of her short sleeves.

I headed over. Because of all the officers, aristocrats, and merchants who went past her every day to spend their stolen wealth, Aylin knew more gossip than a crew of old women. If anyone had work for me, she'd know about it, and I could sure as sugar use a job fast. My pockets were as empty as my belly. Rent had been due yesterday, and I could avoid Millie for only so long. Summer nights promised I wouldn't be cold, but there were other things in the night for a girl sleeping under a bush to worry about. And most of them wore blue uniforms.

I wove through the flow of people coming off the ferry and hopped up on the wall.

"Please tell me you know about some work. I need good news."

"Hi, Nya." She tossed her long red hair and waved at a well-dressed merchant walking by. He flipped up his brocaded collar and ignored her. "Nah, just the usual stuff. Are all the jobs taken already?"

"I got a late start. Think the canal master is hiring leaf pullers?" Water hyacinths clogged the canals every summer and made it tough for the pole boats to get through. Dangerous work, but it paid well.

"Feel the need to dodge crocs?"

"Feel the need to eat."

Her smile vanished. "Oh, that bad, huh?"

"Would I risk becoming a meal to get one if it wasn't?"

Her smile returned. "Hey, handsome, come inside! We have the prettiest dancers in the Three Territories," she called to a muscled soldier in Baseeri blue. He elbowed his friends and waved, but he didn't come over. "No, you're smarter than that. I was telling Kaida the other day how you—"

"Aylin, are they hiring?"

"Oh, no, not anymore. Morning, gentlemen! Come inside, three plays a day, the finest actors in Geveg!" Another set of soldiers went by, all wearing the blue-and-silver osprey emblem on their bulging chests. Baseeri soldiers always lined the streets, but I hadn't seen so many on patrol since the occupation began.

My toes twitched with a sudden urge to be any-where else. "Why all the soldiers today?"

"Verlatta's under siege."

"Seriously?"

She nodded, and her dangling shell earrings

swayed in time with her hips. "I had a Baseeri offi-
cer stop to talk on his way in last night. He's going
upriver today. Said His Dukeship is after Verlatta's
pynvium mines."

Even the late-morning sun couldn't keep my
shivers away. Baseer was two hundred miles upriver,
on the borderlands between the Three Territories
and the Northern Reaches, but it felt like the Duke
was breathing down our necks again. He'd already
conquered Sorille and now controlled most of the
good farming land, but he hadn't had any pynvium
mines until he'd conquered us. We tried to fight
him, regain our freedom, but it hadn't worked. Once
he had Verlatta, he'd rule all three lands his great-
grandfather had granted independence to long ago.
"First our mines, now theirs. You'd think the Duke
would have enough to heal everyone in Baseer by
now."

She shrugged. "It's not for the healing—it's for
the weapons. If he'd stop wasting his pynvium on
weapons, he wouldn't *need* so much. A vicious circle
is what it is. Greedy toad. It's his own fault."

Aylin was right, but it was more sick than vicious
if you asked me. Send your soldiers into battle, use
their pain to fill your pynvium weapons, just so you
could go attack *other folks* and steal *their* pynvium,

so you could heal your people because you used all your pynvium to *make* the weapons in the first place. Stupid. Just plain stupid.

"Sure are a lot of people," Aylin mused, watching the refugees shuffling off the ferry. The Duke had long since set up checkpoints on all the mainland bridges and roads, and without proper Baseeri travel seals, you didn't get to pass. Getting proper travel seals wasn't as hard as you might expect—it just cost you everything you had. Folks had tried forging them, but checkpoint soldiers were *very* good about spotting fakes.

"Too many people," I agreed. Families in tailored clothes with the bright embroidered collars popular in Verlatta shuffled beside families in sewn-together rags. Each person carried a bag or basket—probably all they could grab before they fled Verlatta.

And every last one of them would also be looking for work in Geveg.

I glanced at a pain merchant's shop down the block, its sign swinging in the breeze. Teasing. Taunting. Tempting. Maybe I could risk it. Plenty of refugees around I could sneak some pain from, and one sale might get me through a few more days. I just had to find someone who looked bruised or cut, nothing too serious that might make a Taker suspicious that it wasn't a real injury of mine. Their lack of real training might be a lucky catch for me.

Maybe Aylin knew which Takers couldn't sense? She'd want to know why though, and much as I liked Aylin, I wasn't sure how good she was at keeping secrets. With five pain merchant shops in Geveg, the chances of one having a senseless Taker were—

A man was watching us, almost hidden behind a hibiscus bush two shops down. Dressed fancy too, in smooth yellow and green silk. He wasn't carrying anything, so he wasn't off the ferry. An aristocrat's son? He glanced from me to Aylin, and his lips wrinkled in a vaguely familiar frown.

"I'd better get going, see if anyone needs a hauler in the market," I said. The show house was Baseeri-owned, so I didn't care if my stained shirt and wild curls scared away its customers, but I didn't want Aylin to lose her job over it. "You'll let me know if you hear of any jobs?"

"Of course."

I hopped off the wall, and the world spun around my head.

"Easy there." Aylin grabbed my arm and kept me standing. "You okay?"

"Just a little dizzy. Moved too fast."

"You're so skinny I could wear you in my belt

loops. Do you need money for something to eat?" She reached for a pocket.

"No, thanks, I'm all right," I said quickly. I couldn't pay her back, and Grannyma always said a debt owed was a friendship lost.

She frowned as if she didn't believe me but cared too much to call me on it. "Tell Tali I said hello."

"I will."

Things were still a little swirly, but I tried my best to walk straight and not worry her further. At the farmer's market, a heavyset woman with a basket full of bread caught my eye. Not an aristocrat, but her pink shirt matched her patterned skirt and looked neither worn or patched, so she probably worked for one. Kitchens most likely. She was looking at mangoes, picking up one at a time and sniffing it. My stomach poked at me again, pain caused more from guilt over what I was planning than from hunger, but no one would hire a girl who kept fainting.

I swayed as I walked by and lightly shoved her into the mango bin. Mangoes wiggled, and several rolled off the top of the yellow-orange stack. She cried out and grabbed the table edge, dropping her basket and the fruit onto the rough street stones.

"I'm so sorry!" I knelt and picked up her basket before it could roll over and dump the bread. Good stuff too, warm and cinnamon scented, wrapped in cloth. "Here you go. I hope it didn't get dirty."

She snatched them out of my hands. "Stupid 'Veg!" she swore. "Watch where you're going."

"I'm so sorry. You're right, I should watch where I'm going. There's no excuse for such clumsiness." I tucked two mangoes into my pocket and handed her three others. "I think these are the last of them."

She glanced at my blond hair and scoffed. "Useless, all of you."

"Fine day to you." I dipped a bow.

She harrumphed and turned back to her shopping.

I waited a heartbeat, then two. No cries of alarm rang out, no angry farmer raced at me demanding payment. I slid into the crowd, letting it take me downstream of the market district and into the tradesmen's corner.

Knees quivering, I settled down in the grass under the palm tree in front of Trivent's Leathers, leaning against the trunk with my legs out straight. Madame Trivent didn't care for folks resting under her tree, which is why no one was there. Not much open space in Geveg was empty anymore.

I bit through the mango's skin, sucked the juice up, ignoring the pinch in my stomach as I tried to gobble. The first went down fast and I started on the second, slower this time.

I'd missed all the morning work, but there'd be more after lunch. The fishing boats returned midafternoon, so if I went now, I could get work unloading today's catch. The *Sunset Runner* was on a good streak this week. They'd kept me almost two hours longer than any other loader on the docks the other day. Said I'd done a good job too.

I stopped mid-chew. The fancy man was back, watching me from behind a fence. Me, not Aylin. No good reason why any man would be watching me, unless he was from the League. The League! *That's* where I'd seen him, passing behind the Elder and the wards.

The mango soured in my mouth. A League man overhears that I can shift and starts following me? What if he was a tracker? I'd hadn't heard talk of any since their kidnapping spree during the war. Rumors said they tracked for us *and* the Duke, so the Healers they grabbed never knew which side they might wind up healing. Folks whispered about trackers like they whispered about marsh spirits and the haunted barge wreck. Only trackers were real.

Keep chewing. Don't let slip you've seen him. Too close to the marshes to risk another dip in a canal.

Would he try to grab me in the open or—

"Shoo, girl!" Two more words that always meant trouble for me. Madame Trivent thumped me on the head with her broom. The straw bristles stabbed behind my ears and yanked some hair out.

My mango dropped to the ground. I snatched it back and scrambled to my feet, ducking her wide swings. "I'm going, I'm going."

"Filthy 'Veg. Don't you be bothering my customers." She swept me down the walk like trash and shoved me into the street. "Don't come back!"

Folks put extra steps between me and them as they passed. The soldiers didn't like fuss, and trouble had a nasty way of sticking to other folks like flung mud.

I turned a slow circle but caught no glimpse of yellow and green silk behind bush, tree, or corner. Hunger'll play with your mind, but I didn't think I'd imagined him.

Slouching, I slipped into a wave of refugees. Home sounded like a good idea. If I stayed low, stayed quiet, maybe the fancy man would leave me alone.

That was a foolish dream. Trackers didn't let you go. They dragged you off in the middle of the night, and no one ever saw you again. Made you heal the soldiers. Keep the rebellion alive. Fight the Duke. Chase him out of Geveg. Keep the pynvium *in* Geveg.

None of it had worked.

But I was useless to the League, and Geveg had no more soldiers to heal and fight. The League didn't even know who I was. I rarely spoke to anyone there except Tali, and she wouldn't reveal me. How could—

I sucked in breath. The north gate guards. They knew me. They'd seen me run out earlier, scared as a cat.

I ran the last block to Millie's Boardinghouse. It sat on the edge of Pond End Canal, not far from where the chicken ranchers tossed their garbage. The view wasn't bad and the smell kept it cheap. I climbed up the stairs to my room on the third floor.

My door was pegged shut.

I was only a day late on my rent. Millie had never pegged me out for being a day late before.

"You have your rent money?" Millie stood on the landing at the end of the hall, her skinny brown arms folded tight across her chest. The woman had ears to make a bat jealous.

"I will by this evening, I swear."

She tossed her hands up and huffed, then started

back down the stairs. "I've got your gear. Come get it before I sell it."

"Millie, please, give me a few hours. I'll pay soon as the boats come in."

"I have three families wanting the room."

"Please, I'm good for it, you know I am. I'll pay double tomorrow."

"Got folks willing to pay that now." She shoved my clothes basket into my hands, then wiped her palms on her apron. White flour clouds puffed outward. "Go stay with your sister in her fancy dorm room."

Millie knew the League did bed checks. She rubbed my nose in it 'cause the League had turned her son away. Not enough talent, they said. Couldn't heal a scraped knee. He'd even been turned away by the pain merchants, and Takers didn't need much talent to work *there*. Some of the new swears I'd learned came to mind, but I stilled my tongue. Millie had the cheapest rooms. Throw me out today, take me in tomorrow, and she'd never think twice about either. She was also the only boardinghouse owner in Geveg who believed me when I said I was seventeen and old enough to rent.

I shuffled back to the street, my fingers gripping the basket filled with everything I owned. Two shirts, a pair of pants, and three unmatched socks. I lifted my chin. Tears dripped off onto my hands. I had half a day to find work. Maybe I could untangle nets through the night. Barnikoff might let me sleep in his shed if I tidied it up. And there was always—

Breath died in my throat.

Saints save me, the fancy man was back.

THREE

Strength left my legs, and I flopped into the weeds at the edge of Millie's walk. I sat cross-legged, basket in my lap, chin on the basket. The tears hadn't stopped, and they dripped *tap tap tap* on the wicker.

The fancy man kept watching from across the street. Watched me sit and cry. Open my basket and pull out a sock. Blow my nose on it. Put it back. Watched me watching him. He never moved. I'm not sure he even blinked.

Gave me shiverfeet.

"Nya?"

I yelped. So did the pigtailed girl I hadn't noticed walk up beside me. A flock of bright waterbirds at lake's edge took flight, dozens of tiny wings flapping like sheets in a windstorm.

"Enzie!" I scolded. She'd shared a room with Tali at the League for a while until a bed opened up in the wards' area, the orphanage part of the League where they took in potential Healers. But I'd never seen her without her League uniform on. She looked more like a little girl with her brown hair bound in ribbons and a simple gray shirt and pants like mine. Hers were newer, though, and didn't have patches on the knees and elbows. "For the love of Saint Saea, don't sneak up on folks like that."

"Sorry, Nya." Enzie settled into the weeds beside me. "Tali asked me to give you a message."

My chill returned. "Is she okay?" If she got into trouble because of me, I'd throw myself to the crocs right there.

Enzie nodded. "She wants you to meet her at the pretty circle at three. Under the tree."

The flower gardens. Tali had called it "the pretty circle" when she was four. We'd had picnics there and sat on a soft blue blanket under the biggest fig tree I'd ever seen.

"What's going on, Enzie?" Tali had never been sneaky before. She either spoke her mind clear or didn't speak it at all.

"I don't know." Her green eyes looked away and she sucked in her bottom lip.

"You can tell me."

"I don't know, honest. But I'm scared anyway."

I leaned over and hugged her. Poor girl. She was only ten. She had talent, even if she couldn't use it for two more years. It hummed in her like the shimmy of a bridge when the soldiers marched over it. "It's okay, Enzie."

She sniffled and clung to me. I rubbed her back in small circles. The fancy man kept watching. I stared at him hard, putting a dare into it, though I couldn't say what the challenge was.

Whatever he saw in it, he declined. He turned and walked away.

I hugged Enzie tighter, suddenly just as scared as she and not knowing why.

I walked the full three miles across Geveg to the gardens, on the opposite side of the island from Millie's. Though the gardens were public property, they were inside the aristocrats' district. Powdered women with pearls braided into their black, piled hair glared at me as I headed for the gates. Baseeri soldiers stood watch at all four entrances and kept out the folks aristocrats didn't like seeing—which pretty much meant everyone who wasn't from Baseer. They weren't supposed to by law, and sometimes you could talk your way in if you looked clean and sharp and didn't mumble your request, but nobody went in carrying a clothes basket. Squatters were not allowed under any circumstances.

She'd picked a lousy place for a secret meeting.

I dipped a sock into the lake and washed as best I could, then hid my basket under a leafy hibiscus bush not far from the eastern entrance. Clean? Somewhat. Sharp? Not at all. At least I didn't mumble.

The soldier watched me walk up. I didn't slow when I neared him, making it clear I planned to go inside and did it often.

"Pardon, miss." He stepped forward and held his arm out across the walk, looking a lot like some of the trees that grew inside. Tall, wide, brown, with a mess of gold on top. Unusual to see a blond Baseeri. Most had glossy black hair that shimmered in the sun like raven's wings. But he also had the Baseeri sharp nose and chin. Maybe he looked more like a bird than a tree. Or a bird *in* a tree.

"Yes?"

"Your business here?"

"I'm meeting my sister."

He looked me over, and reluctance flashed in his

dark eyes. Kindness too, if I could make use of it.

"It's her birthday."

"I don't think—"

"Our parents used to take us here every year for our birthdays." The truth popped out on its own and I couldn't stop talking. "We'd walk down from the terraces, and if the wind was blowing just right, the whole bridge would be covered in pink flowers. They'd fall like rain, and the air smelled so sweet it made your eyes water." Mine were doing it now. I hadn't thought about those birthday trips in years.

His stern expression wavered a little, then he dropped his arm and nodded. "Go on in. You tell your sister Good Birthday."

"Thank you, I will."

The gardens welcomed me back. The cool, green-tinted shade kept the rest of the city out, and the air smelled exactly as I remembered. No carpet of flowers this time, but the grass looked thick as a rug and softer than any bed I'd slept in for a long time. Branches above shook as monkeys chased one another through the treetops, whooping in high-pitched frenzy. I passed under arches of brown, and the trees whispered in the way that always made me feel they had secrets to tell me. This time, Tali was the one with something to say.

She waited on a red-veined marble bench under the big fig tree at the edge of the lake, a bright speck among the softer greens and browns.

"I got in, can you believe it?" I called. My smile was almost genuine.

"Oh, Nya." She jumped off the bench and hugged me, her tears soaking the same shoulder Enzie's had. I went cold. Had she been kicked out of the League?

"What's wrong?"

"Vada's gone."

For a terrible, guilty instant, I was glad. Tali's apprenticeship was still safe. Vada was her best friend at the League, and too many of our recent visits had ended short with "Well, I gotta go. Vada and I need to study. . . ." Wouldn't bother me any if Vada left the League, except I'd prefer it if it didn't happen when apprentices were already missing. "Are you sure she didn't go home for a few days?"

"She would have told me. We tell each other everything."

Everything? "Did you tell her about me?"

"Of course not!" Tali wiped her eyes and dropped with a huff onto the bench. "This doesn't have anything to do with you. Something's wrong, I know it. She's the fourth apprentice to vanish this week."

Saints save us, it *was* happening again. But why would the League kidnap their own apprentices?

Tali twisted her skirt, her knuckles white as the fabric. "People are asking questions now. Four girls don't just leave in the middle of the night, and some of the boys say their friends are missing too. They're even limiting the number of people healed because we're so shorthanded. The mentors tell us not to worry, but they act as if something's wrong and they don't want to tell us."

My shiverfeet came back. Apprentices missing. Trackers following me. Verlatta under siege. Just like the war, only this time, no cries of independence rang in the streets. Tali needed to be careful. We all needed to be careful. "Tali, there's a—"

"I'm scared. I hear things from the first cords." She leaned closer and cupped the side of her mouth with one hand. "They say the Slab sometimes turns Healers away. Like it doesn't want their pain."

"What? Tali, you can't trust first cords. They're barely older than I am. Listen, there's—"

"But they've finished their apprenticeship. They *know* things."

"They don't know that much or they'd have earned more than one cord."

"They're also talking about you."

"The first cords?" How many people knew about me? No wonder trackers were on me like fish stink.

"No, the *Elders*. Not by name, but a rumor's been running all day in the dorms about a girl who can shift pain. That chicken rancher came in for healing at first light and told a story too good to keep quiet. The Elders even asked me about you. Interrupted rounds to do it, too."

"Why didn't you tell me this *first*?"

"They were asking everyone, and they called you Merlaina, so why worry you over nothing? No one knows who you are but me."

And the tracker. Even if he had my name wrong, he knew my face—and now he knew Aylin's.

A strong gust blew my curls around, and Tali's hair jingled. We looked up in unison and gazed out across the lake, so large we couldn't see the other side. Blue-black storm clouds darkened the horizon, mirroring the jagged mountain range on the other side of the city. The same mountains that made Geveg rich in pynvium, and a target for greedy men like the Duke. Several fishing boats were hauling anchor. Lakeside storms were the worst kind, and we got our share every summer.

Tali handed me a roll and half a banana, wrapped in what looked like a page from one of her schoolbooks.

"I smuggled this out for you at lunch. I'm sorry, it's all I could get."

"Thanks." I gobbled the food, hoping it would make it easier for me to think. "What do the Elders want with me?"

"They didn't say. I wanted to find out, but I was afraid they'd get suspicious if I asked questions."

I swallowed the last of my bread. No butter or cinnamon, but still delicious. Shame there were no answers tucked inside like the special cookies we used to get on All Saints' Day. "Tali, you need to be careful. There's—"

"I know. They can't find out about you. I was stupid to think the League wouldn't care that you weren't normal. They'd lock you up, or send you to Baseer so the Duke can turn you into an assassin."

"Wait." I held up my hands, palms out. "What are you talking about?"

"This morning's history class. Elder Beit was acting odd, telling weird stories, checking over his shoulder the whole time like he thought someone might come in. He said the Duke used to use Takers as assassins—that's why it was important to report them right away if you found one. He said the Duke discovered a way to make them hurt people. I thought of you right away." Her eyes grew bright.

"Do you think there are others like you and that's why he wants different Takers so bad? Maybe you're not alone!"

Thunder rumbled soft and low, and a fresh gust rustled the leaves. More like me? Saints, I hoped not, but if that were true, then the fancy man might be tracking all of us. "Tali, you didn't ask anything in class that might make them suspect me, did you? Or say anything that hinted you knew someone like that?"

"Nya! You *know* I'd never do that."

I chewed what was left of a thumbnail. Maybe the fancy man was a Baseeri spy. There'd always been spies in the city, and they'd no doubt have some freedom about what they spied on. Just my luck he'd been there when those wards pointed me out.

How much danger was I in?

"Tali, a tracker is following me."

She gasped and looked around frantically. "Here? Now?"

"No, earlier today." I grabbed her shoulders and the panic dimmed in her eyes. "He left when Enzie came."

"He saw Enzie?"

"She wasn't wearing her uniform and he was

too far away to hear what she said. I don't think he knows I came here." Not for certain anyway, but I doubted I'd see him if he didn't want me to. "Be very careful who you trust."

"I will, I promise." Tears spilled from her eyes and left streaks on her cheeks. "Do you think he took Vada? And the others?"

"I don't know."

She hugged me, her head tucked between my shoulder and chin. "Like trackers took Mama."

No, she'd gone willingly, like Papa, to fight, but by the end of the war, the trackers hadn't just grabbed unimportant Takers anymore. They took Elders from the League, personal healers from the aristocrats—no Taker had been safe.

Honeysuckle and rain scented the air, and in the empty space under the fig tree, I imagined a blue blanket held down against the wind by bowls of spiced potatoes and roasted perch, and Mama spooning out her special bean salad while Papa buttered the bread.

Another war. Another need for Takers. What about Takers who could do more than heal? If they came for *me* this time, would I wind up on the front lines healing or get stuck in the dark doing something far worse?

The storm drove the boats back in early. Wind-blown drops stung my cheeks and soaked my clothes. That didn't keep me from the docks and a chance to get my room back any more than the fancy man who wanted to turn me into an assassin did. Sadly, the rain didn't keep anyone else away either. Dozens of folks stood in line by every unloading berth, some with baskets in their arms. A few even had children clinging to their legs or cowering in their arms. No one complained when parents were chosen first, but more than one scowled. At least here, a tracker couldn't snatch me without someone seeing. Whether they'd care or not was anyone's guess.

The jobs filled up fast. By sunset, only one boat was out, but at least forty people jostled one another to catch the berth foreman's eye. I'd kicked the foreman once after he'd pinched me nowhere proper, so I walked away, shivering in the rain as the last of the sun's warmth faded.

Where could I go? I retrieved my hidden basket and sat in the dry lee of the ferry office, half hidden behind a drooping hibiscus bush. On the lake, now-empty fishing boats packed the canals leading to the docks, and two ferries with more people looking for work and rooms waited for the dockmaster's signal to come in. One was an overloaded river ferry from Verlatta, its flag whipping around on its stern. The other was a small lake ferry that took folks from the docks to Coffee Isle, the largest of the farm islands. Every few seconds a sharp crack echoed across the lake as waves knocked the ferries into each other. The urge to scream "go away" at the refugees stuck in my throat. Lot of good screaming would do me.

A screech ripped across the lake, and for a confused heartbeat I thought maybe I *had* screamed. I dropped my basket and it rolled into the rain, gaining speed down the sloped bank toward the lake's edge. Thunder rumbled as I scrambled away from my dry spot under the awning. My feet slipped in the mud and I fell to my knees, but I caught the basket before it rolled into the water.

Another grinding squeal, like pigs gone to slaughter. The smaller ferry dipped hard to starboard, its side crushed against the bigger ferry. Muffled screams mingled with the splattering rain. The wind howled, and another crack rang out.

I clutched my basket to my chest as a chunk of deck broke off and plunged into the churning waves. Crates followed. Lightning flashed, illuminating people falling into the water. Saints be merciful! I turned, scanning the shore, though I couldn't say what I hoped to find. Rescue boats? Lifelines?

The crowds on the docks surged forward, but none did more than gawk and point.

"Do something!" I shouted. Wind swallowed my words—not that anyone was listening anyway. The ferries chewed at each other. Passengers staggered across the decks, slipping on the wet wood. Waves and wind slammed the smaller ferry farther under the water. It hit the canal wall and bounced off. Waves sloshed against the walls, the ferries, the shore, getting higher and higher.

And still, people did nothing.

Dropping my basket, I raced to the ferry office and banged on the door.

"Help! People need help out here!"

No one answered. Had they left already to do whatever they did in this situation? They *had* to have a plan; they just had to.

I raced along the bank back to the shoreline, slipping on grass and trampling reeds. Lightning lit the sky, silhouetting three people as they fell overboard and slipped into the black, swirling water. Before their heads reappeared, the ferry swung back, blocking the surface. Wood ground against rock. I tried not to picture bodies crushed between them, but I couldn't picture anything else.

Off to my left, a smaller fishing boat crashed through the waves, fighting its way toward the sinking ferries. The crew struggled with oars never meant to propel the boat through rough water. Waves hit the side and the boat listed heavy to port, and kept tilting. I held my breath, stepping closer as if I could pull the boat upright from the shore.

Wind ripped along the docks and the boat righted itself, but its angle said it had taken on too much water to stay afloat. Half the crew was already swimming, fighting against the current dragging them deeper into the lake. Swells chose victims randomly, lifting one man toward shore, sucking another under the darkness.

"Hang on," I hollered, squishing through the reeds. Pale hands shot above the water beyond my reach and were swept away. Red flashed amid white foamy waves, but the bloody arms weren't close enough to grab. Screaming. More screaming. So much screaming.

I had to get closer! Water swirled around my waist, tugging at my legs, trying to drag me out where the screams were. My heart made it farther than my hands ever could.

A splash to my right.

I turned, searched the water. Orange flickered

for an instant, and I lunged for it. My fingers found softness and warmth, cloth and skin. *Please, Saint Saea, let them be alive*. I grabbed, held on with both hands, and yanked.

A crewman rolled out of the waves, coughing and sputtering. So much blood on his forehead. A deep wound for sure, maybe even a bone bruise. I dragged him out of the water, through the reeds, and up the bank. My hand covered the gash in his head and I *drew*, not a lot, but enough to close the wound and stop the bleeding. My head throbbed above my left eye.

Fishermen and dockhands appeared on the bank beside me, forming a chain with a thick rope wound around their middles. The largest man planted his feet in the muddy bank near where I had huddled behind the bush. I darted over and grabbed the rope a foot in front of him.

"Stay back." He pushed me away, and I nearly went down.

"I can help!"

"Help the injured."

Men thick from hard labor jostled me aside and extended the chain out into the water. I moved away, scanning the shore for survivors, but the men hadn't brought any back.

More flashes of color and snippets of screams

caught me. I ran down the bank, away from the men and their rope chain. Ferry passengers neared the shore, fighting to keep their heads above water.

I went back in, bits of wood and debris banging against my hips as wreckage started washing up. A dark shape loomed ahead and I lunged sideways, swallowing a mouthful of water. A crate swept by and slammed into a barrel behind me. Coughing water from my lungs, I found a woman whose arm would never bend again and dragged her to shore. My fingers were stiff as I pulled out a man who would limp. My heart went numb when I touched a boy too still, too cold, to heal.

Rain fell harder, as if trying to flatten the waves so we could save more, but it hindered more than helped. A horrible snap, louder than the thunder, caused heads to turn. The smaller ferry broke in half and disappeared under the water. Seconds later, the larger ferry ground itself over the wreckage. The hull cracked, wood tore away from beams. People clinging to rails toppled to the angled deck and slid into the lake.

I kept going, pulling them out, dragging them in.

Even after the screams stopped and the crying began.

I walked slowly, achingly, unsure where my own hurts began and the ones I'd taken ended. League Healers were rushing past me with stretchers slung between them, splashing through puddles and muddying their uniforms. Most were apprentices and low cords. I looked for Tali but didn't see her. My basket had disappeared. Stolen, kicked away, I didn't know, but it didn't matter. I had nothing left but pain.

Tali would be busy tonight and exhausted tomorrow. With so many injured, the Slab might even fill before the night ended. Did they keep extras for emergencies? Two hay-bale-sized pynvium Slabs was more wealth than I could imagine, but would even *that* be enough for so much pain?

Music and laughter drew me to Aylin's show house, but she wasn't there. Happy, dry faces shone through the windows, oblivious to the suffering at the docks. The blacksmith's was closed, but heat radiated off the chimney in the back. I stood against it under a roof that kept most of the rain off me.

"I have nowhere to go." The words slipped out, startling me. Could I go to the League? Maybe they'd take my pain before realizing I couldn't pay for it. Or at least give me a dry place to sleep. I pressed closer against the bricks. Foolish thoughts. If I went to the

League, those wards or even the Elder might see me. Too big a risk just to stay dry for one night.

I watched for Aylin, but she never appeared, not even when the rain stopped and the moon came out. So I walked. Almost dry, I listened to cicadas and music. Tomorrow, I'd go to the pain merchants. I had pain to sell, lots of it. If they sensed what I was, I could run. I was getting good at it.

And if they told the League?

Then I'd run faster. Or let them catch me and force them to tell me why they were following—

Hands shot out and dragged me into the darkness between the buildings. One hand clamped over my mouth while an arm wrapped around my chest and pinned my arms at my sides.

"Don't scream."

I couldn't think of doing anything else.

FOUR

"Don't hurt me," a low voice said matter-of-factly, as if he knew me and what I could do to him. He sounded familiar, but I couldn't quite match a face to the voice. Then hesitantly he added, "And I'm not going to hurt you, I promise."

My fingers couldn't reach his arm, but they tingled, ready to *push* every hurt into him the moment I could get my hands on his skin. Yet his fear seemed real, and no one had ever been afraid of me before.

"I just want to talk." He took his hand off my mouth but kept the other arm tight around me.

I was too angry now to scream, but indignant I could manage. "What do you want?"

"I need your help. If I let you go, promise not to run? Or hurt me?" His tone sounded desperate.

"Yes."

He dropped me like a live snake. I spun around, fingers splayed as if I could flash the pain out like an enchanted pynvium weapon. A handsome boy stared at me nervously, even sheepishly, and in the moonlight he almost looked like . . .

"You're that night guard!"

He nodded and smiled. A real smile this time, and I didn't see a rapier anywhere. "I'm Danello. I'm really sorry—"

"Why did you grab me like that?"

"I was afraid you'd run, thinking maybe I'd want to arrest you again."

I folded my arms across my chest. "What do you want?"

"I need you to heal my da."

Every inch of my sore body flared protest. I couldn't hold any more pain, not even a blister. "I can't."

"Yes, you can. You healed *me*, twice."

No, just once. The other was a shift I never should have done. Mama's terrified face flashed across my mind. *Don't ever put pain into someone again, Nya. It's bad, very bad. Promise me you won't do it.* I'd tried so hard to keep that promise.

"Go to the League. They probably have every Healer on duty tonight."

"We can't afford the League."

"Then go to the pain merchants." If his da's injuries were obvious, they'd probably be okay. Hard to pretend to heal a broken leg. Trouble came when they only half healed it. One of the fruit vendors couldn't walk again after he went to a merchant and they healed him wrong.

"I did—they turned us away. They're turning everyone away."

That left me mute. The ferry accident should have been harvest day for them. No one would argue over the pittance they'd offer with family members bleeding and broken. People might even be willing to pay *them,* and they'd make money off the healing *and* selling the pain-filled trinkets later. With so many refugees around, pynvium security rods were in higher demand than usual. You thought twice about climbing through a window if the sill might flash pain at you.

"They can't *all* be turning folks away," I said. "Did you try the ones by the docks?"

"I tried all five in town. Three were even charging, not paying, but by the time I got there, they said no more heals."

Not good at all. If they were turning everyone away, they'd also turn *me* away, and this time I had plenty of pain to sell.

Danello took a hesitant step closer. "Please—my da was on the ferry. He's seriously hurt, a broken arm and leg, maybe a rib or two. He can't work and he'll lose his job."

I couldn't do it. I already carried too much pain, and who knew when Tali would be able to take it from me. "What about you? Can't you pay your rent if he can't work?"

"Heclar let me go." He didn't say it was my fault, but I heard it anyway.

I glanced away. "Well, you can work in your da's place 'til he's well. Most foremen'll let you do that."

"I can't. My da's a master coffee roaster and I don't have the training. You can bet someone from Verlatta does though. If my da can't work, the landlord'll peg us out. My little brothers just turned ten. My sister's only eight."

Too young to be tossed out on the street, even with Danello to look after them if their father died. And he could if the merchants weren't buying. Some old soldiers could set bone, but I'd never heard of one who did it well. Danello might be able to find one of the herb sellers from the marshlands, but you couldn't trust the powders and poultices they sold. Better to risk an untrained pain merchant Taker than *that*. Even if the Taker missed an injury, they'd probably heal most of it. My throat tightened and I coughed to clear it. "I don't have any pynvium."

"But you don't need it! You healed me and gave my pain to Heclar. You can do the same for my da."

"Who's going to take his pain after? You?"

He nodded. Actually nodded! "Yes."

Even if it wasn't a crazy idea, it wouldn't be enough. Not if his da had that many broken bones. "Taken pain doesn't heal like a natural injury does. It doesn't belong to you, so it just stays in your body. Once you take it, you need a trained Healer to get rid of it."

"I can manage it until the merchants are buying again."

"No you can't. You'd hurt bad as he does now. Don't you need to work too?" Even master roasters didn't make enough to support a whole family. Not many jobs in Geveg did—at least, not the ones Gevegians could get.

"Then we'll all take some, me *and* my brothers and sister. It'll be okay if we spread it around like that, won't it?"

"It'll be awful." My stomach soured at the thought. "I can't do that to them."

Pleading, he grabbed my shoulders. "You *have* to. We don't have anywhere else to go for healing. We don't have much, but we can pay. A little food, a place to stay for a few days if you need it." He looked me over, then smiled, an odd mix of hope and pity in his eyes. "Looks like you could use that."

More than he knew.

"I can't," I said. "I was there, at the ferry. I . . . I pulled folks out. I . . ." Wanted to cry. Wanted to run. Wanted to say yes and sleep somewhere dry. Shame settled on me like a damp chill. Hundreds had died tonight. Was I really thinking about hurting children for a bed? If I could consider that, I might as well work for the pain merchants, trading on misery for my own comfort.

"I'm sorry, I can't help you."

He stepped back a pace and looked at me, critically this time, reaching out and lifting one aching arm, then the other. Noticing every time I winced and bit my lip. "How much did you take?"

"More than I should have."

I'd seen despair before, but it never looked as bad as it did on his face. I could get used to seeing that face, too. Shame we kept meeting in the dark, twisted up in our own problems. "What if we also took that pain?"

"No. You don't understand what you're asking me to do." I folded my arms again, trying to keep what little warmth—and self-respect—I had left. Without my terror keeping me alert, exhaustion tugged at my sleeves. I needed to find a place to sleep; preferably somewhere that didn't ask me to give pain to children. "I'm sorry, I really am. I hope—"

"Give me some, right now."

"What?"

"Pain. Let me see what's it like; then I'll decide."

"You're insane."

He held out a hand. Not even a quiver. "Just do it."

No, not insane. Desperate. Willing to do anything to save his da and his little brothers and sister. Would I do anything less crazy to save Tali if *she* were in trouble?

If I showed him what it felt like, he'd change his mind. I checked the alley and the street. A few folks were chatting outside the taproom, but no one was close. I took his hand and *pushed.*

He cried out and his hand flew to his temple over the left eye. Groaning, he pulled his fingers away and stared at them, a surprised look on his face. "I expected blood."

"There was a lot on the man I took that from."

Danello inhaled, blew it out slowly, nodded. "Okay, give me another."

"No!"

"You need—I don't know, room—to hold more pain if you're going to help my da."

The boy was crazy as a guinea hen. The pain should have ended it. Should have made him realize what a stupid idea this was, and not something you did to children, no matter how desperate you were. Refusing was the right thing to do. I took his arm, prepared to take back the headache.

Memories made me pause. I was ten when we were orphaned, Tali seven. The orphanage had taken us in, but kicked us out when I turned twelve 'cause I was old enough to work and they needed the beds for the younger ones. Tali was scared, wanting to go home and barely understanding why we couldn't. Danello's siblings wouldn't be considered orphans, not with him old enough to care for them. They wouldn't even get a *chance* at a real bed or a hot meal. All four would be out on the street soon as their rent came due. Sweet as Danello was, he sure didn't know how to live like a river rat.

He'd have to learn fast, or they'd all die. He'd have to become the kind of person who would consider shifting pain to children to sleep in a bed. He'd have to become me.

I gave him more pain. A little in the arm, the leg, a twinge in the shoulder. Nothing in the hands or back. Nothing that might keep him from working.

Danello closed in on himself, sucking in his breath and falling back against the wet wood of the building behind him. "It feels different from getting hurt."

"The body has defenses for injuries, but it doesn't recognize another's pain the same way."

"Oh." Another deep breath and he stood straight, defiant. If I didn't know pain, I wouldn't have seen anything wrong with him. Crazy, yes, but he had iron in his bones for sure.

"Better?" I asked.

"Yes. How do you feel?"

"Sore, but not bad." At least on the outside. Inside? Like maggots on a dead crocodile.

"Good enough for my da?"

"I think so." Unless he was dying. If so, I wasn't good enough to do anything but steal his kindness the way Tali and I stole heals. And Saints save me, I wasn't sure which was worse.

Danello lived in one of the better boardinghouses on Market-Dock Canal, in a neighborhood I could only dream of affording. His family had three rooms to themselves—two bedrooms attached to a small kitchen and dining area. Though a woman's touch still showed, it had been a long time since it showed strong. Two dying plants—possibly coriander—sat on a shelf near the window, holding back faded and singed curtains bunched on one side. A rack of worn copper pots hung above a small stove, its skinny pipe chimney snaking up the side wall. They did have a view, though it was only a grassy corner of a market square. Two people were huddled under a bush, a ratty blanket tucked around them. I looked away.

"Did you find her?" a boy called, running out of the room on the left. "Oh, I guess you did." His mouth wiggled as if he was unsure whether to be happy I was there or scared that I had come.

"This is—" Danello turned to me and laughed sheepishly. "I don't even know your name."

"Nya."

He nodded. "Nya, this is Jovan. The other two are with our da."

Not knowing what else to do, I waved, and the smaller version of Danello waved back. Same rich brown eyes, same pale hair, same determined yet sad set to the chin.

"Da's unconscious now," Jovan said in the measured tone of someone trying very hard to sound grown-up. Saints, he was so young. Too young to carry pain that wasn't his. "Do we need to wake him?"

My stomach twisted, but I shook my head. "Don't wake him. I can do it while he's asleep."

We moved into the back bedroom, small but cozy. Paintings of flowers hung on the walls, some painted on wood, others on squares of cotton. By the bed, Jovan's twin brother sat on a yellow stool, his unhappy face pale and tight. Their little sister sat on the floor at his feet. Her blond head rested on his knee and her arms were wrapped around his shin. Neither looked up.

"That's Bahari, and Halima there on the floor."

I backed away. No bed was worth this. I wasn't healing, I was deciding who suffered. Saints did that, not me. "I can't do this."

"Yes, you can. So can they." Danello squeezed my hand, drew me forward. "What do we do?"

"Change your mind, find a pain merchant who's buying, drag him here by his hair if you have to, just please don't make me do this."

He took both my hands, held them tight. They were warm, and for one irrational moment I felt safe. "*What* do we *do*?" he asked.

What we had to, even if we didn't like it. Hadn't I always wanted to be a Healer? It might not be what Tali did, but I *could* help them. The shift was only for a few days, until the pain merchants were buying again. It wasn't as if I were *permanently* hurting them. I gulped down air and reluctantly pulled my hands away.

"Nothing yet," I whispered. "I have to see how badly he's hurt first."

His da's forearm bent the wrong way, so that was broken for sure. The thigh was bloody and gouged, but the leg was straight. I glanced at Jovan and my stomach rolled. *Just think about their father.* I went to the opposite side of the bed and placed my hand on his forehead. Cold, wet strands of the same pale hair as his children's stuck to my fingers.

Tali's voice echoed in my head. She'd been teaching me what they taught her, claiming it was in case the League ever let me in one day, but I wasn't so sure of that. I figured it was just her way of making it up to me 'cause she got accepted and I couldn't.

I took a deep breath. *Feel your way through the*

body, to the injury. My hand tingled as I felt my way through blood and bone. Broken arm, as expected. Three broken ribs. Torn muscle on the leg, but not broken. Cuts and bruises all over, but he'd heal that on his own.

"It's not as bad as you thought." I explained his injuries as best I could without scaring the little ones. Bahari already looked ready to bolt.

"I'll take the arm and leg," Danello said as if ordering dinner. "They can each take a rib. That won't be too bad, will it?"

Spoken like someone who'd never *had* a broken rib.

"It'll hurt to breathe deep. Bending and stretching will be hard." Three sets of brown eyes went wide. I almost smiled, but figured my grin would scare them more than the pain. "No roughhousing 'til the pain merchants are buying again."

Bahari jumped up, his fists clenched at his sides. "I don't want to do this."

"We have to. It's for Da," Jovan snapped back.

"I'll"—Bahari looked around the room—"do something else to help. Go to the herb sellers."

"Bahari!" Danello gasped. "Half the time they sell you poisons. I'm not risking Da's life like that."

I shuffled back against the wall. I wasn't sure I

wanted to do this either, and I didn't want to shift anything to Bahari if he didn't want it.

"It'll hurt," he said.

"Yes, but you can handle it for a few days."

"But—"

"Do it, Hari," Jovan said in a voice too old for such a small boy. "Da's never let us down, and we're not letting him down now."

Bahari didn't agree, but he didn't say no again either.

"Fine, then it's settled. Me first." Danello dragged over a chair from under the window and sat down, grabbing the arms tight.

"Danello . . ."

"Do it."

Just set the arm, heal the pain, and sleep in a dry bed tonight. Gritting my teeth, I tugged on the broken arm and *drew.* I swallowed my gasp and tugged harder as the bone knitted, setting the arm back straight. My eyes watered, blurring the already spinning room.

"I'm right here, Nya." Danello took my hand. The other was entwined in his da's fingers.

I gathered the pain like Tali taught me, held it in a tight ball churning in my guts. "I'm okay. Are you ready?"

He leaned back, grip tight on the chair again, and nodded.

I *pushed*, a little at a time, letting him take some in and make peace with it before another shaft of pain sliced through him. My hands burned to my elbows, especially on one side. Danello shook, his skin pale as mist. His breath came in short gasps at first, then lengthened.

I slid to the floor, my back against the bed.

"Danello, are you okay?" Jovan tentatively reached out a hand and cupped his brother's shoulder. No one asked how I was, but Bahari glared at me.

"I'm fine." Danello puffed a breath and grinned. Pain tightened the corners of his eyes, but he hid it well. "Now the leg."

I gave him half. Who knew how long he'd have to carry it. I'd never carried pain for more than two days, and by then I'd been good and glad to be rid of it.

Jovan stepped forward, hands clenched at his sides. "I'm next." His determined face challenged me to say no.

If only I could.

"It'll be sudden," I warned, "and sharp. Breathe through it, and squeeze something. That helps."

I *drew* quickly, moved slowly, the needle stabs along my belly hot but not unbearable. I kept a little. Maybe he'd be okay with what was left.

Jovan yelped as I gave him his da's pain, but sucked in his bottom lip, hissing as he inhaled.

"Shallow breaths, Jovi," Danello cautioned.

"That wasn't so bad," Jovan said as I let him go. He wiped his sweaty forehead and grinned at his brother. "I bet you cry."

Bahari shifted his glare to his brothers, but he stepped forward anyway and grabbed the bedpost. He nodded sharply at me, like I'd seen the boxers do when the Fair came to town. "Do it fast."

"Are you sure?" I whispered.

His eyes softened a little, and he nodded. "Yeah. It's only for a few days, right?"

"Right." I kept a lot of his. He didn't cry, but he came close. He also didn't yelp, or make a single sound beyond the same teeth-gritting hiss Jovan had made. Bahari shot a smug grin at his brother. "I did it."

"The bravest twins in Geveg," Danello said, ruffling their hair.

Halima stepped forward, a handmade doll clutched in her arms. "I'm brave too!"

"I'll take hers," said Jovan. Bahari looked as if he

wanted to argue but kept his lips tight together.

Halima glared at them like a mountain cat guarding a kill. "I can do it myself."

"No you can't."

"It's too hard," added Bahari.

"Yes I can! You never let me do anything you do."

"Halima," said Danello softly, a shaking hand on her hair. "They're right. It's too hard."

Tears spilled down her cheeks. "I wanna help Da too."

"Your brothers will need you to take care of them," I said. I could handle another rib. It'd be a rough night, but I'd have a bed and Tali could take it all tomorrow first thing. I could even come back after and get the rest. Stealing a few heals was better than hurting folks, and worth risking a trip or two back to the League. "Do you think you can run the house for a while?"

"Uh-huh." She sniffled, wiping her nose with the arm of her shirt. "I'll take good care of us."

"Danello, I can—"

"No," he said. "I *know* you kept some pain. Our deal was we take that from you too. You can't heal well if you're hurting."

I nodded, even though I didn't know if that was true or not.

"We can share it," Jovan said quickly, giving me

that stare again. "Don't tell us we can't. She's not your sister."

I glanced at Danello, and he nodded. "Okay, who's first?" Jovan stepped forward and dragged Bahari with him.

"Together?" he asked, clasping hands. Bahari looked at his sister and nodded.

I *pulled* the last rib from their da, then placed a hand on each of their hearts. Under the pain, a faint hum like the one I'd felt in Enzie ran through them.

They were Takers!

Weak though, probably not even strong enough to work for the merchants, or I would have sensed it when I first touched them. I glanced at their hands, gripped so tightly ten knuckles shone bright white. Linked twins. Did their talent grow stronger when they were linked? I'd never heard of that before, but then, I'd never heard of shifting until I first did it, and neither had Mama. They probably didn't know what they could do yet. *Couldn't* know or they'd try to take more pain from their father. Jovan would anyway.

Danello touched my shoulder. "Nya? What's wrong?"

"Nothing." Just that his brothers were now at risk from fancy trackers and the Duke's new war.

Most Takers started sensing pain at ten, and were ready to start taking it by twelve. But with the siege on Verlatta, the Duke would need more Healers. He'd lost a lot of them fighting us, and he'd have no problem stealing children to conquer yet another city that didn't want his rule. Just like he'd stolen from Sorille to conquer us.

"Are you sure? You look funny."

I didn't have to tell them. If no one knew, they weren't in any danger. Even if someone checked them, they wouldn't sense it unless the twins were linked. "I'm fine, really." I turned to the twins, trying not to let Danello see my lie. "You two ready?"

They nodded, faces white as their da's.

Neither made a sound this time, their eyes and cheeks bulging as they held back even the hiss. The lines of their da's face had smoothed, and he shifted a little in his sleep. The twins settled down on the floor, gingerly prodding their middles. Halima watched them like they might suddenly turn inside out.

"When do you think our da will wake up?" Danello asked.

"Not 'til morning. He'll be stiff and sore for a while, and probably mad as marshflies when he finds out what you did."

"He'll understand. Come on, I owe you supper."

My stomach growled and he laughed.

Equal parts hunger and guilt twisting my guts, I followed him back into the kitchen. I hid my slight limp. He didn't hide his and also kept one arm tight against his chest. He wouldn't be chasing any chicken thieves for a while.

"Danello, let me help you with that." Ribs throbbing, I reached for the coffeepot shaking in his hands. He jerked it away and winced. What a pair we made.

"No, I got it. Least I can do is make you supper. We owe you so much more than we can give. Thank you for this." He smiled, and my cheeks warmed faster than the pot.

"Are those fish cakes?"

He loaded up a plate for me, then set the pot to boil. About halfway through my fish, I realized my gobbling looked a lot like a hyena with a fresh carcass.

"Um, sorry."

"It's okay." He chuckled and poured us both coffee. "I don't know how you do it."

"Don't eat for three days," I mumbled around a mouthful of fish. "You'd be surprised how fast you can shovel it in. You don't even need to breathe."

"No, I mean holding pain. But your eating is impressive too."

I shrugged and tried not to glance at the twins. "It's only healing."

"It's more than that. I hurt so much I don't want to move, but you seem fine."

I kept my eyes on my fish cakes. "I'm used to it, I guess. Or Takers have a naturally high pain threshold. I don't know. I never thought about it."

"Well, you're really good at it."

"Good at it?" I looked up in time to catch his grimace.

He looked away fast and fiddled with the edge of his plate. He was really cute all shy like that. Even cuter than he was in the moonlight.

"You know what I mean," he mumbled.

"Hmm," I said, suddenly aware of my dirty hands, damp clothes, and a smell I prayed wasn't me.

He stayed quiet for a long time, slipping glances at me and looking away again. I kept eating, fighting the urge to smooth my hair and trying not to think about how much it was frizzing. When the weather was this humid, my curls puffed like a frayed rope.

Finally he said, "Are your parents Takers?"

I chewed the fish a bit longer than necessary and

swallowed. "My mother was. Grannyma too."

He nodded. "So it's just you and your da now?"

"Sister. Just me and my sister."

An understanding pause. "Did she work at the League? Your mother, I mean."

"Since she was twelve, same as my grannyma. My father was an enchanter. He worked the forges mostly, and prepared the pynvium to absorb pain. His great-grandfather staked the first pynvium mine found in Geveg."

Danello's shoulders slumped like he'd heard bad news. "You're an aristocrat."

It surprised me that still mattered. It used to, back when Geveg was wealthy and there had been a lot of aristocrats. You didn't see fishermen or farmers invited onto the Terraces. Such distinctions vanished when the war came. All had gone to fight when needed, even aristocrats. They weren't like the Baseeri nobles, who paid others to die for them.

"Not since the Duke took it all away." I gulped my coffee and singed the back of my throat. "After the Duke arrested Grannyma, his soldiers barged into our home like it was theirs, tossed Tali and me out like trash. Didn't even let us get our clothes, our toys, memories of our parents. Didn't care that we had nowhere to go. Is there more coffee?"

He stared at me, mouth half open, then nodded. "Yeah, let me get it." He poured it, got me another fish cake, and started slicing a pear. "My parents worked at the university, but they weren't full professors or anything high-pay. My ma taught fencing and military history, my da philosophy. She was killed before the war ended. Da says it was stupid for her to fight when everyone knew we'd lose, but she did it anyway.

"They kicked us out too." He set the plate of fruit down between us and eased into his chair.

We didn't talk much after that. Kinda nice really, sitting with someone who understood and could just be. Halima came in and cleared the table, then made me a bed by the window. She fussed over it like any good hostess. Even asked me if I needed an extra blanket. Jovan's brows rose a little and he glanced at his bed, so I declined.

"Good night," the children said as they shuffled into their room. The door thumped shut behind them.

Danello stared at me, rubbing the back of his neck with one hand. Foolish as it was, I kept worrying about my patched knees and mismatched socks. He didn't seem to notice, though, and he had his share of patches.

"How did you find out you were, you know, *different*?" he asked.

I hesitated, but he knew the truth already. "It was just before the war ended. I was ten, and my little sister and I were helping Mama and Grannyma treat the wounded at the League. Tali was running when she shouldn't have and tripped over a sword. Sliced her calf open bad. I saw all the blood, heard her crying, and I just grabbed her leg. I wanted it to stop, you know?" I shivered. "I'm not even sure what I did, but suddenly *my* calf hurt and she was fine."

"You healed her without any training at all?" Danello's eyes widened. "At ten?"

"Yeah. Mama always figured we'd both be Takers—it runs in families—but she kept quiet about it. She was afraid they'd take us away. She was always telling me, 'Don't try to heal, don't touch the Elders, don't get too close to the trackers.' I was so scared I'd done something wrong by healing Tali, I tried to put her pain back. And I did."

That had scared Mama a lot worse than me healing had. I could still remember the terror on her face when Tali ran up, pointing to her calf that didn't have a scratch on it and crying that it hurt funny. Mama had grabbed me by the shoulders and told me to never, ever do it again. Then she hugged me so tight I couldn't breathe, made me *swear* to Saint Saea I wouldn't tell anyone what I could do.

Until tonight, I never had. Only Tali had known.

"Was she—"

"I'm really tired," I said. I was done talking. It wouldn't change anything, and why haul regrets back into the light.

"Oh, sorry. I guess I should let you sleep then."

I fluffed my pillow and fought not to look at him again. It was a lot harder than I'd expected. "Night, Danello."

"Good night, Nya."

Another door thumped closed. His da's room. I settled into the makeshift bed's softness, my mind too full of guilt and relief to sleep, enjoying the lingering smell and warmth from the stove and the quiet murmurs of overexcited boys trying hard *not* to sleep, even though sleep would ease their pain. A quick, not-so-quiet order from Halima shut them both up. Despite my melancholy, I grinned. She was taking to her new role well. I'd forgotten how nice family felt.

Unable to sleep, I sat up and leaned my head against the window. Moonlight washed the market corner in muted silver. Dark shadows cut across the stone in patterns, darker where the pair I'd seen earlier under the bushes slept. It was a good spot, protected from the coastal breezes and usually dry.

A bouncing glow caught my eye—the gentle sway of the night patrol's lantern. The soldiers stopped next to the bushes, kicked the sleeping pair, and scared them off. The patrol didn't chase after them like most did, just continued on their way, passing a man who didn't seem concerned to be out alone at night.

The lantern rocked and a shaft of light spilled across the man's face.

Saints and sinners! My fancy man was back again. I pulled the blanket tighter around me and slumped, even though he couldn't possibly see inside the dark room. What did that sneaky reed rat want? He'd had plenty of opportunities to grab me after the ferry accident, while I was wandering and not paying attention. Danello had certainly been able to do it.

I glanced at the children's room. The twins! What if he came after me tonight and sensed them? After everything Danello had done for me, I couldn't risk putting his family in danger, but if I left now, the fancy man was sure to spot me. I hunkered down, fingertips hanging on the windowsill with my eyes peering over.

Shadows flickered, and another man stepped into the silver light. He spoke with the fancy man, who gestured up and down the street with one hand. Heads shook, fingers pointed as if they weren't sure where I'd gone and were arguing over which direction to look next. The new man nodded and leaned against the wall, watching the street with his arms folded across his chest. The first fancy man walked away and vanished into the dark.

Now there were two of them! I shivered in the dark room that didn't feel nearly dark enough to hide in. I glanced at the door, soothed by the heavy bar across the middle. Good and locked. I was safe for now, and they couldn't know about the twins. Who had sent them after me, the League or the Duke? I slid down and pulled the blanket over my head.

It didn't matter. Trackers were trackers, and I was prey.

I woke feeling like someone had shrunk every muscle in my body while I'd slept. Extending my arms hurt. Bending my knees throbbed all the way to my toes. I should have expected it. I'd hauled too many people from the water the day before to avoid it. Or maybe it was punishment for shifting pain to children. I was just as sore as if I'd slept on hard ground. Served me right. I should have told Danello no. I'd been tired and hungry before—I could have managed like I always do.

I unfolded myself, and my joints popped in the silent house, waking up hurts I'd forgotten I'd taken. I hated to admit it, but I'd probably be a lot worse off if I'd bunked under a bush. Too sore to work at all, let alone make it to Tali.

You're just saying that so you don't feel guilty.

I gritted my teeth and stretched. It didn't matter. As Grannyma said, what's done is done and I—

The too-silent room suddenly felt loud, like it was trying to tell me something. I stopped stretching and looked around, half expecting to see green and yellow silk poking out from behind the curtains, but the room was as bare as it had been last night. Except the children's door was open. My breath caught and I darted to the room, wincing with every step.

All three beds were made. No open windows, no furniture knocked over, nothing that indicated a struggle. I sighed as the clock tower chimed nine.

They were just at school. No tracker had sneaked in and kidnapped them.

Danello's door was closed, and my knuckles itched to knock. He might be sleeping, but I pictured him sitting on the small yellow stool by his father's bed, holding his hand, waiting for him to wake up, Danello's sweet, gentle smile brightening the whole room.

He'd been so kind. I could still make things right with his family. I could bring Tali here and take their pain away. If we split it between us, it wouldn't be so bad. Sure, we'd have a rough walk back to the League, but we could manage it.

Elders and wards and silk-clad trackers slid into my memory. Was it even *safe* to go to the League? I lifted one edge of the curtains and peeked out. No sight of my fancy men, but they were probably out there, multiplying like rabbits. By sundown, I'd no doubt have four of them on my trail.

My stomach rumbled and I headed for the kitchen, my eyes alert for leftover fish cakes. It looked like Danello's family had enough food and wouldn't miss one or two. I'd heard the schoolroom in this neighborhood even gave students lunch. A cheesecloth lump sat in the middle of the table with a note resting on top. I smiled at the slow, deliberate print, the ends of all the letters round from letting the pen sit too long.

Nya, here is your breakfast.
I hope it tastes good.

Inside the bundle was a feast: two more fish cakes, three pears, and a banana. I ate the fish right there and slipped the fruit into my pockets for lunch and dinner. I'd save one pear for breakfast too, just in case.

A glint in the cloth caught my eye. Three copper coins stuck in the bottom, as if someone was trying to hide them from me. I glanced at the closed door. Maybe Danello expected me to take the bundle and leave, and not find them until later.

The food and bed were more than payment enough. I hadn't done much, and I'd hurt the whole family doing it. Still . . .

I picked up a coin and ran my thumb over the etched lion on one side. A Geveg deni, not a Baseeri oppa. In the poorer districts, Geveg coins bought more than Baseer money, just to spite the Duke. Would it be enough to get my room back? Or any room? I'd share if I had to; sleep in shifts with someone who worked nights. I pocketed the money and added "go straight to Millie's and see what I can get" to my list of chores.

I glanced at Danello's door again. It was only polite to say good-bye, but my feet refused to move. He knew I was here, and if he'd wanted to see me off, he'd have been there when I woke up. My hand slipped into my pocket and rubbed the coins again. Why would he even *want* to see me? I was just hired help, and I'd been paid for my services. It was time to go.

My muscles fought me every step down the stairs, burning as if I'd run three times around Geveg. It was tempting to spend one of my coins on a pole boat to the League, but money didn't come easy and the poleman probably wouldn't take a deni anyway. Sore or not, I had good legs and feet to carry me.

I paused in the doorway, scanning every person, every bush, every hiding place in sight. No fancy men. I crept outside, staying in the crowds as much as possible. The sun filtered through a hazy sky, gray as the slate lining the League's antechamber. Puddles of water shone like mirrors on the sidewalk. I continued checking corners and bushes, but if the fancy men were there, they were hiding well; not a flash of yellow or green anywhere. Would they approach me today or keep lurking like a pair of hungry crocs?

I paused across the bridge from the League on the west side of Grand Canal. If the fancy men were from the League, then going inside was as foolish as spending money on a pole boat. Safer to get a message to Tali and have her meet me someplace a lot easier to get into than the gardens. The birthday ruse wouldn't work twice in a row.

A passing Baseeri jostled me, and my rib pain woke up bright and sharp. There'd be no running from Elders today.

So: risk going to the League, or hide and hope Tali came looking for me? Both ideas stank like bilge water.

Laughter from the League's side yard caught my attention. Wards! They played in the small courtyard facing the bay, and a set of boys were knocking a ball around with sticks. Tight bunches of girls stood near the shore talking. I spotted Enzie in a group in the middle.

I waited for another good-sized swell in the crowd and merged with them, making my way toward the League behind a man with a crippled arm. A wrought iron fence surrounded the courtyard; too high for rebellious wards to climb and go wandering, but wide enough between the bars to carry on a conversation.

"Enzie!" I waved, looking out for mentors and fancy men. It took four waves to get her attention. She saw me and froze like a spooked cat. After a few nervous glances around the yard, she scurried over.

"Nya!" She kept checking the doors leading into the League, but stood between me and the building, her hands on her hips. With the puffy sleeves she made a pretty good wall to hide behind.

"Could you get Tali for me, please? I really need her."

She looked at the doors again, a lot more fear in her eyes than normal ward-mentor wariness. "Now?"

"I'm sorry, but it's important."

A pause, then a quick nod. "Okay, but stay out of sight. The mentors are clingy today. Something has them arguing and hovering over us worse than mosquitoes."

More missing apprentices? She dashed off before I could ask. I moved away from the fence, to avoid any mentors who might pop out to check on the wards. It was possible someone might spot me from any of the dozen or so windows. I hoped they didn't look out much.

I kept an eye on the League doors and windows for a while. Too many towers to watch. Tali used to gush about the spires at each of the four corners, even drew me pictures of the intricate leaf patterns carved into the stone along the tops of the pillars. Mama had loved the dome and the way it looked like it was floating over the building. She said the tall, wide windows underneath the dome gave that illusion. Papa had liked the arches, and there were plenty of those. Arches over the windows, the doors, the hallways. Looked like the whole League was stretching up to grab the sun.

Though I tried not to, I looked at the wing where the Luminary's office was. It had the best view of the city, overlooking the lake and the mountains along the shore. Sometimes when Mama had been too busy, I used to sit on the floor in that office, my face against the glass while Grannyma worked at her huge desk. People hadn't been scared when *she* was Luminary.

"Nya!" Enzie raced toward me, and her worried expression said it wasn't good news.

I limped back to the fence. "Did you find her?"

"No, no one's seen her."

The fish cakes turned to rock in my belly. "She wasn't on rounds? Or in her room?"

"No." Lip trembling, Enzie reached through the bars and grabbed my hand. "And I couldn't find any of her friends either. I asked some of the round's leaders about Tali and they said she's fine, but they didn't tell me where she was. And they looked nervous that I asked."

The door banged open and several mentors dashed out. Their dark heads swiveled back and forth over the courtyard. Enzie gasped and squeezed my hand tighter.

"I don't believe them, Nya, not anymore. She vanished, she and the others." She glanced at the mentors again. "You'd better vanish too!"

FIVE

"Wait!" I called after Enzie, but she was already running away, hiding herself in the mass of green with the other wards. Two mentors herded them up while one cut through toward me. He wasn't one of the old ones I could outrun. I limped for the safety of the sidewalk crowd, weaving between fat refugees and skinny day workers. I tripped over a waddling two-year-old and nearly splatted on my face.

"Watch it, 'Veg!" the mother snapped.

"Sorry!" What had I done? The fancy men were supposed to be after *me*, not Tali. How could they have snatched her from the League? The League had real guards with solid Baseeri steel weapons to protect it. Folks couldn't just vanish!

Vada's gone. . . . The fourth apprentice to vanish this week. . . .

I stumbled again, but caught myself on a farmer with a basket of bananas under one arm. He glared and shook me off.

Apprentices were disappearing from the League. Tali made five. For the love of Saint Saea, how could five apprentices go missing in one week and no one notice? Breath caught in my throat, and I ducked behind a pillar past the edge of the League's fence, out of sight from a pair of soldiers. Maybe the Elders *had* noticed and couldn't do anything about it. The Duke could keep them quiet if he wanted to. Was he stealing Geveg's apprentices and sending them to Verlatta?

Oh, Tali!

I risked a look back. The mentor was shooing the last of the wards inside the League.

My chest tightened and I understood how a reed rat felt, squeezed in a python's coils. All my skin flashed hot, then cold. It was my fault. I'd led the fancy man right to Tali. He must have followed her back from the gardens, snatched her before she got to the League. He was even at the League yesterday morning! Probably picking his targets, finding apprentices who would be easy to kidnap.

"Where are you?" I muttered, staggering away from the fence. He had to be close—he'd been close since yesterday, watching me.

I stood in the middle of the bridge between the League and the basic-goods shops, turning a slow circle and scanning the edges of bushes and buildings. So what if the soldiers saw me? They weren't the ones kidnapping Takers—those fancy men were, and when I got my hands on one, I'd make him tell me where Tali was or else—and I had enough pain left to make that "or else" something to reckon with.

No yellow or green silk flashed in the bushes.

Or at the corner of any building.

Or anywhere that I could see. I climbed onto the wall of a bridge. Gray water rushed under me, while folks with nervous stares hurried past me. One of the soldiers glanced my way, nudged his partner, and pointed. My muscles gave out, and I sagged to the damp stone road. Thankfully, the soldier looked away.

"Oh, Tali." I had to find her, and my best chance to do that was to find a fancy man. It all made too much sense to be a coincidence. He *had* to be a tracker.

Aylin! Maybe she'd seen him again. All the

Baseeri went to the show house. They were the only ones left who could afford it.

I jumped down. My thigh flared hot, shooting needles down to my toes and up into my belly. I paused, letting the pain subside, then limped my way to the show house.

Aylin was there, dressed in blue with long feathers dangling off her skirt and sleeves. Her hair was piled on her head, with a few long strands left free to blow in the wind as she twirled and danced.

She smiled as I approached. "Morning."

"Tali's missing." Tears blinded me, and I wiped them away.

"What happened?"

"I don't know. I went to see her, but she wasn't there. Enzie said she was gone, and no one would say where." I kept wiping my eyes, but there were too many tears. And now my nose was running.

"Maybe she went on a heal call?"

"No, something bad is going on. Have you seen a fancy man in yellow and green silk here today? He was here yesterday, over by the pain merchant's shop. Did you see him?"

Aylin blinked at me, her dark red lips a wide circle of confusion. "A what?"

I told her about the fancy man and all his watching. About the missing apprentices, Tali's fear over Vada, and the Duke's assassins. It sounded crazy, but Aylin had lived through it all before, just as I had.

She rubbed one of the two beaded bracelets she always wore. "Nya, you have to be careful. People don't follow other people for fun."

"I know that, but I have to find him."

"No you don't. You have to make sure he doesn't find you." She hugged herself and glanced up and down the street. "You have no idea what he wants."

"He wants Healers."

"Then why is he following you?"

I bit my tongue. I'd all but admitted I was a Taker, though with luck, Aylin wouldn't realize what my slip really meant.

"Because of Tali," I said. "He knows I have access to Healers. He's seen me with them."

"But he can get all the Healers he wants at the League. There's no reason for him to—"

"Aylin, I don't know!" I said, probably more harshly than I should have. I took a deep breath. "All I know is that there's a good chance he knows where Tali is. He has to tell me. I'll force him if I have to."

"If he's a tracker, you can't force him to do anything."

But I could. I snapped my mouth shut before something else stupid spilled out. "I have to find her, Aylin."

She twirled a loose strand of hair and stared upward, brows wrinkled, lips mashed. "Are you sure she isn't on a heal call?"

"They would have told Enzie that."

"Not if they didn't want anyone to know. Maybe she had to go heal someone important, or in secret—like the Governor-General."

"He has his own Healers from Baseer. And what about the other missing apprentices?"

"Maybe they didn't tell her. Maybe it's all secret."

"Three maybes don't sound like truth to me."

She put her hands on my shoulders. "Don't panic—let me ask around and see what I can find out. Maybe you're worrying for nothing."

"That's four."

"Stop that. None of this makes any sense, so we're missing something. I know a guard at the League. Maybe he knows something." She stabbed one finger in front of my nose before I could say "five." "He'll be able to get me inside either way, and I can ask around."

"Won't you lose your job if you leave?" Tough as it was for me to find work, Aylin would have it tougher. People didn't like any Gevegian who worked for a Baseeri, and even worse, the owner of the show house was the Governor-General's brother. Aylin pretended not to care, but I saw the hurt look in her eyes when folks called her names. Probably wouldn't be so bad if they'd let her work inside, where only Baseeri would see her, even if Aylin did insist she was a lot safer outside.

"I'll be fine. My lunch break is coming up. I can go early."

"Be careful."

"I'll be okay." She hugged me, and I caught a whiff of jasmine. "It's you who needs to be careful. Whoever this man following you is, he's up to no good, so stay hidden."

"But I need to talk to him."

"Not alone. Wait for me to get back, and we'll look for him together." She grabbed my face in both hands. They trembled against my cheeks. "Promise me, Nya? Promise me you'll stay out of sight?"

I nodded.

"Wait for me in the Sanctuary on Beacon Walk. You should be safe there."

I doubted it, but it gave me more time in the open to spot my fancy men.

No one had jumped out at me by the time I reached the Sanctuary. I cast one last look around before slipping inside. My footsteps echoed in the marble hall, forcing me to an embarrassed tiptoe. The low ceiling loomed above me, reminding me to show proper respect to the Seven Sisters. The builders had sure done their job, 'cause by the time the hall opened into the domed centrum, I wouldn't have spoken above a whisper if the room were on fire.

I crossed the geometric flower gracing the middle of the room—six overlapping circles centered under a seventh. The glazed tiles sparkled even in the weak light from the arched windows. Curved wooden benches radiated outward, two rows facing each of seven alcoves, in which statues of the Seven Sisters stood, staring with blank eyes.

On the left, Saint Moed had her twin swords crossed above her head, though she'd done nothing to defend Geveg against the Duke when we needed her. Beside her, Saint Vergeef had one hand in a basket of pears, the other outstretched in offering. Cruel when so many went hungry. Saint Erlice had the smug look of one who never told a lie, not even to make someone feel better.

The right side wasn't any better. Saint Vertroue planted her staff in the marble block at her feet, both hands gripping it and daring anyone to try to get past her. So much for her fortitude. Many had passed her, and she'd never once pulled her staff from the stone to stop them. Saint Gedu patiently leaned against her alcove, clearly in no hurry to save anybody from anything. Saint Malwe smiled modestly, lids and eyes cast down as if embarrassed to have folks worshipping at her feet.

In the center of the six was Saint Saea, hands open as if apologizing. The mother of mercy, the grannyma of "sorry it had to turn out this way," the one who made you think that this time it would be different.

Saints and sinners, this was the creepiest place in Geveg. All those blank eyes watching and judging you, even though *they* did nothing when people needed help. I couldn't help but wonder what they saw in me.

I grabbed a seat by Saint Saea between an old man with far too much hair in his ears and a box of water-soaked prayer books. Shame, 'cause I could have used a prayer.

So I made one up.

Please let Tali be okay. Please let her be off at a heal call, standing in the bedroom of a snooty Baseeri aristocrat who thinks he's too good to go to the League. Please let me be wrong about the fancy men.

Uneven footsteps echoed behind me, and I glanced over my shoulder. No fancy men, just a bent and twisted woman who had no reason to think the Saints cared. Another dumb soul like me, hoping for answers. If she could remember her prayers, maybe *she'd* find some. I closed my eyes and the murmured words of others drifted to me, gentle reminders of what I used to say when I was small, and Tali smaller.

Saint Saea, Sister of Compassion, hear my prayer.

Nothing else came. I sighed and prayed from the heart.

Bless me with the wisdom to find Tali. Guide me to a fancy man who . . . who knows what I need to know. Give me the strength to choke it out of him if I have to.

I winced. Maybe I should have asked Saint Moed that part.

The polished white face of Saint Saea kept staring over my head, making sure no one walked into the room too loud. Footsteps rose, then fell quiet again.

And still she stared.

"You never listen," I mumbled, sliding forward to kick the statue where her shins would have been. It left a muddy green-gray smear on her marble robe.

The hairy old man harrumphed at me and scooted farther down the bench.

I hung my head, hands in my tangled hair. Why had I let Aylin go to the League? She wasn't going to find out anything Enzie hadn't, and she might get into trouble herself. If no one outside the League noticed missing apprentices, they sure wouldn't notice if one dancer vanished.

My guts said only one person could tell me where Tali was, and if I couldn't find that yellow-green sneak, then I'd make sure he found me. He'd seen me near Danello's home, Aylin's corner, and the boardinghouse. I'd keep making circles between them until he showed his blank-as-a-Saint's face, then confront him. Demand to know where Tali was. Make him take me to her.

More footsteps tap-tap-tapping. And tapping . . . and tapping . . . like everyone in the room had suddenly up and left.

I lifted my head and glared at Saint Saea, who was doing a piss-poor job keeping her Sanctuary quiet.

Someone sat down on the bench next to me. Yellow and green flickered at the edge of my vision.

Saints and sinners, she *did* listen!

It was the second fancy man, the one from last night. This close he was even fancier, his black hair stark against the colorful silk. Pressed silk too, and not a speck on it, despite the rain and muddy puddles.

"Are you Merlaina?" he asked.

For a moment I blinked, confused. Oh! Merlaina was the name I had given the Elder yesterday morning. So even though they'd found me, they didn't know who I really was. I lunged, muscles screaming protest, and grabbed a handful of perfect silk.

I shoved him down on the bench. "Where's my sister?"

"What? I don't know—get off me."

Shocked gasps and worried cries drowned out the echoing footsteps as the few remaining folks ran

from our scuffle. I had to threaten quick. Some-
body was bound to get their wits back and go find a
patrol.

"Tell me where she is!"

"I don't know what you're talking about." He
shoved back, lifting me off the bench like a sack of
coffee beans. He grabbed both my arms tight, and
my eyes watered. "Settle down, girl."

He loosened his hold on my arms. I twisted and
gripped his now-mussed silk shirt. He grabbed my
wrists this time, but I'd worked two fingers under
his sleeve and felt flesh beneath. "Tell me where she
is or else."

He paused for a heartbeat, then glanced upward
and sighed. "Stop being difficult and come with—
aarrhhcck!" he cried, collapsing as I *pushed* the last
of my pain into him. He released me and grabbed
his thigh.

"Where is she?"

I heard chuckling coming from the entrance. I
snapped my head around as Fancy Man One strolled
in. He wore red today. No wonder I couldn't find
him. "Take it easy, *Merlaina*," he said, keeping a row
of benches between us.

I backed away and bumped into Saint Saea. Her
outstretched hands fit my shoulders perfectly.

"You're safe—you don't have to run."

As if I could run anywhere with a Saint holding me down. "Where's my sister?"

"I don't know."

"Liar!"

Fancy Man Two groaned and sat up, his face pale and sweaty from the pain. "Did you see what that 'Veg did to me?"

"Quiet, Morell. I said she was dangerous." Fancy Man One smiled, but I couldn't tell if it meant humor or disdain.

"You're an ass, Jeatar."

Fancy Man One laughed, but at least now I had both their names. In the bedtime stories Mama used to read us, names gave you power over things. I could sure use a little of that.

"We have no interest in your sister," Jeatar said. "Just you."

My hot anger chilled. If they didn't have Tali, then who did?

"Now come along quietly before the patrol arrives and they find out what you can do. I'm sure both the Governor-General and the League would be very interested."

It could have been an empty threat, but it didn't seem wise to test Morell, even if he was having a hard time getting to his feet.

Despite my trembling, I elbowed Saint Saea in her cold marble gut. It was stupid, but somehow this felt like it was all her fault.

SIX

We left the Sanctuary and turned right, toward one of the richer neighborhoods. The closer we got, the more dark-haired people we passed, and more than a few shot a glare my way. Jeatar kept a hand on my upper arm, gripping it tight, but not enough to hurt, while Morell limped close by without touching me. Was this what had happened to Tali? Had they grabbed her on the way home from the gardens and threatened her with exposing me? A scream quivered in my throat, but Morell looked like he might welcome a reason to shut me up with a smack or two.

"Where are you taking me?" I glanced around, but no one would meet my eyes.

"My employer is interested in meeting you."

"Is he with the Duke or the League?"

Jeatar frowned and shot me an odd look but didn't answer.

"Does *he* have my sister?"

Jeatar sighed, and for a second I thought I saw pity there. "We have nothing to do with your sister. We simply have a job opportunity you might be interested in."

If they didn't have Tali, then I didn't need to keep gulping down my fear and playing along. Besides, this looked less like a job offer and more like a kidnapping. I stopped walking, tugging him to a halt. "So what's the job?"

"Sorry, but I'm under strict instructions to bring you in first."

"What if I don't want to go?"

"Then we'll throw a sack over your head and drag you," Morell snarled into my ear. He was sweating heavily now, and the silk around his collar was dark and damp.

I kicked him, jerking my arm out of Jeatar's grasp. Morell swung a fist at my head. I stumbled back, slipping on the wet street and landing on my butt. A few folks turned; one even laughed.

"Help!" I called. The ones who'd looked over

glanced away fast. I scrambled to my feet, legs sliding every which way like a newborn lamb's.

Jeatar picked me up, pinning my arms to my sides. He shook me once, hard, and my head snapped back. "Settle down," he whispered harshly. "I'm sorry, but it's my job to bring you in, and it will reflect poorly on me if I don't. You're not in any danger, but it's important that we not discuss the details in public."

For all his reassurances, there was only one job I knew of that started with a kidnapping, but I'd be useless healing soldiers in Verlatta. It would, however, get me closer to Tali if they *did* have her.

Jeatar continued. "I'd apologize for my colleague, but he's not my responsibility."

Apologies? Trackers were never polite, never protective, and they didn't whisper reassurances, scary as those reassurances were. Maybe this wasn't about Tali, or the League, or anything I'd considered since I'd first seen him.

"You're not a tracker, are you?" I said low so Morell wouldn't hear.

Something flickered in his blue eyes, but I couldn't quite catch it. "No, *Merlaina*, I'm not."

I hesitated over the odd way he said my "name," as if he knew it wasn't mine. "Where are you taking me?"

"Would you like to eat today?"

I blinked. It was an obvious distraction, but a good one.

"Maybe find out something about your sister?"

"Yes."

He smiled, and it almost looked trustworthy. "Then come with me and hear what my employer has to say. That's all I'm asking."

"Except you're not asking at all."

Two merchants deep in conversation nearly bumped into us. They looked up, mouths open, the beginnings of "pardon me" already coming out, then snapped them shut and hurried past, peeking back over their shoulders at Jeatar.

They recognized him! Who did he work for? The Governor-General maybe?

"Coming, Merlaina?"

Could I trust him? Did I even have a choice? If I said no, he'd drag me there. But if I could find out something about where Tali might be, it was worth the risk.

I swallowed and nodded. We walked, his hand on me like a clamp, his manner as cool as a lake stone. I hadn't been this scared since the war, though my guts said I was in more danger now.

Maybe they were mercenaries. Lots had come

at the end of the war, some for fighting and others offering paid protection to folks trying to escape. Some had stayed, protecting the Baseeri from those who'd fought even after the rest surrendered. But no one tried to fight anymore. It was too hard to rally folks when they were more worried about food than freedom.

"Are you mercenaries?"

He raised an eyebrow. No denials though. Morell kept glaring and limping, pale as milk now.

We turned down Hanks-Baron Street and stopped in front of a stone building with a high wall around it. The kind of wall you built when you wanted to protect what was inside. My guess was it was something other than the fruit trees sticking out over the top.

Jeatar opened the gate and extended his arm. "After you."

He let go of me and for a heartbeat I considered running, but if this really was about a job and they could also help me find Tali, then I had to give them a chance. I glanced at Morell, who looked minutes away from passing out. Maybe I could sneak some pain back to use if I needed to make a fast getaway. I edged closer.

"I wouldn't." Jeatar frowned and nudged me

inside a medium-sized room with shelves along two sides, like a shop.

Spices and a bitter metallic odor hit me—raw pynvium? Old, though. The smell stayed in my nose, but it didn't coat the back of my mouth like ore right from the ground always had. Objects of various sizes lined the shelves: silverware, cubes, thin rods, balls, figurines, wind chimes. Most were painted, but some had that distinctive blue I'd so recently had waved in my face. Expensive trinkets full of someone's pain, ready to be enchanted to trigger and flash.

My shiverfeet returned. "You're pain merchants." New ones too, or I would have recognized the shop.

"We work for a pain merchant, though I can't say how much longer Morell will."

Morell frowned but kept his mouth shut.

"Announce our guest before you run off to the on-duty Taker," Jeatar told him, though it sounded more like an order than a request. "I don't think it's safe to leave you two alone."

Morell limped over to a plain yet forbidding door in the back, tucked behind a slate-topped counter running almost the length of the wall.

"Why have you been following me?" I asked Jeatar.

"To make sure your abilities were authentic,

which you so helpfully confirmed there in the Sanctuary. My employer will be pleased. He was already impressed after what the boys at the League and Rancher Heclar had to say."

Saints! How could I have been so stupid? Denying it now would be just as foolish, and probably wouldn't help me anyway.

"I'm sorry we scared you, Nya," he continued, "but we had to be sure before we approached you."

He'd talked to someone besides Heclar if he knew my real name. Had Heclar told him about Danello? He must have, but I couldn't see Danello telling anyone about me. I sucked in a breath. Bahari? Maybe he'd talked out of revenge, for forcing him to take pain he didn't want. But what did *Jeatar* want? Why keep my real name a secret?

The door opened and a man stepped out, so well-dressed he made the fancy men look like refugees. Mountainous in brocaded silk hemmed with small jewels, and black hair that curled without the slightest frizz. He smelled like a forge. Like Papa. An enchanter, sure as sugar. Though I couldn't imagine this puffed and pressed man standing over the refining flames, enchanting white-hot pynvium as he shaped it into whatever would sell best.

"Is this our girl?" he asked.

"Yes, sir." Jeatar stepped aside. A twitch of distaste flashed across his face. I guess even rich folks didn't like their bosses sometimes.

"Merlaina, please come inside and sit down. You look exhausted." The enchanter wrapped an arm thick as a tree trunk around my shoulders and led me through the door. Wealth dripped from beaded tapestries lining the walls and pooled in carpets thick as pudding. "Sit, sit. Jeatar, bring her some tea, would you?"

That same request-as-an-order tone.

I sat on a couch so soft I almost disappeared into it. "Why am I here?"

"I'd like to offer you a job." He smiled. "I find myself in need of someone with your skills."

"I'm not an assassin."

His eyes went wide and he gaped at me for a moment, then laughed. "Quite the imagination, hasn't she?" he said to Jeatar, who was returning with my tea. Again, the flicker. That quiet disapproval sent my nerves twitching more than Morell's threats.

"Sugar?"

"Yes, please."

He spooned it in and stirred. "No, dear, I don't

need you for anything so crass," the enchanter continued, handing me my tea, then reaching for his own glass. "I need a Taker who can transcend the limits of pynvium."

"That doesn't make any sense."

"It means to rise above—"

"I know what *transcend* means, but what good is a Taker who can't get rid of her pain?"

"You misunderstand. I'm not concerned with getting rid of it, only shifting it." He grinned and sipped delicately. "Although I have more mundane requests we can discuss later, my most pressing need is for a client whose daughter was injured in last night's accident. The child is dying and the League can't help."

The twins' pained faces flashed through my mind, and I shuddered. "Then I can't do any better. Their Takers are trained Healers; I'm not."

"I didn't say they didn't *want* to help. They *can't* help. They're out of pynvium."

The glass slipped in my hand and tea spilled on my shirt. No pynvium? That was impossible! They had the huge Slab, big as a bale of hay. Something that big could hold the pain of hundreds. . . .

"The ferry accident," I whispered. "They used it all up? How could they use it all up?"

"They're expecting more, but my clients can't wait for a new shipment to arrive. Their little girl will be dead by then."

Not just the child. How many had been injured last night? How many were injured every day? What would folks do if they knew healing was unavailable? Panic for sure, possibly even riot. Maybe worse than the food riots when the Duke's soldiers had first captured the marsh farms and tried to starve us into surrender.

Bile stung my throat. Was that why Tali wasn't on rounds? She'd been healing last night. What if she wasn't able to dump the pain before the Slab filled up?

"Merlaina?" The enchanter rapped his knuckles on the table. "The girl?"

"You . . . you have to have some pynvium left, right? Why can't your Takers help?"

He glanced at Jeatar and cleared his throat. "My pynvium shipment is also en route, delayed due to the Duke's recent interest in Verlatta. I don't have enough on hand for this kind of healing. Just a few scraps really, hardly good for anything but holding a few broken bones."

The cold tea I'd spilled on my shirt seeped through to my skin, but I was already chilled. That explained their secrecy and why they had kidnapped me. If folks thought I could help, they'd be on me like barnacles on a boat. Still, Jeatar could have been less scary about it. As long as he hadn't lied about getting information on Tali. "So they want me to heal their daughter and shift the pain to them until the League gets resupplied."

He laughed and my weak calm vanished. "Oh, no, dear, not at all. They have *another* recipient for the pain in mind." He stood and motioned me up. I set my glass down on a table worth a year's earnings and followed.

We stepped into yet another room. A small, dark-haired girl lay on a table to one side, her limbs bent and bloody, her skin gray. Beside her, a silk-draped woman sobbed into the shoulder of a man dressed even finer than the enchanter. He looked up as we entered.

"That's her?" A flash of disgust rose above his despair. "Did she agree?"

An untidy blond man stood behind them, clutching a worn fisherman's cap in his hands. A weed in a vase of flowers.

Every street-honed instinct said I should run as fast as I could. Baseeri aristocrats didn't associate with fishermen, not unless they wanted something they couldn't easily take. This man had only one thing to give.

"Dear, this lovely family is willing to pay you thirty oppas to heal their daughter and shift her pain to that man there."

Everything after "thirty oppas" was a little fuzzy. I could work six months straight and not earn that much. If I did this, I wouldn't have to worry about looking for work while I searched for Tali.

I glanced at the fisherman. Faded cap, faded pants, faded shirt. Were they paying him or forcing him to do this? "I don't know. . . ."

"You told us she'd do this, Zertanik," the father cried.

Zertanik the enchanter held out his hands, bobbing them like he was putting out a fire. "Give her a moment—we did spring this on her. Dear, the child is dying. This is no time for waffling."

"She just wants more money. Fifty oppas."

I bet they heard my gulp in Verlatta. *Fifty* oppas! With that much I could *hire* someone to look for Tali and have enough left over to last me months. Still . . . "I'm sorry, but this isn't right. He won't be able to work after I shift the pain."

"He's being well paid, dear," Zertanik murmured.

Maybe, but it felt all wrong, like they were buying us the same as any other sack of goods. "I have no idea what that much pain will do to him."

"But we *do* know what it will do to *her*," the mother wailed. The father hugged her, patting her back.

"You'd let our daughter die?" he said, glaring as if threats would convince me. The guilt was far more likely to.

For the love of Saint Saea, this wasn't my fault. It wasn't up to me who lived or died. I had my own family to take care of, and Tali was all I had left. "I'd do it if you two took some of her pain. Spread among three will be easier to bear until you can get a League Healer to heal it."

The mother cried out again, this time sounding horrified. The father looked at me like I had asked him to eat a live mudsnapper. "Us? We have important obligations to the Duke, young lady. Obligations we can't fulfill if we're bedridden."

A pinch of my guilt vanished. No wonder they thought their daughter's life was worth more than a fisherman's. Just like every other Baseeri aristocrat who'd thrown families out of their homes when the Duke's occupation began, ensuring we'd behave ourselves and not interrupt his flow of precious pynvium. Hard to rebel when you were scrambling for food. I folded my arms across my chest. "Sorry, the answer is no."

Voices exploded. The father yelled, the mother wailed, Zertanik hollered over everybody. For a moment, he succeeded in forcing calm, and a small voice rang clear in the room.

"Please? For me?" said the fisherman.

So much sadness in his words I almost cried. "You don't know what you're asking."

"I do. Please, miss, I lost my boat a few months back. I can't get work no more and my wife is carrying our fourth child." He tipped his head toward the parents. "They offered to pay our rent for a full year if I'd help them. My oldest boys have been scraping barnacles since they was six, so they can get work while I'm down. And they can fish, so we won't go hungry."

Saints no, I didn't want to do this again. "You could die."

He nodded. "I know. Either way my family has a year to get back on their feet. We could sure use that right now."

I looked at the dying child and her family. The enchanter and my fancy man. Jeatar looked hesitant, his unreadable eyes on the dying child; then he leaned over and whispered into Zertanik's ear. The enchanter's eyes flared wide for half a breath; then he nodded.

"Dear, if you do this, I'll ask my sources at the League about your sister. My contacts are *very* influential."

Five faces stared at me, all hopeful, but for different reasons.

"Please, miss," the fisherman said again in that soft voice.

He was trying to save his family. They were trying to save their daughter. I needed to save Tali. This wasn't so different from helping Danello and his family, was it?

My guts still said no, but fifty oppas! And I didn't even have to dodge crocodiles to get it.

I nodded, and the mother started sobbing again. I placed my hands on the child and tried not to think about the fisherman's chances. It was hard once I felt how injured she was. How injured *he'd* feel once I healed her and shifted all that pain to him. It wasn't real injury anymore, but could so much pain kill?

"You're sure?" I asked the fisherman. "This is"—I glanced at the parents—"bad."

"I'm sure."

I turned to Zertanik. "Do you have another cot or table?"

He flicked a hand at Jeatar, who slipped out and returned with a cheap vendor table like the shop-keeps used at the market.

"Put it next to her," I instructed, "with me in between. I'll need to do this at the same time." Though they didn't deserve the sparing, the fisher-man did, and I didn't want to say the child was so injured that I didn't think I could hold her pain long enough to shift it. Some things folks were better off not knowing.

I put one hand on each, gritted my teeth, and *drew*. Agony raced into my arm, cut across my chest and down my other arm, faster than I'd *drawn*, like it wanted out before something caught it. Bright specks flashed around my eyes, shifting to red, pale at first, then darkening, tinting the room. Then the pain poured into the fisherman, and nothing I tried would stop it.

Struggling to stay on my feet, I blocked out his screams and thought of Tali.

Jeatar set a damp cloth on my forehead while Morell mopped up my puke in the front hall. I'd almost gotten his shoes in my rush for the door, but that didn't make me feel any better. Jeatar had carried me to the couch after I'd emptied my stomach, and even lying down, I felt the room wobble.

"Feeling better?" he asked, real concern on his face. Morell glared at me, but he looked better, so there had to be a little pynvium somewhere if they were able to heal him.

"Some." The fisherman had finally stopped screaming. I'd tried to keep some of his pain, but it had poured through me fast as the Cyden River and I couldn't dam it. Closest I'd ever come to feeling death, and the poor man had to live with it now. *Please, Saint Saea, let him live.* "What's going to happen to him?"

"Zertanik made arrangements to get him home. He'll be taken care of."

"He can't hold that much pain for long. Even if you only have a few pynvium items left, take some of it from him, please. It was so much worse than we thought. He can't take it." My stomach rolled again.

"Easy." He put a steadying hand on my shoulder, but I spotted doubt in his eyes. He masked it quick. "In a day or two the pynvium shipments will arrive and we'll buy the pain from him."

"How can you be sure the shipments are even going to get here?" He couldn't promise anything with Verlatta under siege.

Jeatar glanced at Zertanik's door. "He pays very close attention to those things. Don't worry, the fisherman will be fine."

He wouldn't be fine. Who could be fine with all that pain? Enough to kill a child, maybe enough to kill a man. I closed my eyes, but that made it easier to see his agony. I opened them again. This was all for Tali. I could stand it if I remembered that. "He'll ask his sources about Tali?"

"I'll make sure he does, I promise."

"When will you know something?"

"There's not a lot of information coming out of the League right now. Might take me a day or two to hear something."

Would the fisherman still be alive then? What had I done?

The door opened and the Duke's rich couple walked out, the sleeping little girl clutched in her mother's arms. The father reached into his pocket, then dropped a handful of coins on my chest. I flinched, but they didn't burn. They should have after what I'd done to earn them.

Ten oppas.

I sat up and they slid down into my lap. "You said fifty."

"You didn't help her for us—you did it for that

man and for yourself. You're lucky I gave you anything at all." They stomped out of the building and slammed the door shut behind them.

Jeatar frowned in disgust. "They should have paid you double," he muttered.

"I have to get out of here." My shirt suddenly felt too small, keeping me from taking more than tiny, shallow breaths. I pocketed my coins quickly, not wanting to touch them longer than necessary. "Find me the instant you hear something about Tali."

"Where will you be?"

I hesitated. I had no home anymore. Would he even keep his promise, or would he trick me like the Baseeri had? "I'll find you. I'll come back every day."

He glanced again at the door to the fancy rooms. "No, don't come back here. Send in a note and I'll meet you somewhere. You pick."

"I will. I need to go."

"You should rest longer."

"I can't stay here."

Zertanik appeared as I started for the front door. "Well, dear, your attitude was certainly uncalled for. Those people offered a fair price for a service only you can provide, and you treated them most terribly. I hope that doesn't happen next time."

Jeatar cleared his throat. "Sir, I don't think we should—"

"Nonsense, she's a natural."

My heart banged against my chest. "I'm not doing this ever again."

"Think of all the money you could make."

"Yeah, ten whole oppas." Papa used to say principles were a bargain at any price, and I'd sold mine for cheap.

He frowned and smoothed his sleeves. "Well, they *were* a bit stingy there at the end when you refused to help. If you'd been more agreeable, I'm sure they would have paid more."

I grabbed the front door latch, but he snatched my arm and stopped me.

"We have other clients willing to pay dearly for this service."

"No."

"You'd never go hungry again. You could get a place with your own washroom."

My old house flashed through my mind. A room of my own, two washrooms, rooms for eating and cooking and sitting by the fire reading. A yard out back, small but ours. Without Tali, without family? Meaningless.

How had I been stupid enough to think this was

real healing? Real healers didn't hurt people. Ever. Blood rushed in my ears, but not loud enough to drown out the screams in my head. "I'm not doing this ever, ever again."

"Oh, I'm certain you will, my dear. Not a doubt in my mind." He smiled like a man who knew things I didn't.

I yanked my hand away and pushed out the door, running as fast as my quivering legs would go.

SEVEN

I got as far as the bridge before I stumbled against a
wall. The street swirled around me, and I sagged
to the ground.

Something cold touched my head. I looked up,
and the usual afternoon rain tapped my forehead.
Just a drizzle. Saint Saea's crocodile tears.

What if the fisherman couldn't handle the pain
until more pynvium arrived? What if he died? What
if I'd *murdered* him? I couldn't breathe.

I squeezed my eyes shut. He had *begged* me to
do it. He knew the risks, and he was willing to take
them to save his family.

You didn't argue all that hard.

I clamped my hands over my ears. I *had* argued.

I said it was wrong. I said no. They didn't listen. And he *begged* me!

Was it worth it?

To find Tali? Yes! I sniffled, wiped my nose on a damp sleeve. Jeatar insisted the new pynvium shipment was on its way. The fisherman would be fine once it got here. Everyone got what they wanted. No one was forced to do anything.

Is having no choice the same as choosing?

I shook the thought away. He begged me. They begged me.

Cold washed over me, then hot, then blackness. Cold again, and hardness, rough against my hip and shoulder. I opened my eyes. The world had shifted sideways.

No, I was slumped over. Fainted? I'd never fainted before, not even from hunger. I sat up, my body sore, my skin clammy. It stung a little as the rain dripped on it.

People looked at me as they walked by, some in pity, others in disgust. One woman started to move closer, concern on her wrinkled face, but three Baseeri soldiers came over the bridge and she scurried away, her head low. The soldiers didn't even glance down.

No one was going to help me stand up, let alone

save Tali. Certainly not a Baseeri, and not even one of my own people. They were all too scared they'd get noticed, too scared to raise a fuss, no matter how small. People who got noticed got hurt. People who fussed, disappeared. That was just how things were.

We'd heard the same stories from those who'd escaped Sorille before the Duke had burned it to the ground, and by the time the Duke was done with Verlatta, they'd understand it too.

I took a few deep breaths and things steadied. I could do this on my own. I would find Tali and together we would save the fisherman. I struggled to my feet and started back toward the Sanctuary. I was nearly there when a hand landed on my shoulder.

I screamed and turned around, braced for soldiers or worse.

Aylin yelped and threw her hands in front of her face.

"Saints, Nya! I thought I told you to stay hidden."

"Aylin, I'm such a horrible person." I clung to her, sobbing on her already damp feathers.

"No you're not. What happened?" She leaned her head away and wrinkled her nose. "Were you puking?"

I covered my mouth and nodded. "I did something terrible. I—" Couldn't tell her without telling her I was a Taker. Not without getting her involved in this more than she already was. I still didn't know who had Tali and couldn't risk Aylin getting kidnapped as well. "I stole ten oppas from the charity box at the Sanctuary."

Her worried frown twitched at the corners. "You need it more than anyone I know. You're not a bad person."

Yes I was. Monstrous. But money and information could help me find Tali, and I needed both. "Did you find out anything?"

"A little, but I don't think it's much help." She glanced around. "It's too open here. Let's go to Tannif's, and you can buy us coffee with your stolen wealth while we talk."

Tannif's was crowded, stools and benches along the walls crammed with people. Baseeri were seated at the larger tables with padded chairs. Aylin managed to grab us a small table in the back near the door to the kitchen. Every time a serving girl swished by, scents of coffee and fried perch wafted out.

"Tell me everything," I said, hands tight around a mug of coffee. My first hot meal in months was cooking in the back. The money felt tainted, but I couldn't find Tali if I was half starved. Common sense saves more lives than swords, as Grannyma used to say. *And liars and thieves are never happy.* I shoved *that* thought away.

"My friend said the Elders have been carrying a lot of people away from the main treatment rooms. Somewhere higher inside the League, but he couldn't see exactly where the stairs led past the second floor." She leaned in closer across the table. "Nya, he swears every person he saw carried upstairs was wearing green."

"Apprentice green?"

She shrugged. "He wasn't sure, but he thought so."

"Did you talk to any Elders about Tali?"

She scoffed. "They wouldn't talk to me, but I found a few fourth cords who said Tali quit because it was too hard. They said she went home."

Fear stole my hunger away. "That's a lie."

"I know, but they believed it, so someone they trusted must have told them that." Aylin looked around the coffeehouse. "Nya, I asked the son of one of the show house regulars about the people being carried upstairs. He's a guard at the League, and he didn't seem that worried, said the *Luminary himself* told him they were exhausted because the ferry heals were so draining. They were just being taken somewhere to rest."

The Luminary was lying? It shouldn't have surprised me, but it did. He had a lot to hide. No pynvium, so many injured, apprentices being carried upstairs and not coming back down.

Saint Saea be merciful! They *couldn't* be. . . . No, it was too unthinkable . . . but . . .

What if they were healing without the pynvium? If there'd been more injuries like the little girl's, folks so close to death the pain leaped right out of them, the apprentices wouldn't have been able to stop it. I doubt even the Luminary could have stopped it. Was that why he wanted more Takers? Because he couldn't get any pynvium and needed more bodies?

How could the League do that to them? The apprentices couldn't know. No one would agree to that if they knew.

The fisherman did.

Not Tali. She wouldn't sacrifice herself to help a Baseeri aristocrat.

"Aylin, I think the Luminary is using apprentices as pynvium," I whispered, hardly believing anyone could be so horrible. "When they can't heal anymore, he's taking them upstairs and out of sight."

Aylin's eyes went wide. "What are you talking about?"

I told her what I'd learned at Zertanik's, and her eyes went even wider.

"I have to get Tali out of there. I have no idea how much pain she's taken or how long she's carried it. A day at least. Probably since the ferry accident."

The serving girl came and thunked our perch and sweet potatoes on the table. I gave her one of my oppas and she handed back my change. Wasn't much, but I could get another meal for it. She scowled at Aylin and walked away. Aylin picked up a few chunks of potato that had rolled off and set them back on her plate. It never seemed to bother her when folks treated her badly for working for a Baseeri.

"I have to go," I said, rising.

Aylin gripped my arm and held me down. "No, you have to sit and eat. You can't lay siege to the Healers' League without food in your stomach. Eat. Now."

"But—"

"No, be practical about this."

I ate fast, speaking between bites. "Can your friend get me inside?" I doubted I had time to wait for Jeatar to get back to me.

"I don't know—I can ask. Nya, you'll need more than that to get to Tali, though."

"I'll figure that out when I get inside."

"No, you won't. You'll get caught and thrown out—if you're lucky. If not, you'll get arrested. Or worse." She lowered her voice, even though the chatter in the room was loud. "Do you think they want people to know there's no pynvium?"

"No. There'd be panic."

Aylin nodded. "Bad as anything in the war. Maybe even more riots."

"I *have* to get inside somehow."

"If they're doing this, they'll never let you in. It's amazing *I* got in. They started turning people away as I was leaving. Have you seen the crowds in League Circle?"

"Then I'll wear a disguise. I'll steal some clothes. Something green. Can you make me look like an apprentice?"

Aylin hesitated only a heartbeat, then squeezed my hand. "Come back to my room. I know exactly what to do."

I'd forgotten how nice a bath felt. By the time Aylin finished scrubbing me with the floral soap she splurged on, I looked almost respectable. Her room was next door to the washroom, and some of the steam crept in through tiny cracks in the walls.

"I appreciate the help, but what about your job?" I asked, combing out my wet hair. "You can't still be on lunch break."

"I told them I had a family emergency."

"What if they fire you?"

"Then I'll find a new job."

She made it sound so easy. But then, that was just her way. We'd met scrubbing out the bilge on a Baseeri skiff two years back. Taking work from a Baseeri bothered me a lot more than the smell had, but Aylin smiled her way through the job and even made it fun. The owner liked her so much, he recommended her for more work. I didn't get the same offer, but then, I'd made it pretty clear how I'd felt about Baseeri.

"Here, put this on." She pulled a simple yet pretty white dress off a line strung up in one corner and tossed it at me. Six more dresses bounced on the line, and she had two clothes baskets on the floor underneath. "I don't have any green vests, but it should get you inside."

"They're not going to let me walk upstairs just because I'm clean," I said as I pulled the dress over my head. My voice sounded muffled through the cloth.

"You're realizing that *now?*"

I frowned at her, but she was right—I had no idea what I was doing. A plan simmered, though, and I just needed a few more ingredients to make it palatable.

"I *can* get your hair right," she said, opening a jewel box on a small table by her bed and pulling out a green beaded necklace. She snapped the string, spilling beads into her palm. "Hmm, not exactly League green, but close enough. No one's going to be looking that closely at your hair anyway."

The beads sparkled like hope. "Tali has three uniforms. If I can get to her room, I can change into one and look like any other apprentice. I'll get there just after classes have let out, so I should be able to blend in."

"And then you can go wherever you want! Great idea. Better hope they don't ask you to heal." She flinched as if sorry she'd mentioned it. I'd let slip once how jealous I'd been of Tali getting into the League when I couldn't, and she probably figured this was harder for me because of that. She grabbed the hair iron heating on the stove. "Let's straighten out those curls, shall we?"

Steam hissed as Aylin tugged my hair into shape. I tried to remember the fastest route to Tali's room. I'd go in through the north gate for sure—or maybe not—the skinny guard might recognize me and I needed to look like an apprentice. West gate then, with the public, and I'd blend in with folks wanting heals. I could do this. I could make it to Tali's room. And after that? I needed a plan I didn't have.

Aylin held up a mirror. "You look perfect."

I looked like Tali. Tears blurred my vision. I caught myself before I wiped them on Aylin's dress. I blinked them away instead. She tied a white scarf around my fake Healer's ponytail, beads and all.

"Thank you, Aylin."

She flashed a grin, then solemnly pulled the two bracelets off her wrists. "Take these."

"I don't need jewelry—I'm good enough."

She grabbed my hands tight. "They have pynvium beads in them. I painted them to look like regular beads, but they'll trigger if anyone grabs your wrists hard. They won't flash a *lot* of pain—I couldn't afford the ones to knock someone out—but these'll sting hard enough to make them let go so you can run away."

"Aylin, I—"

"Take them." She slipped one on each wrist. "Healing is big money. People kill to keep big money. If you're right about what they're doing to the apprentices, think about what they'll do to hush *you* up."

I was trying my best *not* to think about that. I hugged her, focusing on the badly framed landscapes all over her walls to keep from crying. "Thank you, Aylin. Thank you so much."

She clung to me, trembling. "You be careful. You're the only real friend I have. You know that, right?"

I didn't, though I probably should have. "I'll be careful."

She wiped her eyes, smearing dark streaks across her cheeks. "Okay, let's go."

"What? No, you're not going."

"Who's going to introduce you to my guard friend?"

"No, I changed my mind. You're right about the danger, and I won't risk getting anyone else in trouble if I'm caught. I have to go alone."

She bit her lip but nodded. "Good luck. Saint Moed be with you."

"Thanks." I needed all the courage I could get. "I'll be back soon with Tali."

She smiled, but it was forced. Like she never expected to see me again and didn't want to think about it.

I turned before I started crying again, and headed for the League.

Seven Sisters, hear my prayers, 'cause I'll need every last one of you to get my *sister back.*

EIGHT

The League had never looked so *mean*.

Like an arched cat, hissing and spitting. A bold crab, claws at the ready. A mama croc, guarding a nest full of eggs. And I was the one about to poke it with a stick.

I tugged my damp scarf down over my hair and drifted into the people flowing toward League Circle in the softly falling rain.

The main door loomed ahead. Had it always been so high? So wide? It swallowed me with a half dozen others, and we milled in the antechamber. The usual shafts of late-afternoon sunshine from the dome's windows were nothing more than pale gray light today, veiled by the rain. Bleak light.

Bleak mood. Bleak chances.

But not as bleak as Tali's if I couldn't get her out.

I held my breath past the soldiers, but none looked at me. I waded through the battered and bruised people hoping for heals, not one of them aware that if the League let them in, it would cause some poor apprentice more pain than she could handle. If screaming the truth would've saved anyone, I might have hollered to the cliffs, but I'd had enough reminders lately of what desperate people were willing to do.

Slinking right, I headed down the hall toward Tali's room. A dark-haired League guard leaned against the doorframe, looking bored. His interest kindled as I approached.

"Excuse me," he said, "but this area is restricted."

In the eternal pause between heartbeats, I mustered my best smile and most of the confidence I'd faked at Aylin's. "I know, and thank you for keeping my room safe." I almost winked, but it might have come off looking like a nervous tic.

"You live here?"

"Since last Moedsday." I took a step to pass, but he moved and blocked my way. Did all guards have broad shoulders? Must be all that rapier thrusting.

"Can I go now? I'm already late for rounds."

"I don't recognize you."

"I'm new." I tossed my head so the beaded braids slid over my shoulder.

He hesitated, his jaw working as if chewing it over. "Where's your uniform?"

"In my room." Oh, for the love of Saint Saea, all that work and I was going to fail *here*? Tali deserved better than a sister with a half-simmered plan.

"So you went out earlier?"

"Exactly."

He smirked like he had me. "Then why didn't I see you leave? I came on this morning—*early*, and I've been here all day."

My mind flailed faster than a spooked chicken's feet. "I wanted to watch the sun rise" wouldn't work. Why would a girl be out before light? At least an apprentice girl—an ordinary girl would—

"Listen." I stepped in close and glanced around as if looking for Elders. Which I was, but not for the reason I wanted him to think. "I didn't come home last night," I lied. "This boy I know lost his mother in the ferry accident and needed comforting." All dressed up, I looked old enough to go sneaking off to meet a boy. I hoped.

He stared back for three agonizing heartbeats;

then a sly smile cracked his face. He looked me up and down and nodded. "Be careful with that. The mentors'll boot you if they catch you."

"They won't catch me." Saints willing.

"Hurry up then." He stepped aside, and I forced myself not to run all the way to Tali's room.

I ducked inside and collapsed on her bed. The shakes started, and it took me a good five minutes to get my courage back. Should've taken less time with so many reminders of Tali all around me, but being in a room she might never see again scared me more than any guard I'd ever crossed.

Nerves finally steadied if not calmed, I stripped out of Aylin's dress and into Tali's white uniform. It was too short, and tight around the waist and hips, but the green vest hid it well enough. I folded Aylin's things and hid them in a drawer in case anyone looked into the room.

I left, trying hard not to sneak, and strolled toward the treatment ward. After a few odd stares from various first and second cords, I picked up the pace. An apprentice late for rounds wouldn't be strolling.

The general treatment ward looked just as I remembered as a child, when I'd helped Mama on her rounds. I hadn't done much—held some towels or small bowls of warm water for cleaning up blood—but I'd felt important. It was the life I'd hoped to have, back before I discovered my dreams were hopeless. The room looked smaller now, maybe 'cause I was bigger. Beds were arranged in neat rows with gauzy curtains hung between them for privacy. Most of the folks who came here were mildly injured or sick, or couldn't pay as much as a full healing required. The rich and the really hurt ones were taken to private rooms.

I turned and headed that way, sweat dampening the hairs along my neck. I hadn't been in one of *those* rooms since Papa died, killed by one of the Duke's soldiers a few months before the war ended. Mama had tried to save him, but by the time the other soldiers in his unit had gotten him to the League, he was gone. No one ever told us where Mama died; they just returned her in a box, like some unwanted gift. Baseeri men were running the League by then, helping to squash the last of our rebellion.

Closed doors lined a hall almost as intimidating as the Sanctuary. At the end, wide stairs spiraled up and into shadows. I grabbed the copper handrail and took a step closer to where I hoped Tali would be.

"You there!"

I froze, fingers tight against the cold metal, then took another step. Maybe he wasn't talking to me.

"Apprentice! Get down here—you're needed in the ward."

I turned, mouth open, but couldn't think of a single believable reason to refuse. A short, bald man with six gold cords on one shoulder and two silver ones on the other stared at me. A Heal Master.

"Now, girl." He folded his arms across his chest. "We have injured waiting."

Saints save me! I walked over, and he took me by the back of the neck. Not hard, but like someone used to herding disobedient apprentices around. He guided me back into the general treatment ward and stopped between rows of beds. Four beds had people on them, some sitting, some lying down, all injured.

"What's the first step in determining an injury?" He spoke in a teacher's voice, and probably wouldn't take kindly to me answering wrong.

I swallowed, but my mouth was dry. "You, uh . . ." My hands hovered over the woman on the bed. Well-dressed despite the rips and bloodstains on her clothes.

The Heal Master's toe started tapping.

"You put one hand on the head and one on the

heart, to feel the extent of the injury."

He nodded and the tapping stopped. "Go on."

I glanced down at the patient. She was awake, and though her eyes were glassy and unfocused, she didn't look too badly hurt. I placed my hands on her and sensed around inside, like Tali had taught me. "Bruised ribs and skull, no breaks."

"Any bleeds?"

Bleeds? Tali'd never taught me how to feel for bleeds. "I, uh, can't tell."

"Did you pay *any* attention in class?"

He put his hands over mine. A faint tingle slid through me, passing into the woman underneath. The bruises became brighter, sharper in my mind. Then something else, a dark spark, like spots behind your lids after you stared at the sun too long.

"Do you see it? There, along the base of the cranium?"

I did. "Yes."

His hands pulled away, and the spot dimmed. I reached for the spot again, and it blazed. A guilty giddiness bubbled in my chest. Tali learned things like this every day. Real healing.

"Are there any others?" The Heal Master sounded pleased, and I almost smiled.

"I don't see any."

"Then proceed."

"What?"

His disappointed frown returned. "Heal the patient. Internal bleeds are closed same as external."

He really wanted me to heal! I could run, but then I'd never get back in, never find Tali. He'd stared at my face long enough to know me if he saw me again. Since I had to pass right through his domain to get back to the stairs, he'd sure as sugar see me at least once more.

I moved my hands over her ribs and *drew*. Then to her head. Closed the small bleed at the base of her skull but left the bruising. The bleed would have killed her, but she could live with a headache for a few days.

"Done." I pulled my hands away, my head and ribs throbbing a little.

He put his hands back, then frowned at me again. I cringed. "You missed one."

"Sorry." I took the bruise, accepted the shame. If I'd really been an apprentice, would he have kicked me out of the League for such a mistake? Probably not.

It didn't matter. If I *had* belonged here, I wouldn't have left the bruise in the first place. I'd have been eager to prove my worth, and to impress him I would have mentioned the knuckleburn I sensed starting around her hands and toes.

But I didn't belong and never would. For the first time in my life, it didn't hurt to say that. If I belonged, I'd be locked in a room somewhere with Tali and no one to help either of us.

"Now, what about this gentleman?" The Heal Master took my elbow and led me to the next bed. I didn't need to touch the patient to see both arms were broken. I couldn't help carry Tali with aching arms.

"I can't."

"Can't?" His eyebrows arched higher than the windows. "Are you refusing to heal a patient?"

An apprentice at the next bed jerked up and stared at me, horror clear on his pockmarked face. He sure didn't know what was going on here or he wouldn't be so quick to judge.

"No, I . . . um . . . I . . ." Couldn't stay there because I had to save my sister. Not something that would get me out of this or help Tali. "I don't feel well."

The apprentice glared, his spiky black hair puffed around him like a sooty dandelion. The Heal Master flicked his hands out as if he'd had enough of me. I could only hope.

"A Healer's job is to heal, girl—otherwise you're just a useless Taker, fit for nothing but filling some half-pure pynvium spoon with pain. I know it's scary, and it hurts, but if you want to make your first cord, you'd better remember what we endure to help others. Or maybe you're not strong enough to mend bone?" He said it like a challenge. I bet it worked on the boys every time, chased away their fear so they could do their jobs.

"I, uh . . ." Two Elders walked in, each scanning the room like soldiers on watch.

The Heal Master grabbed my hands. I gasped, and a cold tingle shivered all over my body. He harrumphed and let me go, but a flicker of appreciation flashed in his eyes. "You're plenty strong. You could make a good life for yourself here if you wanted it."

Words I'd wanted to hear my whole life, only now they had no value.

One of the Elders walked over, and my heart stuck in my throat. It was the same one I'd kicked when I was Merlaina. "Problems, Heal Master Ginkev?"

"Oh, no, not at all," The Heal Master twitched and flashed an uncertain smile. "First-time jitters, I think."

"She refused to heal the patient, Elder sir," the

151

apprentice said, butting his pointy Baseeri nose in where it didn't belong.

"Refused?" The Elder glanced at me, then doubled back and stared. "What's your name?"

"Tatsa." It wasn't really a name, but an old swear Grannyma used to use when we'd jump out at her from behind the furniture. Said it came over with *her* grannyma from the mountain folk.

He peered closer.

Saint Saea, please don't let him recognize me.

"Refusing to heal a patient is grounds for expulsion," he said at last.

"I, uh . . ." Still couldn't figure out what to say. I had some pain now. I could hit them, run up the stairs, grab Tali, carry her out past guards and Elders and Heal Masters. Please, who was I kidding?

"Oh, I'm sure once she sees there's nothing to fear, she'll be fine." The Heal Master patted my shoulder and tried to turn me away. What color had *his* hair been before it fell out? I'd bet anything it wasn't black. "Don't want to push her too fast."

"No?"

The Heal Master hesitated. "No, not one to waste here."

A smile slithered across the Elder's face. "So she's strong?"

Even my hair wanted to scream.

"She's, um . . ." He looked at me and gulped. "She's quite strong. But untrained," he added quickly.

"Perhaps I've been too hasty," the Elder oozed. "I'll reconsider your expulsion if you help us with a high-priority heal. Refuse, and you're expelled from the League. Out on the *street*."

An effective threat, if I was really an apprentice. Even a first cord would say yes and be thankful for the second chance. A job, food, and a room were too hard to come by to throw away out of fear. Of course, a real apprentice wouldn't know what that second chance really meant. I didn't have much of a choice. Tali once said high-priority heals took place "upstairs," and she'd rolled her eyes afterward, like mere apprentices weren't good enough to go "upstairs."

I guess *that* had changed.

Saying yes would get me upstairs, but if this heal was as bad as the little girl, it could fill me with so much pain I couldn't help Tali. Saying no would get me thrown out, and there was no guarantee that I could get back in. My best chance to save her was to do it now, but it would be a *huge* risk.

The Elder flashed a cat's grin. "Choose wisely."

Two impossible words.

NINE

"**A**re you a Healer or not?"

Is it worth the risk or not?

"I'm a Healer," I said, not bothering to hide the tremor in it. Scared was good. Scared meant pliable, and Elders liked pliable.

"Excellent." The Elder tapped his fingers against my back, nudging me in a direction I really didn't want to go. "The Romanels will be so pleased."

"But Elder Mancov, she's needed here."

The Elder narrowed his eyes at the Heal Master. "Surely you don't think these broken bones and cuts take precedence over serious injury?"

"No, sir. We're just so shorthanded, you know." Again the false grin. "If you could send her back this time—quickly, when she's done?"

"Of course."

We walked between beds filled with hurt, past closed rooms holding anguish, up the stairs toward agony. Footsteps tapping away the seconds I had left before I couldn't run, couldn't escape anymore, and maybe even ended up like Tali.

We stopped at a door. From this side no one would ever guess what waited behind it.

I tensed, ready to bolt up the stairs.

The Elder opened the door and pushed it inward. Three people. A man, standing to the side, and two women, lying on beds shoved next to each other.

"You said one heal." I winced. My mouth never knew when to stay closed.

"It is. Sisters. The one on the left was conscious when the brother brought them in. She refused to let go of the other sister, even though we can't help her."

"Is she dead?" She didn't look it. Pale, but not the waxy sheen of the newly dead.

"So close it doesn't matter. Brain was crushed. Nothing we can do."

A gift, *if* I was strong enough to take it. I glanced up the stairs. Tali was up there, somewhere, and I needed a way in. What better way than with a personal escort? I looked back at the sisters, clinging to each other even in that half step from death. Her sister could save mine.

I walked in, heart pounding, skin sweating, bones trembling. *Be strong for Tali.* It almost sounded like Mama's voice, but I knew better. Mama would have told me to run. Save the child she could and grieve for the one lost. Grannyma would have said to grab a chair and whack someone over the head—but she'd have said it with a proverb so it wouldn't sound so mean. Papa would have been here himself, and folks would have listened to him. He had *very* broad shoulders. I had to be all three at once.

The brother stepped forward with that same hopeful, desperate expression I'd come to resent over the last few days. "Can you save her? Can you?"

"I can."

The Elder's eyes widened; then he smiled softly, soothingly. A smile for the brother, not for me. I was nothing but walking pynvium to him. "Tatsa here is one of our finest. She'll do her best, but remember, not every injury can be healed."

"Please save her. Please?"

I blocked out his fear, his hope. I had enough of my own.

The Elder watched with waiting eyes as I placed one hand on the head and one on the heart, like any apprentice would do. I cringed a bit, and not just for show. Multiple broken bones, crushed in some places. Several bleeds, now that I knew how to sense them. Severe injuries, even worse than those of the little girl I'd saved mere hours ago.

I didn't need to check the dying sister. From here, I could see the shattered dent in her head, and the grayish-pink ooze seeping out. Amazing she wasn't dead yet. Or maybe just a mercy.

Both Elder and brother leaned forward as if expecting me to speak.

"It's bad, but I think I can heal her."

The brother started weeping; the choppy, gaspy kind where relief and hope are so great they trample over the fear. The Elder tried to hide his grin, but I could see it there at the corners of his thin mouth. *They must be paying a fortune for this.* He turned to the brother and placed a comforting hand on his shoulder.

While his back was turned, I slipped a hand under the almost-dead sister's shirt and pressed my fingers tight against her cooling skin where the Elder couldn't see it. The other I kept on the living sister's heart. I had to shift her pain into the dying sister fast, before he turned around again. A deep breath, a quick prayer, and I *drew*.

Hot pain and blinding agony raced into me. I funneled it through a small corridor I fought to maintain between sisters—a human sluiceway of hurt. Whimpers bubbled up, and I let them out as screams. No children to scare here, and the Elder expected me to scream.

One sister saved. One sister dead. I needed a better outcome for Tali.

Still screaming, I dropped to the ground and curled into a ball. Forced my fingers into claws. Made my legs twitch. Put on a good show, like the Elder expected.

"Saints have mercy!" the brother cried in horror. For that, I was glad I healed his surviving sister.

"Hu . . . hurts . . . help . . . me . . . ," I whimpered, moaned, writhed. How much was too much?

"No, no, this is normal on a heal of this magnitude," the Elder lied, hands on the brother's shoulders. Holding him back? He seemed like the kind of man who would run to my aid. "She'll be fine."

"She doesn't look fine!"

I screamed again for emphasis.

The door opened, and two boys ran in with a stretcher. Neither had gold cords dangling from his shoulders, but both had dark, glossy black hair. As did the Elder. And the guard outside the dorms, I realized with a chill. There were all Baseeri. Where were the Geveg Healers and guards?

The guards lifted me with none of the care a trained Healer would have had, and plopped me on the stretcher. I moaned again and silently urged them to hurry.

"These gentlemen will take her where she can release the injuries into the pynvium."

"Are you sure she'll be okay?"

"Good as new. Ah look, your sister is waking up. . . ." His words faded as the hired thugs bounced me up the stairs. I moaned while they grunted and panted, but hope raced through me. Wherever they were taking me, it was high, close to the top of the League, maybe even near the dome.

Please, Saint Saea, let them take me right to Tali.

"Wonder how much that one paid," the boy at my feet asked.

"I heard a thousand oppas."

For a heartbeat, I forgot to moan. *One thousand?!*

"We should demand a bonus."

"And lose this job? Not me. I like easy work for high pay."

"Bet we could get a lot more if we threatened to talk."

A dry laugh. "You think anyone cares what happens to these Takers? Nothing but war orphans. Bunch of useless 'Vegs."

I cared. If only I'd kept some of the pain. I would have made these two respect what an orphaned Taker could do, and fast. Maybe I'd even give them Tali's pain, see how much they cared when they were lying on the floor screaming, suffering like the Luminary was making Tali and the others suffer.

We stopped and a third boy spoke. "Another one? Didn't think they had any left."

"Scraping the bottom of the barrel now." The one at my feet laughed. I clenched my fists tighter. No time to teach lessons—Tali could be on the other side of that door.

"Bring her in."

The room smelled of urine and damp face powder. No whiff of Tali's lake violets and ginger. Was she here? She *had* to be here. My carriers dumped me on a squeaky cot and walked away, thumping across a hard floor.

"Hey, Kione, want to play cards later? There's a spot open."

"Um, sure. I'm through here at sunset."

"See you in a few hours then."

A soft thud and silence. No, not silence. Just a

hum so low that it mimicked silence. Moaning, quiet sobs, sniffles.

I opened my eyes. Blond hair stuck out above the blanket in the cot on my right. Tali? I squinted. No, not her. I scanned the other nearby cots for blond hair, but Tali wasn't in any of those either. Where was she? Soft light burned in lamps widely spaced along the walls, making it hard to pick out blond hair in the cots. No windows either, and only one door. But it had beds—lots and lots of beds.

Saints be merciful.

Twenty, maybe thirty beds were laid out in neat rows like a wartime triage ward. Only a few were empty. No wonder I'd seen hardly any apprentices downstairs. There couldn't be that many left. How could I find Tali when I couldn't see the faces across the room?

Footsteps echoed to my right, soft but quick. I closed my eyes again. Someone draped a blanket over me and tucked it under my chin. Snatching the blanket and tackling this person flashed across my mind, but who knew how many were in the room.

"Easy now," a girl said softly. "I know it hurts, but it'll be over soon. The Luminary will get more

pynvium and take all the pain away. He promised."
She sounded young, maybe one of the low cords.
Gentle fingers stroked my brow. "You hang in there,
you hear?"

When the girl's footsteps faded, I opened my
eyes again and searched the beds farther away for
Tali. Five blond heads had their faces turned away;
any of them could be her. Several more on the far
side of the room also looked blond, but in the dim
light, I couldn't be sure. I couldn't see anything
from this stupid cot. If Gentle Fingers would go
pee or something, then I could get up and do a real
search.

A sharp gasp split the quiet, followed by low
moaning. Footsteps tapped across the room.

"There there, go back to sleep. It's easier if you
stay asleep."

Hot anger flashed though me. How could the
Luminary do this to them? It was worse than anything the Duke had done in the war. The League
was supposed to heal folks, not hold them in agony.
Some of these people were children! They trusted
the Elders, trusted the Luminary to take care
of them when no one else did, even if he *was* just
another Baseeri appointed by the Duke. They didn't
deserve this. Tali sure as spit didn't.

The door opened again. My stomach and fists clenched. Another poor apprentice threatened into service?

"Hey, Lanelle." I recognized the door guard's voice. "Are you allowed breaks?"

She giggled. Didn't any of this mean anything to her? Didn't it make her mad enough to throw bedpans at the Elders?

"I get meal breaks."

"Can you get one now? The sun's come out and there are double rainbows over the docks. Come see."

My breath caught. *Yes! Go run off to flirt with your heartless boy.*

"I can't. They're my responsibility."

"You can take fifteen minutes, can't you? Might do you some good to see something pretty for a while. I know it would help *me*."

"I don't know."

"No one will see you. I promise."

"Well, okay, but only for a teeny weeny while. I don't want to leave them alone too long."

The door thudded shut. I leaped from the cot and ran for the nearest blond head. Not Tali. I darted for the next. . . . Still not her. Three cots up. . . . Not Tali, but a boy with long hair. Two rows over, a girl I

163

recognized, though I didn't know her name. Where *was* she?

I ran to the far wall where the shadows were the darkest. A girl's familiar nose caught my eye, but as I dropped to the girl's side, her hair was red, not blond. Hair! I glanced around the room. Not a single head of hair was Baseeri black. No wonder I hadn't seen any Geveg Healers. Even those waiting for healing downstairs had been dark-haired. Of course. The Luminary *would* use Geveg lives to save Baseeri ones. He was the Duke's man to his rotted core.

Anger heated my cheeks. Tali had to be here. I'd check every bed twice if I had to.

Another blond head in the far corner, top of the row. I knelt, found a face I knew as well as my own.

"Tali!" I cupped her cheek. She trembled, hands clenched and arms pulled close to her chest.

"Nya?" Her eyes fluttered open, and the pain shone right out of them like beams of dark light. Almost as dark as the circles under her eyes and the hollows in her cheeks.

"I'm here. I'll get you out." I moved a hand over her heart.

"No!" she cried. I stopped as she started

coughing, wincing with every hack.

"Tali, I'll take half, and we'll sneak out of here."

"You can't. . . . Too much."

"No, it's not. We can do this together."

"Look . . . for yourself."

I felt my way in, to the agony, the crushed organs and broken bones she'd healed, the bleeds and the bruises and the horror.

"It's too much." I wanted to check again, but I knew. I'd felt it, same as Tali knew and felt it. I couldn't take half. A quarter, maybe, but it wouldn't be enough to let her sit up, let alone walk out. Even if I tried to take a little, I wouldn't be able to stop the pain from pouring into me, just as it had with the little girl.

I wiped the sweat from her brow, struggled not to hug her tight. She couldn't handle the pressure on her ravaged body.

"Oh, Tali."

"Run, Nya."

"Not without you."

"You . . . can't help . . . me."

"Yes, I can. All I need to do is . . . I have to find . . ." What? There had to be a way. "Pynvium! I need pynvium."

"None . . . left."

"Not here, but there has to be more somewhere." Enchanter Zertanik's words slithered back into my ears. *Oh, I'm certain you will, my dear. Not a doubt in my mind.* Saints, he knew they were doing this. That filthy vulture *knew! Just a few scraps really. . . .* He'd dangled the pynvium carrot right in my face.

Was that why Jeatar had been at the League yesterday morning? Gathering information? Making deals? He *was* the one who'd told Zertanik about me. He'd acted like he wanted to help me, but I'd bet that wasn't what he'd whispered in Zertanik's ear. Probably a lot closer to "Her sister is one of them, sir. We could use that to control her, make her do what we want and make so much money."

And he'd been right. I was hungry enough to grab that carrot.

"Tali, I think I know where I can get some pynvium." If people were really paying a thousand oppas for a heal, they'd probably pay just as much for a shift. Maybe more. I could trade shifting for whatever pynvium he had left.

She smiled a little, and tears slid from the corners of her eyes. "Nya. Go."

"I am *not* leaving you here. I'm going to get you

166

out of here and out of pain." Even if I didn't like what I'd have to do to keep that promise.

The door opened. Two people stood silhouetted in the light. I tensed like a clock spring.

"What are you doing here?" a girl asked.

Lanelle and her boy. I couldn't help but wonder what color their hair was.

I tucked Tali's blanket under her chin, stroked her cheek once more. "Easy now, go back to sleep," I said, loud enough for Lanelle and the guard to hear. "It's easier when you sleep." To Tali, I whispered, "Hold on a little longer."

"You shouldn't be here." Lanelle stalked toward me, but she looked more scared than authoritative. She twisted the ends of her braids nervously. Brown hair, but dark. Nothing marked her as either Gevegian or Baseeri.

"I'm relieving you for dinner break," I said, as if she should have known this.

She gaped, worked her open mouth a moment, then snapped it shut. "But that's not for an hour."

I shrugged. "I came early. Didn't want to be hanging around in the ward in case they chose *me* for some priority healing, you know?"

Even in the dim light, I could see her pale two shades. "I know. Okay. I'll be back soon."

"Take your time. Not like they're going any-where."

She glanced at the guard waiting by the open door. Light kept him in silhouette, masking his face and features. "Thanks," she said. "I owe you."

Yes, you do.

And I knew how to collect that debt. The only question was when.

When Lanelle returned from dinner, I told her I'd be back to relieve her at breakfast, right after the rounds bell. She thanked me again and didn't even look up as I left. The door guard winked at me. Gevegian for sure. He was even cute, with wavy blond hair and big brown eyes, but inside he was ugly as a half-eaten rat. Traitor.

"You have a good night."

Though it would have ruined everything, I wished I could grab a chair, or even a bedpan, and whack him a good one. Maybe being with Lanelle was punishment enough. Leaving Tali with those two twisted my guts into knots, but I needed pyn-vium and help to get her out of there, and I had only until morning to find both.

Sneaking out was a lot easier than sneaking in. With everyone at dinner, only the guards and a few cleaning staff wandered the halls. Most of the apprentices were locked away upstairs, so the dorm halls were mentor-free. I retrieved Aylin's dress without anyone knowing I was there, tucking it under my arm like a wrap in case the night grew cool. The hall guard gave me that same knowing smile as I left, and warned me not to stay out too late.

I went to Aylin's first, the last of the sun's light slipping below the horizon before I got there. Work was done for most folks in Geveg, but my day wasn't over yet. Seemed like weeks had passed since I'd woken up at Danello's, though that had been only this morning. I wouldn't be getting much sleep tonight.

"It was awful!" I collapsed in Aylin's arms and hugged her as tight as I'd wanted to hug Tali. "There are so many of them, and they're all in such pain, but that's not even the worst part. The Luminary is only hurting apprentices from Geveg."

She swore one even *I* hadn't heard before. "Someone needs to feed him to a crocodile. Did you find Tali?"

I nodded, though I couldn't bear to describe how she looked. "She's bad, real bad. I need pynvium or I can't get her out."

Aylin paled. "How are you going to find any?"

"I'll buy it."

"Nya! You don't have that kind of money."

"I know." My guts said I wouldn't be buying it with money anyway. *Oh, I'm certain you will, my dear. Not a doubt in my mind.* He'd drawn me in like a fish, tricked me into doing exactly what he'd needed. And all for profit. "But I have to try."

"I have a little saved up—I could—"

"No, Aylin, you've done so much already. I'll be okay. You have to trust me on this."

She hesitated, then nodded. "What are you going to do?"

"Don't worry about it."

She frowned but didn't push it. "Is there anything I can do to help?"

"Your friend at the League. Can I meet him tonight? I'll need his help in the morning." And maybe a stretcher, but I'd seen one in the corner not far from Tali's bed.

"I'll try. He works sunrise to sunset, so he's probably off now. I should be able to convince him to talk to you."

"I'll meet you at Tannif's in three hours."

"Three hours. Right." She hugged me again, and I sniffled.

I changed out of Tali's uniform and back into my own clothes, then left Aylin's small yet comfortable room, a hollow gnawing in my guts that wasn't from hunger.

I headed for Zertanik's. The rain had stopped, and the damp streets shimmered orange in the setting sun. In the darker corners, the stones seemed to bleed. Zertanik didn't care about the apprentices, but he did care about how much money I could make him. That had to buy me something.

His imposing wall and fruit trees appeared ahead, and my courage slipped. Would Tali really want me to do this? Trade her pain for someone else's?

"Nya?" A small voice came from the shadows ahead.

"Halima?"

She stepped out and ran to me, throwing her tiny arms around my waist. "I found you! I found you!"

"What's wrong? Is it Danello? The twins?"

"All of them." She looked up at me with those giant brown eyes, red around the rims. "Come quick, Nya. You have to come quick."

I glanced at Zertanik's shop and the League's brightly lit dome rising above its roof in the distance. I was running out of time, and who knew how long it would take me to get enough pynvium to save Tali? "I can't right now—my sister really needs my help."

"So do my brothers." She sniffled and grabbed my shirt, pulling me closer. "I think they're dying, Nya, and I don't know what to do."

TEN

No! It couldn't be true. Curling into a ball and crying 'til dawn wouldn't help me, but it sure sounded like a good idea. "Halima, they can't be dying. The twins barely took any pain." But Danello had. A lot of it.

"They hurt. Danello won't wake up unless you shake him really hard."

"Where's your da?"

"Working double shifts so we can get them healed at the League."

I winced. Without pynvium, those extra shifts wouldn't help. "Halima, I can't right now."

"You have to! You put it there. You can take it out."

I glanced at the clock tower in the market square, the face still visible in the setting sun. I had to meet Aylin and her friend at the coffeehouse in a few hours. Danello's house was a fifteen-minute walk from here, back toward Tannif's. Tannif's was half an hour from there. Not enough time to check on them, unless I stopped on the way back.

I dropped to one knee and placed a hand on each of her shoulders. "Halima, I need you to wait right here until I'm done."

"They need you now."

"I know, but so does my sister, and I can't help both at once. I *have* to talk to someone here first, then we'll go straight to your brothers."

I never should have shifted their da's pain. Was this really better than being pegged out and on the street? What if she lost her brothers? Who would take care of her while her da was working?

I hugged her. "I'll be right back, I promise."

"Okay." She sat on the first step of the shop next door, arms wrapped around her small knees. We'd had a puppy once that used to wait on the front steps for us to come home from school. He had that same look in his eyes every morning when we left.

I walked into Zertanik's shop, one of the few places still open that didn't serve food or drink. A well-aged blond woman looked up from behind the counter. Another traitor. She smiled a shopkeep's grin, fake as the jeweled trinkets the merchants sold in the summer.

"Can I help you?"

"I need to speak with Zertanik."

"I'm sorry, he's unavailable. Is there anything I can do?"

"Tell him Merlaina's here."

Her smile vanished, and she jumped up like her seat was on fire. "Wait here."

I did, my stomach sour, my mood more so. Tali's face flashed through my mind, but Danello's sweet smile floated in as well.

The woman returned. "This way, please."

I went into the same opulent room, this time lit by blue and yellow glass lamps flickering in the corners. Zertanik sat in his chair, smug as sin.

"How lovely to see you again, dear. The braids look quite fetching on you."

"I need pynvium." I also needed to smash all four of those pretty lamps over his head, but that would have to wait.

He grinned, but I couldn't tell what was behind it this time. "Pynvium is rare now, dear. How much are you willing to pay for it?"

"I have nine oppas." Plus the three deni Danello paid me, but here all that would get me was a laugh.

He laughed anyway and I squirmed; a lizard under his paw. "I could get nine *hundred* for what I have left. Probably more."

Not that he'd sell it. It was more valuable as a carrot. "Who do I have to heal?"

"Does it matter?"

It didn't. I wasn't a real healer, but I was good enough for the pain merchants. Good enough to save Tali. That was the only thing that *did* matter. "How much pynvium do you have?"

His eyebrows shot up. "My my, now who's the greedy one?"

"How much can it hold?"

"*They*, dear, and not much. The pynvium's not pure. It's not even molded, useless for sale. Nothing but a box of chunks left over from the forge."

"How much?"

"A small injury each, I'd say. You'd need two for a broken bone, maybe four for a crushed organ."

Four broken bones, two crushed organs, and a bleed for Tali. Three ribs for the twins. One leg and an arm for Danello. Multiple cuts and bruises for all of them. Thirty at least. Thirty-five to be safe.

Tali might have other injuries I couldn't see, like how I couldn't see the bleeds before the Heal Master showed me how to find them.

And the fisherman?

I couldn't think about him right now. "I get the pynvium equivalent of what I heal. I want three dozen pieces total."

He barked a laugh. "Three dozen? Dear, I don't know if there's that much in the entire scrap box."

"Check. I'll wait." But not for long. I had to get to Danello's while I still could.

Zertanik lifted a bell on the table beside him and clanged once. A door opened and a small man scurried in.

"Sir?"

"Count the pynvium scraps and bring me the total, please."

"Yes, sir."

Zertanik stared at me, his fingers drumming slowly on the padded arm of his chair. "And what could you possibly want with all that pynvium? More than I expected you'd ask for."

"More than my sister needs, you mean?"

He chuckled. "Such a smart girl. You should come work for me. I can always use smart people."

"I think I'm being used enough."

"Temper, temper. This is business, dear, and negotiations are always challenging."

"I don't like your business."

"Such a shame. You're uniquely suited to it."

The servant reappeared. "Sir. I counted thirty-three pieces, sir."

Close enough.

"Will that suffice?" Zertanik waved the servant away.

"I'll need it all tonight. Line up your vultures and I'll be back in—" I totaled the runs between Danello's, Tannif's, and here, leaving enough time to work out a plan for tomorrow—Saints, it would be after midnight before I returned. Would people be willing to come here in the middle of the night? "Three hours to do the heals."

"Done." He stood and offered his hand. I shook it, wiping it on my pants afterward. He grinned at that and gestured toward the door. "Think about my offer, dear. I could make you rich."

He probably could. After all, he'd already made me a monster.

Halima and I hurried through the silvery darkness to her brothers, our way lit by the moon above and corner streetlamps bathing the evening-shift soldiers in yellow light. To keep my mind away from the big things, I focused on the little ones: Halima's scuffed shoes, shop-door jingles as the last of the shopkeeps locked up and went home for the night, muddy flower beds. Brighter yellow lamps glowed in the League's dome, a lighthouse for the lost and hurting. A prison for the forgotten.

Little things weren't working.

"Halima, when did they start getting bad?"

"This afternoon. Jovan and Bahari were sick at school so they sent us home."

Less than a day. Maybe this was how their bodies adjusted to the pain. Maybe it was all perfectly normal. Maybe they'd be better by morning. Too many maybes. I was starting to sound like Aylin.

We hurried up the stairs and inside. The twins sprawled on their bed, faces pale, eyes wet. Jovan offered a faint grin as I approached. Bahari wouldn't look at me.

"How are you two doing?" I put a hand on Jovan's head. Cool and damp.

"Don't feel good," he muttered.

He didn't to me either. The rib pain bubbled inside him, but I sensed others things that shouldn't have been there. His blood felt wrong, but not like a bleed or a crushed organ. It felt . . . almost thick. His heart beat too fast, his breathing was ragged.

Bahari fared no better. In this, they were also identical.

If they were a few years older, they'd be able to handle the pain better, but their talents hadn't developed enough to help them yet.

I turned to Halima. "Where's Danello?"

She took me to him, and I bit my lip to hold back the gasp. Danello lay still as death on the bed, his skin beyond pale. His fingers twitched in time with his panting. I'd swear he'd lost weight. My heartbeat skipped, and I rushed to his side.

"Danello?" I brushed damp hair off his forehead and felt my way in. Same thickness in his blood, and his liver seemed wrong. So did his stomach, with dark blotches almost like bleeds splattering it.

Halima tugged on my sleeve. "Is he gonna die?"

I didn't want to say yes, but I couldn't say no. "I hope not."

"Take it back."

"I can't, not yet. Tomorrow, early." Saints willing. I'd done this to him. To them. *Please, Saint Saea, give me time to fix this.*

She sniffled. "Promise?"

"I promise." If I wasn't arrested, or killed, or locked away in a high room with too many beds and not enough conscience.

I gave Danello's hand a gentle squeeze and ran down the stairs and back into the street. Even the big things couldn't distract me from my guilt—the families huddled in doorways, folks with stretchers heading for the cemetery, the hungry eyes watching me, noting my League braids—none of it blocked out the horrifying truth.

Oh, no. Shifted pain must kill if it doesn't get healed right away. Even worse—it killed them fast. And I'd just agreed to do it for thirty-three pieces of pynvium.

I stumbled, catching myself on a fence. Or had I already fallen? How many would Zertanik bring me tonight? How many lives was I willing to trade for Tali and Danello? For Jovan and Bahari?

I glanced toward the Sanctuary, though I couldn't see it in the darkness. *Saint Saea, I don't have the right to choose. Please tell me what to do.*

She didn't answer. I hadn't expected her to, but it would have been helpful.

Mama had told me never to shift again. I'd thought she just didn't want me to get caught by the trackers, but was there more to it? Had she known it would kill? Had any Healer known?

I pushed off the fence before soldiers grew wary enough to question me and continued to Tannif's, searching my memories for Grannyma's advice. One kept jumping out. *She who has a choice has trouble.*

An aromatic cloud of roasting coffee wafted over me, and a second bit of wisdom echoed in my ears. *Don't fear what you can't change.* But I could change this one. I could tell Zertanik no. Tell him shifted pain killed. I didn't know why it thickened the blood and organs, but it did, and they had to believe me. None of the folks who accepted their loved one's pain were likely to survive until more pynvium arrived.

If I said all that, five people died, one I loved, and the others—my stomach went tight just thinking about losing them, even though I hardly knew them.

I shoved the thought away as I pushed into Tannif's. Few people were there this late. Aylin was sitting in the back, across from a blond boy with broad shoulders. She looked up as I hurried over, but he didn't turn around.

"Thank you so much for meeting with me—" I gushed, then dammed my gratitude quick. "You're Lanelle's boy!"

He gaped at me. "Do I know you?"

I stabbed a finger at him. "*This* is the boy who told you he *thought* apprentices were being carried upstairs?"

"Wait a minute—"

"Yes, this is Kione. Nya, why are you yelling at him?" Aylin glanced around and smiled nervously. "People are staring."

I plopped on the bench beside Aylin and lowered my voice to what I hoped was a threatening growl. "This *friend* of yours lied to you. He was standing guard outside the room they're holding Tali in."

"Kione? Is that true?"

"Of course not!"

"I saw you there when I relieved Lanelle for dinner."

"Oh." His pretty brown eyes darted for a way out faster than a trapped rabbit; then he smiled. I'd bet my nine oppas that grin had never failed him before. "I was trying to help, Aylin. I told you as much as I could without getting into trouble. You know I can't give away League secrets."

Aylin snorted. "How stupid do you think I am? You brag all the time about your League secrets."

He laughed uneasily. "Some things you can't talk about. What do you think the Luminary would do if I talked about"—he glanced around—"*that*. Tukel said he was going to tell, and he wasn't on duty this morning. I bet he lost his job."

Or worse, though Kione didn't act as if that thought had occurred to him. Probably better for me that it hadn't. I doubted he'd help at all if he knew the real dangers.

I gripped a fork so tight it bent. "'Another one?' I quoted him. "'I didn't think they had any left.' Sound familiar?"

"Hey . . ." Confusion wrinkled his face. "How did you know . . . you weren't there. . . ." His eyes lit up. "You were on the stretcher?"

"I heard every word!"

"And you're calling *me* a liar? You tricked League Elders to get inside. I should go to the Luminary right now and report you."

Me and my big mouth. Anger felled more fools than sticks. "If you do, I'll tell him you left your post to go watch rainbows with Lanelle."

Aylin put a hand on each of our arms. "Stop it, stop it. This isn't helping."

"Sorry, Aylin," said Kione, sliding off the bench. "I'm not going to listen to anything she has to say."

She leaned across the table and grabbed his hand before he could walk away. "Kione, please. This is serious. Her sister is one of the apprentices in that room. She's trying to help her."

"Her sister's in the *League*, for Saint's sake. She has the best care she can get. I'm sure they'll find whatever disease is causing this."

I jumped up and stood in the aisle, blocking his escape. A few people looked over, but I didn't care. "Disease? Is that what they told you?"

He shrugged, eyes flicking to Aylin, as if he didn't want to admit he didn't know everything he claimed.

"Those apprentices aren't sick. They're dying because the Luminary is using them like pynvium."

"What? Why?"

"There's no pynvium left, Kione." Aylin's soft voice floated up between us. "The Luminary is lying to us all."

He went pale, and that can't be faked. His mouth opened and closed as he sat back down.

"That can't be true."

"It is." I pushed my hair back and sighed. "I need to get Tali out of there, and I need your help to do it."

"Me? No, I can't."

"I need help carrying her out. There's a stretcher in the room. We can carry her out the side gate and take her to Aylin's."

He shook his head. "I'll lose my job."

"She'll lose her *life*."

He flinched. "This isn't my fault."

"No, all you did was look the other way while they did it. How many apprentices are up there, Kione? How many did the Luminary use and toss away?"

"Thirty maybe, in that room."

His pause yanked the heat right out of me. "In *that* room?"

"It's the largest one, but there are two others. Maybe fifteen people each. Mostly second and third cords who were healing at the ferry site. Elder Mancov said the disease came from the Verlattan refugees, and that's why so many got sick so fast." Kione leaned closer. "You're saying that isn't true?"

Sixty people. Two thirds of the League at least, if not more. And I'd bet every last one of them was born in Geveg.

"No," I said, voice tight, "it's not true. There is no disease."

Aylin gasped a sob and covered her mouth with both hands. "Kione, you have to help us."

"I can't!"

"But we have to stop him."

"You can't take on the League—that's insane."

"Can you continue to do nothing?" I asked softly. It was about more than just saving Tali now. I had to get her out for the others, the sixty who didn't have a sister willing to do anything to save them. I couldn't accuse the Luminary on my own. The Governor-General would never listen to a homeless, useless Taker about what the Luminary was doing. He might listen to Tali, a credible League apprentice who'd been through it. Who'd escaped it. If the Governor-General listened, he might stop the Luminary and demand enough pynvium from the Duke to save the rest.

If, if, if. Just as bad as maybe.

But there was hope there as well. The governorship of Geveg may have been a reward for ending our rebellion, but even I had to admit the Governor-General had treated us fairly ever since, Baseeri man or not. Besides, he'd have quite the riot if word spread that he'd let his pynvium run out and his Healers die, and the Duke wouldn't stand for that. He might even march his soldiers our way after he finished with Verlatta. He'd done a lot worse to the folks in Sorille when they refused to stay quiet.

Kione just stared, his jaw clenched.

"Can you continue to do nothing?" I asked again.

"I'm not risking—"

"I'm not asking you to. When I show up just after sunrise, will you do nothing when I walk in, no matter what I'm carrying?" If I couldn't get Tali out, I'd have to take the pynvium *in* and risk an Elder sensing it. Thirty-three pieces probably filled a mighty big sack.

Aylin shook her head. "You can't go back in there alone."

"Kione? Will you?"

He wiped the sweat off his upper lip and nodded. "Yeah. I'll even go in a little early and keep Lanelle at breakfast long as I can, but that's all. I'm not crossing the Luminary for anybody."

"Thank you."

He scoffed and rubbed his palms on his thighs. "If you get caught, you don't know me."

"Fair enough."

He slunk away without another word, not even a look back. As Grannyma used to say, sometimes you had to kill a cow to save the herd, but did I have the right to do it? I ordered coffee to keep me awake a few more hours, and enough supper for

Aylin and me. There was still time before I had to leave for Zertanik's and make a choice for those who couldn't.

I prayed I was making the right one.

ELEVEN

"Punctual as well as smart," Zertanik said as the clock tower chimed midnight. He held the door open for me and I walked past him, leaving my conscience on the porch. It curled up next to my principles.

The front room was empty, save for the same blond woman, who counted oppas in neat stacks on the counter. An awful lot of stacks.

"This way, dear." We slipped in the same door as before. The same softly lit room and out through the servants' door. The same hall I'd walked earlier. The same room where I'd sacrificed a fisherman to save a rich man's daughter.

They were the only things that felt the same.

"You know this will kill them," I said. "The

ones who take the pain."

"Speculation."

"People I shifted to are dying. The fisherman might already be dead. These folks need to know that before they agree to this."

"If any leave, there won't be enough healing for all that lovely pynvium you want."

I swallowed my objections. "How many are there to heal?"

"Nine."

Acceptable losses. The war had taught me all about those.

"Let's get started then. I haven't got all night."

Zertanik grinned, and for a horrible second I thought he might ruffle my hair. "As you wish, dear."

He brought them in like guests at one of the Duke's balls.

"The Jonalis. The husband broke both legs, and they'll be dividing it among the four uncles.

"Kestra Novaik. She'll be taking her son's crushed shoulder this evening.

"The brothers Fontuno, paying an undisclosed amount to this young lady who prefers to remain anonymous."

Most were Baseeri, which made it easier. Two

looked Verlattan, who had probably traded every-thing they'd escaped with for this. Those were harder. One family was Gevegian, and I really wanted to tell them to run.

I didn't. Instead, I *drew*. I *pushed*. I tried not to look at their faces, but every heal started with my hand on their foreheads and their hearts. Pain in the eyes of one, fear in the eyes of the other. Each stared at me, then looked away. I didn't want to think about what they saw.

A snapped back. A shattered hand. Hurt after hurt slid through me. Chunk after chunk of pyn-vium plinked into a bag near my feet.

"The Mustovos, with their son and, well, some-one whose name isn't important."

Two men in night-guard's uniforms carried in a man dressed not as fine. His wrists and ankles were bound, and a rag flopped from his mouth. They'd kidnapped someone off the street?

Shiverfeet raced down my back and out the door, leaving me numb. "What's going on?"

"Number seven, dear. Wensil Mustovo suf-fers from multiple knife wounds and a severe head injury."

"No." I pointed at the bound man. "He didn't agree to this. I didn't agree to this."

"You agreed to the heals. You never specified the terms."

"I'm *not* shifting into anyone who didn't agree to it." That was no better than cracking a stranger over the head and stealing his money to *buy* pynvium. No, worse, it'd be murdering him for it.

I folded my arms across my chest. "I'm not doing it."

The Mustovos watched me without the tears and the wails expected of worried parents. No one had gotten *knifed* on the ferry. Whatever this man had done came after, and he'd grabbed his own thorns.

The father leaned closer to Zertanik. "Corraut promised us you'd cover this until our pynvium arrived. That was the deal. I'm not giving you the boat if—"

"We'll work it out—no need to get hasty." Zertanik patted him on the arm, then turned back to me. "Dear, you agreed."

"Not to this. Not to those without a choice." I had maybe twenty-one pynvium pieces in my bag. Was it enough to save Tali, Danello, and the twins? Save them all?

It had to be. "I'm done." I grabbed my bag and slung it over my shoulder.

"Dear, this is unprofessional." Zertanik placed

his hand on my arm, a lighter touch than hands that big ought to have. "The Mustovos are doing a *lot* for this heal."

"Then pay them back." I shoved past him. The light touch turned to steel on my arm.

"We had an agreement. Other people have agreements with me based on your cooperation. You simply cannot change your mind."

I'd be a fool to miss the threat in his tone, but I was a fast learner and he'd taught me well. "We agreed to the pynvium equivalent of what I healed. I haven't taken anything I didn't earn."

"We agreed on thirty-three pieces."

"Consider me on sale." I yanked my arm away and slammed the door behind me.

I'd managed to grab a few hours' sleep, but my fingers were shaky as I wrote Danello's address on a scrap of paper in Aylin's room. The sun was just starting to rise, so if Kione kept his promise, he'd be showing up to take Lanelle to breakfast soon.

I handed Aylin the address. "If I'm not back by midmorning, fetch a Taker from one of the pain merchants for him and the twins. I have the pynvium for it now, so they can't turn you away this time. Pick one of the ones on the docks, not the fancy ones the aristocrats use, and *definitely* not the new one near the market."

Aylin shook her head, her face suddenly pale. "Not the pain merchants, Nya. You can't trust them."

"Right now we can't trust the League. The merchants are Danello's only hope."

"They'll probably kill him, and his brothers."

The anger and fear in her voice made me pause. Aylin rarely ever got annoyed, let alone angry. "It'll be okay, I promise."

"No, it won't!" Aylin bit her lip and looked down at the handful of pynvium chunks I'd given her. The smallest was walnut sized, the largest big as a tangerine. "What if they *don't heal* them?"

"All they have to do is take the pain. Any Taker can do that."

She looked at me in horror. "You don't care if the injury isn't healed?"

"Aylin." I groaned, frustrated. I didn't have time for this. "They're not really injured. The pain they're carrying is from their father."

"That's not possible."

"Yes, it is," I said.

"What do you mean?" Aylin stared at me, and though I'd spent my whole life hiding what I could

195

do, lying to her now would end our friendship. "I . . . uh . . . shifted it into them."

"You did *what*?"

I explained the whole thing: the chicken rancher, the ferry, the desperate plea in a moonlit alley. Aylin's eyes got bigger and bigger, and her anger grew with them.

"How could you not tell me?" She paced in her small room, fists balled at her sides. "I *knew* you were hiding something about that tracker. That's why he was following you, wasn't it? It had nothing to do with Tali or the Healers."

"Um . . . well . . ."

"You'd better tell me you *healed* their father." From her expression, if I hadn't, she'd have probably smacked me with a chair.

"Of course I did. Aylin, what's wrong?"

"They killed my mother," she said softly, squeezing the pynvium tight. "She was at the market, waiting for those stupid rations they made us beg for. Some men beat her up because she wouldn't give up her space in line. We didn't have enough money to go to the League, so I took her to a pain merchant. He said he healed her, that she was all better, but he lied." She closed her eyes, and tears slid down her cheeks. "He took her *pain* away but left the parts that were hurt. She didn't even know. Just kept getting weaker and weaker, and then she was gone."

"I'm sorry, Aylin." I sat beside her and gave her a hug. I felt guilty, but I couldn't stay there comforting her. "I really need to go. Will you find a pain merchant if Tali doesn't show up?"

She nodded and sniffled. "Won't you need these for Tali?"

"I have enough for her to fill." *Please, let me have enough.* I got up and wrapped the now-lighter sack to look like a bundle of clean clothes from the laundry. It was still bulky, but at least it made it easier to sneak into the League.

"Where did you get so much?"

"I bought it."

"Not for a few oppas you didn't." She rolled the chunks around in her hands. "This has to be worth a fortune."

"It's worth three lives, Aylin. Two of them children's."

"How did you—"

"Later. It's almost sunrise. Do my braids look right?"

She checked and nodded, looking a lot more like her old self. "A little frayed, but fine."

"Tali will need food when we get here." I handed

her three oppas. "Buy enough to last a few days."

"This is too much for a few days' food."

"I need you to stay here and wait for Tali. You'll miss work. The extra should cover it."

She chewed her bottom lip as if she hadn't thought about that. "Thanks."

"Thank *you*." I hugged her. She smelled like coffee. "Remember what I said about Danello. Don't forget about them." *And don't run off and sell the pynvium yourself.* I didn't mean to think it, but it popped in there anyway. Aylin wasn't a bad person, or a desperate one. She'd do as I asked, despite her distrust of the pain merchants, even with a year's rent, food, and maybe even a new dress in her hands.

I hoped.

"I won't."

"I'll be back in a few hours. I'm getting Tali out this time if I have to carry her past the Luminary on my back."

Sunrise cast Geveg in pale gold. I hurried along with tavern cooks and kitchen mistresses on their way to market 'til the street forked, then crossed the bridge and found myself alone except for the always-present soldiers. League Circle was unusually empty of the hurt and hopeful. Maybe they'd all been turned away yesterday and had accepted there'd be no healing for a while. Except for those willing to pay a Duke's ransom through the back door.

Of course, no one else knew that part; otherwise there'd be lots of people here, shouting and waving rakes and fishing poles, or whatever weapons they could find. I'd seen such anger before. *And* seen how little it mattered.

I pulled the white scarf off my head and shifted the "laundry" to my hip. Just a simple apprentice returning with her clean clothes. I'd put Tali's uniform back on, so the gate guard nodded with little more than a glance and yawned. I nodded back and walked through the gate.

Without people in it, the antechamber seemed twice as big, my footsteps twice as loud. I struggled against tiptoeing. Apprentices didn't need to sneak into their own house, but I stepped as lightly as I could anyway. Past the guard outside the dorms. Through the treatment ward, down the hall of closed doors, and finally to the stairs that led to Tali. I grabbed the rail and started to climb.

"Where are you going?"

Oh, for the love of Saint Saea, did they have people watching these steps? I turned. A stern-faced woman stood at the base of the stairs, four gold cords coiled on her shoulder.

"What?" I asked.

"That way's restricted."

"I'm relieving Lanelle for breakfast." I tried to look bored, look normal, look like this was the most natural thing in the world for me to do.

"What's your name?"

"Tatsa." I winced. Did they keep records about who they sent upstairs? "I'm running a little late. Lanelle must think I forgot about her." I chuckled and waved a hand toward the upper levels. "Can I go now?"

The reasonable request battled with whatever lie the Elders had told everyone about letting folks up the stairs. Her brows wrinkled and she glanced around.

"No one told me Lanelle had a replacement." The clock tower rang seven, its bell sharp in the quiet morning. "Come with me while I verify this with an Elder." She glanced down the hall, then grabbed my wrist.

Whoomp. The pynvium beads of Aylin's bracelet triggered under the pressure and flashed. My wrist and hand tingled, but whoever had enchanted the beads had done a good job. The pain flashed up and out, over the fourth cord's hand.

She yelped and snatched her hand away, staring at me with wide eyes.

"Why do you have—"

I tackled her, leaping off the stairs like a frog from a tree. She squealed as I knocked her to the floor; then her cry shifted to a wheezy gasp. It was only a matter of seconds until she caught her breath and fought back. Running I was good at, but fighting? I swung the sack, slamming it against her head. Her head flew back and cracked against the tile. She stilled.

For a terrible second I thought I'd killed her, but then she groaned. I felt my way in real quick and sighed. Just unconscious, not even a bone bruise. She'd be out for a bit, but not nearly long enough for me get Tali.

I scanned the hall, but no one dashed into view to see what all the noise had been about. Moving her would take time Tali might not have, but I couldn't leave her there. Folks might be willing to overlook a lot of things in the League these days, but an unconscious fourth cord on the floor wasn't likely to be one of them.

Trembling, I dragged her to one of the empty treatment rooms down the hall and plopped her behind a cot. Doubtful anyone would be using the room this early. I bound her hands and feet with her cords, which seemed pretty fitting to me, then shoved Aylin's scarf into her mouth. With luck, no one would go looking for her until Tali and I were gone.

I slipped out of the room and resumed my climb. Kione leaned against the door at the end of the hall, same as before. He stood straight as a soldier as I stepped onto the landing, then slumped his shoulders when he saw it was me.

"I'd hoped you weren't going to show up."

"Well, I'm here." I fought the urge to look behind me.

He eyed my "laundry" but didn't say a word, like we agreed. With a deep breath, he opened the door and walked inside. "Hey, Lanelle, your relief's here. Let me buy you breakfast."

Lanelle yawned and smoothed the wrinkles in her white uniform. Behind her was a cot with a green vest lying across the foot. She'd slept here?

"I'm starving," she told Kione, then turned to me. "Do I have time to wash, or do you need to get back soon?"

Take all day, you horrible, heartless rat. I forced a smile. "You have time. They don't need me in the ward until this afternoon."

She grabbed her vest and slipped it over her skinny shoulders. "They've been quiet all night. The two under the lamp there are looking rather waxy, so you might want to check on them more often. They might not last the day."

I gripped the pynvium tighter. "I'll check them."

"Come on, Lanelle, I'm hungry." Kione tugged at her arm.

"And if Elder Vinnot comes by early, my symptom report is on the table there. Three of the symptoms he asked me to watch for have manifested. He'll want any bodies too." She paused and glanced at the beds. "For dissection, I mean, so they can figure out what's causing this." She spoke in a rush, as if trying to convince both of us that was the truth.

She had to know they were lying. Impossible for her to spend time in this room and not figure out what was wrong. I fought the urge to shove her through the door and out the nearest window.

"And if—"

"I'm starving here, Lanelle."

"I'm coming, I'm coming."

Kione gave me a quick nod as he shut the door.

I ran to Tali. She was still breathing, still pale,

and still alive. I ripped open my bundle. "Tali? I have pynvium. Wake up, Tali, you have to dump the pain. Hurry, we don't have much time."

Her eyes fluttered open and she cried softly, like a kitten.

I grabbed her hand and shoved a chunk of pynvium into it. "Feel it? Fill it up."

She whimpered and shook her head slowly.

"You can do it, Tali. *Push*, please, for me." For an instant, I felt it, a quiver under my fingers as she *pushed* her pain away. I handed her another. "Now this one."

A sob burst from her lips and broke my heart. Her hands shook, barely able to hold the pynvium, let alone grab it.

"Please try."

Another tingle, another injury thrown away. One by one I passed her chunks of hope, begged her to find the strength to shove the pain away. Prayed that no one would find the fourth cord tied up downstairs anytime soon.

Her hands stopped shaking on the seventh chunk. On the tenth, her color returned. By the twelfth, her sunken cheeks had filled in a little. I handed her the thirteenth chunk, hardly bigger than a chicken's egg. "Last one, Tali. Push as hard as you can."

She did, and though pain shone in her watery eyes, awareness did too. "Where. Get this?"

"A pain merchant. I'll explain later, but we have to get out of here right now. Can you stand?"

She struggled to sit up, then fell back with a pained yelp. "No. Hurts."

I touched her heart and forehead. Still so much pain, but I sensed something else—something worse. The thickening of her blood, like Danello. Saints have mercy. Takers weren't immune; they only needed more pain over more time before it killed them too.

I was out of pynvium. She was out of time.

"Tali, listen to me carefully, because I may not be able to tell you afterward. When you leave here, go right to Aylin's."

"Leave?"

"Do you remember where Aylin lives?"

She hesitated. "Yes."

"Go to her right away. She'll have food for you, and clean clothes. She'll take you to a boy named Danello and his family. You'll need to heal them. She'll have pynvium to hold it."

"How?"

I took her hands. "Get to Danello's as fast as you can, Tali. They don't have much time left before their pain kills them."

"Nya. Don't." Tears flowed across her temples toward her ears.

Eyes closed, I pressed my forehead to hers. "I love you, Tali."

I kissed her cheek and *drew.*

TWELVE

Agony swiped my knees out from under me. I collapsed beside Tali's cot, knives twisting in my lungs, needles stabbing my belly. Aches I didn't even have names for ate away at my joints. I moaned, and even that hurt. How had Tali withstood so much for so long?

"Oh no, Nya, no!" Tali slipped out of the cot and knelt on the floor beside me, moving gingerly, as if she expected everything to hurt. That was my job now.

"Run," I wheezed. "Hurry."

"Why did you do it? You shouldn't have done it."

"Go. Danello. Needs. You."

She hugged me. "I won't leave you."

"Go!"

"Not without you."

The fourth cord I'd tackled might be conscious by now, and someone would find her soon—if they hadn't already. I gritted my teeth and gathered as much pain as I could in the hollow place between my heart and guts. The pain eased a bit, but I couldn't hold it there long. My fingers tingled, needing me to *push* the gathered pain away.

If only I could.

"Tali, you have to go," I gasped, struggling to hold on to the words. "If they catch you, they might kill you."

Anger darkened her face. "They already tried to do that."

"Then get out before they try again."

"I'm not leaving you."

The door opened and Tali sucked in a gasp.

"Tali," I whispered fast, "tears." Crying would give her away for sure. No one working in this room would cry over a bunch of useless, orphaned 'Vegs.

She cocked her head at me, then her fingers darted up and smeared away her tears. Even in the dim light, I could tell she'd been crying.

"You will never believe what happened!" Lanelle

said in a fearful rush. I didn't hear Kione or another set of footsteps. Was she alone? Moving hurt too much to check. "Elder Nostomo found Sersin tied up in treatment room three. Can you believe it? The guards are everywhere. The entire League has been sealed!"

I shifted my head a little, and fresh pain washed over me. I took stomach-settling breaths and prayed Tali had time to escape.

"Was she hurt?" Tali asked. Sweet of her to care, but now was not the time to worry over folks who wanted her dead. She wasn't a Healer today, at least not until she got out of the League and over to Danello's.

"I don't know. She's still unconscious. I heard there was blood on the floor!"

Blood? How could I have missed blood? Hasty hands do no good, as Grannyma used to say. Tali had to leave, *now*.

"Why would anyone attack Sersin?" Lanelle came into my line of sight and jerked to a stop, a flush across her face. "What happened? Did she fall out of bed?" It almost sounded like real concern.

"Um, she had a seizure."

"Really? That's a new symptom, but it isn't on the watch list. Elder Vinnot says we'll learn enough about pain from watching them to develop entirely new treatments, maybe even some that don't require pynvium at all! He's doing special research for the Duke himself, and he's even letting me help. I've been writing it all down in my notebook. How long did the seizure last?"

"I, uh . . ."

Tali had never been a quick liar. As a child, if she broke a vase, she said the crocodiles had done it. Forgot her homework—the lake wind had blown it out the window.

"Oohhh." I started twitching and moaning, even gurgled up a bit of spit. I barely had to fake it this time.

Lanelle grimaced, and shame flashed across her pink cheeks. "What am I thinking? We'd better get her back into bed first."

"Probably best."

She knelt and reached toward me, then stopped. Her brows wrinkled. "Is this the same—"

"You grab her shoulders," Tali said quickly, nudging Lanelle forward so she wasn't staring at my face. "I'll get her legs."

I slipped a sigh into my next moan. Not much of a liar, but she could think on her feet when she had to.

Lanelle lifted me gently, not putting too much pressure on any one spot. More care than I was expecting, but then she'd been dealing with the pain-filled apprentices for days now. I bet she handled them carefully so they didn't scream and give her a headache.

They got me "back" onto the cot. My skin burned as Tali draped the blanket over me. I swallowed my cry but couldn't stop the shakes.

Please don't let her notice. She had to hold herself together, and she couldn't do that worrying over me. I gathered the pain again, shoved it away best I could.

"Did you, um, need me to stay?" Tali asked. "I could help for a while longer."

Maybe I'd been too fast to praise her quick thinking. I tried to force *Tali, leave* into her brain with a glare, but she wouldn't look at me. Lanelle stood by my shoulder, peering at Tali with that same funny look she'd given me. We looked an awful lot alike, and in the dim light might even pass as twins, but my guts said Lanelle wasn't as dumb as she seemed.

"What was your name again?"

Panic shook loose my hold on the pain. It raced through me, and sweat tickled over my body like tiny spiders. A gasp burst its way out, and a sob followed close behind.

Tali dropped to one knee and grabbed my hand. "Ny—no, no, don't fight it."

"Go," I whispered.

Her eyes widened like I'd given us up. She swallowed and patted my hand. "That's right, let it go."

If only I had enough strength left to kick her.

Lanelle tugged at her shoulder. "Leave her be. She'll feel better once she falls back asleep. It's the only thing that's helped them so far."

"I guess so." Tali stood, gazing at me with far too much worry on her face. Lanelle's had too much suspicion.

My fingers tingled again, clearly seeing what my fuzzy mind had missed. I didn't need pynvium to dump my pain—I just needed a place to put it. Lanelle was helping them. She deserved to know what it felt like to be in one of these cots, didn't she? *They lied to her too—she might not know.* I tried to shut up a conscience that sounded a lot like Grannyma.

Lanelle stood at the head of my cot, a few feet from my shoulder. The distance kept changing, shifting to and fro like waves on the shore. I closed my eyes a moment to squash down the pain again and focus. This wasn't about me but all of them. Lanelle could help them by helping me and Tali escape. The sacrificial cow to save the herd.

"I'm Lanelle, by the way. Not sure we were ever introduced."

"Tali."

I almost heard her gulp. She glanced at me and I curled my fingers toward me as best I could. *Get her closer.*

"That sounds familiar."

"I guess I told you before then. Or maybe we had a class together?"

"Maybe." She frowned and pointed a finger at Tali. "Why is your uniform so wrinkled?"

"I, uh . . ."

I strained to sit up, lunge my crippled body at Lanelle, grab her by the ankles, and get rid of the hurt. My focus dropped again, and pain shattered under my skin.

Tali sucked in her breath and took a small step toward me. I mouthed *no*, gathered the pain yet again, and curled my fingers.

Lanelle folded her arms across her chest. "Okay, what's going on here? You're acting strange."

Tali gasped and yanked her gaze away. "I fell asleep on your cot," she blurted.

"You fell asleep?" Lanelle repeated as if she

wasn't sure what to say.

"Yeah, silly, huh?" Tali chuckled. "So, you were saying before, about Sersin being attacked?"

Lanelle gaped for a moment longer; then gossip won out over suspicion. "Can you believe it? They found her tied up in one of the treatment rooms with her own cords!"

"That's terrible. Are we in any danger up here?"

"I don't think so. Kione's guarding the door." Lanelle took a step toward it—and toward me. My fingers twitched. Almost in reach.

Clink!

Pynvium rattled. The sack!

"What's this?"

"That's, um . . ."

Lanelle knelt and opened the sack, then jerked back as if something with teeth had popped out of it. "There's pynvium in here!"

"Really?"

Even I didn't buy Tali's innocent tone.

The door slammed open and footsteps thudded in. Several people in boots, which meant guards. Lanelle scrambled up, her face pale. Tali went white as her underdress.

"Good morning, girls," said a man with a smooth,

commanding voice. It was almost gentle unless you listened closely—then you heard the edge to it. A serrated one too, not a blade that would cut cleanly.

Lanelle clasped her hands behind her back. "Morning, sir."

"Any trouble this morning?"

"No, sir. It's been quiet." She stepped closer and shoved the pynvium under my cot with her foot. Perhaps Lanelle had a plan of her own simmering in that not-as-empty-as-I'd-hoped head of hers. Like steal it and make a fortune.

"Anything unusual happen?"

"Not really. This patient had a seizure and fell out of bed, but she wasn't hurt."

"Did she now?" Footsteps, then a shadow fell across me. I looked up, my eyes catching immediately on the heavy braided gold bars on his shoulders.

The Luminary stood over me, close enough to touch.

THIRTEEN

I couldn't fail here. Tali wasn't safe. Danello and the twins were still dying. So many Healers were still in agony.

"Sir," Tali said with more respect than I'd ever heard her use. "With your permission, I'd like to return to the treatment ward. My rounds start soon."

Lanelle looked ready to jump out of her skin, but she stayed quiet. So did I, not even a whimper of good-bye. If facing the Luminary finally got Tali to run, I'd stare at the rat all day.

He glanced at Tali, then nodded. "Report to Elder Tyleen."

"Yes, sir."

"You, go with her," he added.

"Sir?" Kione sounded as shocked as I felt. I didn't even know he was in the room.

"I don't want anyone walking around alone today. Make sure everyone has an escort."

"Yes, sir."

I took a deep breath and let some of the panic seep away. Kione was with Tali now, and she was on her way out. Would he let her go? Doubtful, since it meant defying the Luminary, but maybe he'd continue to "do nothing" while she slipped away from rounds. Maybe . . .

I jumped. The Luminary was studying me, staring at me with sky blue eyes as if he knew what was stumbling through my head. He was younger than I'd thought, barely forty. He didn't bother with a Healer's braid and kept his black hair short against his head. I looked away, tried to make my darting eyes look like delirium.

"Has she manifested any of the symptoms?" the Luminary said calmly. Lanelle had mentioned symptoms too?

"No, sir. Only the three I told Elder Vinnot about yesterday. But I can barely go near the Kolvek girl anymore. It hurts from at least three feet away. I had to move her cot away from the others."

My ears perked up despite the pain. Hurts?

The Luminary nodded, studying me. "I'll send someone up to remove her—for your safety." He said the last part as if it was an afterthought.

"Am I in danger here, sir?" Lanelle asked.

"No, just keep watching like Elder Vinnot asked. I'll leave one of the guards outside. If you see anything suspicious, notify him immediately."

"Yes, sir."

One of the guards. So there were several. I tried to remember how many different voices I'd heard, but my brain felt muddy.

I shifted my gaze back to the Luminary, and it was hard to glance away again. From my angle, he seemed tall, but he didn't have broad shoulders. He probably hadn't fought in the war, only healed those who had. On the Duke's side, of course.

"Sir?" a young voice called from the door. "Elder Mancov is asking for you. He says Sersin is awake."

The Luminary's eyes gleamed and he turned away before my panic displaced my calm. The fourth cord. She would describe me, but she'd also be describing Tali.

Tali needed more time to get out. I took a deep breath and . . .

"Aaaiiieee!" Screaming hurt, but I screeched as loud as my lungs would let me. Flailed my limbs, gritted my teeth against the agony my fake seizure caused. I blubbered. Drooled. Thrashed.

"She's having another one!" Lanelle cried, running over.

The Luminary knelt and grabbed my arms, pinning me down and sending fresh stabs of pain where he touched me. A quick twist and I could grab *him*. Send *him* flailing to the floor.

"Have any of the others developed seizures?" A new voice, older, with more curiosity in it than concern.

Lanelle answered. "No, Elder Vinnot."

At least four of the Luminary's people were in the room, maybe more, and they would skewer me if I hurt their precious leader. I grabbed his arm anyway, giving Tali a few more seconds to get away. Danello needed her, and I needed them both alive and safe. I imagined pushing my hurts into the Luminary, the one person who deserved it more than anyone else, even the Duke. At least the Duke had been honest about trying to kill us. I held on to that image while I forced my screaming muscles to move.

A blur moved at the edge of my vision, above the Luminary's shoulder. Then a low voice, maybe Vinnot's. "There might be a problem with the Mus—"

"Not now," the Luminary snapped.

I strained to focus, but pain and despair finally stilled me. I let the tears fall with the cold sweat. My body felt like I'd been writhing for hours, but mere minutes had more likely passed—if not seconds. Was it long enough for Tali to get out of the League?

"Strap her down if her seizures continue," the Luminary said.

"Yes, sir."

He rose and left me in hazy agony. Deep voices muttered too low for me to hear; then the door thudded shut.

Please, Saint Saea, let Tali escape before they realize she was here.

Black and red swirls closed in around me. Surrendering to unconsciousness sounded good, but soft footsteps coming closer kept me awake awhile longer.

Lanelle knelt, her face close enough to grab. I no longer had the strength.

"Who are you?"

I panted, unable to answer even if I wanted to.

"What are you doing here?" She glanced nervously around the room, fingering the single gold cord on her shoulder. "I don't know why you and Tali traded places, and I don't care as long as you keep me out of it. But if you threaten my position here, I'm telling the Luminary everything. I *need* this job, bad as it is."

"Don't. Please." Even whispering hurt, but if I kept her talking, kept her close, maybe I'd get enough strength back to dump it all into her. *Or maybe ask for help.* No, she'd never help me, not if she could ignore the suffering apprentices.

"Are you thieves? Is that where you got all this pynvium?"

"Merchants."

She wiped her upper lip, and I could almost see her totaling up the oppas. "How much is in here?"

"Used. For Tali."

She leaned back on her heels, honest desperation on her face. Did she also have someone who needed it? "It was stupid to try and heal her. You can't stop the flow of pain when it is that bad. How do you think they all got here in the first place?"

"Disease," I said, though I doubted my sarcasm came through.

She winced. "You know that's not true."

"I know."

"Then why do this?"

"My sister."

A flicker of emotion crossed her face, but it

vanished before I could figure out what it was. Couldn't be sympathy, not after what she'd done. "Even stupider. You know they'll grab her again the next time an aristocrat needs healing."

I tried to gather the pain again, but it was slow to pool. Was my blood starting to thicken already?

Lanelle sighed and rolled a pynvium chunk between her palms. "Maybe she'll get out. A few did in the beginning, when the rumors started, but the Luminary's men caught them. Made *examples* of them." She shuddered and gripped the pynvium tight. "After that, no one wanted to try. If we did what the Luminary said . . ."

I tried not to picture what the Luminary did to those who escaped, but images from the war kept popping in. Gevegian leaders tied to posts, their backs whipped bloody. Baskets of severed hands. Bodies cast onto the trash pyres like garbage. Things I'd thought I'd buried years ago when the nightmares had finally stopped.

"What makes you think you won't be next?" I asked.

"Because he needs me. I'm helping him." Her voice cracked.

"Not many left who aren't."

She folded her arms across her chest and stuck

her chin out. "What do *you* know? You're not even *in* the League, are you?"

"No."

"Then shut up. I have it good here. Elder Vinnot said I could go far, but I'll lose it all if they find out you tricked me. They'll do to me what they did to—" She stared off into space, jaw tight, eyes scared.

My fingers crept toward her arm, mere inches off the edge of the cot. Skin brushed skin. My whole hand tingled, and a twinge of guilt tickled my belly. If I did this, was I any better than the Luminary?

"People depend on me," she whispered. "And I can't do anything else."

The door slammed open and Lanelle jerked away. The Luminary was on her in seconds, clearly in a panic. He grabbed her arms and shook her like a child scolding a rag doll.

"That girl who was here before, who was she?"

"Ta-Tali, sir."

"What was she doing here?"

Lanelle glanced at me, then her eyes lowered to the sack hidden under the cot. "I don't know. She said she was here to relieve me."

"Did you verify that with Elder Mancov?"

She shook her head, glanced at me again. "No, sir, I—"

"Stupid girl." The Luminary shoved her back and she fell. Pain and terror crossed her face in equal measure.

"It's not my fault. I didn't think anyone could get up here without authorization. And there was a guard at the door! She got by Kione as well."

The Luminary hesitated, probably wondering how stupid *he'd* been in sending Kione and Tali out together. If Kione was faced with helping Tali or sending her back, I hoped he'd be strong and choose right. "Did you see either of them together before?"

"No, sir."

"Did you see her talking to anyone who isn't part of the League?"

"No, sir."

Relief smoothed his brow, but then it wrinkled again, as if she hadn't soothed him after all. He huffed. "You've been here for days, what could you possibly know," he muttered, turning away. "Useless 'Veg."

Lanelle threw me a look of sheer panic and darted after him.

"Sir, I think she traded places with that girl there!" she rushed. "I was about to notify you. I was, um . . . trying to verify it first before I bothered you. I know how busy you are."

He snapped around faster than a croc eats a duck. "Which girl?"

She pointed at me, finger trembling.

The Luminary darted over and shook me. I screamed, but he didn't stop. "Who are you? What are you doing here?"

"She said she was Tali's sister," Lanelle continued, sounding as desperate as the Luminary. "They look an awful lot alike, which is why they were able to fool me at first, but I figured it out soon enough. I think she healed Tali so she could esca— leave the League. You can probably catch her at the gate!"

His eyes went glassy with fear. "An apprentice *left*?" He stared at Lanelle.

"Wait—" I lunged, grabbed for his arm. Guards or not, I needed to give him bigger things to worry about than where Tali was. The Duke and his heartless men were *not* going to kill the last of my family, not if I could stop him.

The Luminary backhanded me across the face before I could touch him. Pain flared around my head and I fell back, nauseated. From pain, from failure, from dread—I couldn't tell anymore.

He stomped away, but his fear was clearly still there. It was more than worry about the panic that would happen if Geveg knew there was no more pynvium. I'd bet next year's pay no one outside the League knew what he was doing. I'd bet even more the Governor-General didn't know. He paused at the door, but "find that apprentice *now*, before she" was all I heard before it slammed shut again.

No! Images of Tali forced to heal flooded me with strength. I had to get out, find Tali, and warn her.

Lanelle stepped closer, her hands clenched at her sides; she looked as scared as a caught bird. "If this gets me picked for priority healing, I'll—"

My fingers darted to her arm, and I *pushed* into her all the hurt and pain I'd taken from Tali. Guilt fluttered at the edges of pain, but I ignored it. I would *not* feel guilty about hurting a traitor.

"Aahhhh!" Pain twisted Lanelle's features and she toppled over. I clawed closer, *pushed* harder.

And then it slowed, as if she were pushing back.

She snatched her arm away and dragged me out of the cot. We both collapsed on the floor, gasping.

She resisted? How? Could Takers refuse pain, or was Lanelle different, like me? *Different.* A chill cooled my burning muscles. What symptoms were on Lanelle's list? Symptoms of those who were different?

"What did you do to me?" Pale and teary-eyed,

Lanelle scooted away on her butt. "Stay away!"

She'd taken half the pain, and already my strength was returning. Then again, so was hers. Healers knew pain, and the shock of it wouldn't disorient her for long. She grabbed the edge of the cot next to her and struggled to her knees, gasping, still unable to scream more than a rasp, but that also wouldn't last.

"Hel—" Lanelle's scream was cut off as a red-haired boy in the nearest cot rolled off and tackled her. He straddled her, pinning her down and keeping a hand over her mouth.

"Hurry, finish it!" he cried, while I stared open-mouthed. "Come on!"

"Finish what?"

"Whatever you did to her before. It's our only chance to get out of here."

Lanelle struggled under him, whimpering and hollering into his hand. Would the guard outside hear?

"Hurry—I can't hold her down much longer." Sweat beaded across his forehead, and his brown eyes shone with pain.

I couldn't stop now, or Tali had no chance at all. Lanelle would tell the Luminary I'd shifted. I'd be bound and gagged and headed for Baseer before sunset. The Duke was still searching for abnormal Takers, but maybe now he'd found a new way to discover them. Folks needed to know that.

I crawled toward Lanelle and the boy.

Suddenly the door opened and a guard walked in, annoyance on his uncaring face. "What's going on in here?"

I gasped and jerked backward as Lanelle renewed her kicking and muffled screaming. My knee hit something hard and rough.

"Get off her! What are you doing?" The guard ran in, heading for Lanelle. He had black, glossy hair, dark as his Baseeri soul.

The guard yanked the boy off and tossed him aside. I grabbed the pynvium, wishing I could shove my frustration into it like Tali shoved pain.

"Leave him alone!" Childishly, I threw a handful of pynvium chunks at the guard. Throwing all my anger and hatred for what the Luminary and his Duke had done to my family, my home, my *life*, with it.

Whoomp. A low sound more felt than heard. Pain flashed, shimmering like heat waves in the air, as the pynvium hit the guard in the chest.

Whoomp. Another against his thigh.

It flashed like the beads in Aylin's bracelet had

done when Sersin grabbed them. Like every trinket sitting on every shelf in every pain merchant's shop. Hurt sprinkled me like blown sand while the guard screamed and dropped to the stone floor. Lanelle had curled into a ball and lay whimpering, her arms covering her head.

I gaped at the moaning guard. How did I make pynvium flash? Only enchanters could trigger the metal to do that, like Papa had done during the war. I'd inherited his eyes—had I gotten more than that?

What exactly *was* I?

The guard was up on his knees now, crawling away while I gaped, still shocked as a caught fish.

"How did you do that?" he wheezed, reaching for his rapier.

I couldn't let him tell the Luminary while I was helpless. I gathered what pain I had left and scrambled after him, forcing my legs to push me forward and ignoring the ripping aches shooting through them.

The red-haired apprentice was on his feet, stumbling toward Lanelle and the guard. "Stop them!"

I grabbed the guard's shin. He kicked at me but didn't put much force into it. I put *everything* into him. Even my guilt in doing it. He screamed.

My pain fading, I sucked in breath and tried to

focus. The guard was unconscious. Lanelle too, so she wasn't going anywhere. She'd taken half my pain and probably some backflash from the pynvium.

Saint's mercy, what had I done?

"Did you just flash pynvium?" the apprentice asked, dropping to the floor beside me. He looked about eighteen, with tiny freckles across his short nose.

"I don't know." I'd never heard of anyone flashing pain like that before, without an enchanted trigger to release the pain and shape the direction of the flash.

"I'm Soek," he said, pronouncing it with the distinctive lilting accent from Verlatta.

"Nya."

"You're that shifter everyone's talking about, aren't you?"

"Uh . . ."

"Come on, we have to get out of here."

"I know." Still, too many questions spun through my head. "Did you sneak in here to save someone too?"

"No, I'm an apprentice."

My mouth hung open for a shocked second. "Why aren't you suffering in one of those cots then?"

"I heal fast."

"You heal *other* people's pain?"

"I guess so." He smiled, but I saw fear in it. I'd be afraid too. He was better than walking pynvium. He was *renewable* walking pynvium.

"You're different too," I said.

"Yeah. Though your differences are a lot handier in a fight."

Which we'd have more of if we didn't get out of here. "Let's go."

I snatched up the chunks I'd thrown and put them back into the sack. Who knew how many guards stood between us and freedom? A single pain flash would be enough to distract them, maybe even do more than distract if the pain was sharp enough.

If I *could* flash it again.

I paused at the door, even though the hall had to be clear or another guard would have already been there, pointing a rapier at my throat. Soek limped behind me, not saying a word about the pain.

"How much are you carrying?" I asked softly.

He grinned. "As long as we don't have to run, I'll be fine."

"I think running will definitely be needed."

"Do you think you could . . ." He tipped his head at the unconscious guard.

My skin went cold. "No!"

"But you gave him your pain—why not mine?"

Because it was wrong, even if it *was* the only way out. But how could I say that while he limped and I was fine? I glanced at Lanelle and the guard. They both deserved it, but hurting them now when we didn't have to felt worse. Like stabbing them when their backs were turned.

"Give me your hand." I took it and felt my way in. He carried pain, but it was dim. I'd never seen half-healed pain before. I *drew*, taking some away. Aches seeped into my body, feeling a lot like the muscle soreness I'd woken up with at Danello's.

The tightness in his eyes eased. "Thanks," he said. "But it would have been better for us if you'd given it to them."

"Easier, maybe, but not better. Come on."

We slipped out and headed down the stairs. A few strides later, I froze. We wouldn't make it down the stairs, let alone through the hall. At least one Elder who'd recognize me was working in the treatment ward. If by Saea's luck we made it as far as the main antechamber, dozens of League guards and Elders and who knew who else were waiting to nab us like chickens.

There had to be another way out.

"What's the fastest way down from here that

doesn't go through the main halls?" I whispered to Soek.

"I don't know. I only worked here a few days before they . . . put me up *there*."

I searched my memories from when Tali and I had followed Mama around. What about the rooms higher up? Didn't one of the halls cross over to another set of stairs? Voices drifted up from below.

". . . her to the Luminary for further questioning."

"Yes, sir."

Footsteps next, lots of them, echoing off the marble stairs and coming in our direction. We hurried back up, my sandals thankfully quieter than the guards' boots, though my heartbeat sure sounded louder than both. Soek's bare feet made no sound at all. We passed the open door to the apprentices' room, and I risked a pause. The guard was still balled up on the floor, but Lanelle was moving, sluggish and groggy. She lifted her head and our eyes met.

Not good.

"Hurry." I raced up the stairs with Soek close behind as Lanelle started hollering. Raspy, but the guards would hear her soon. Stairs, there had to be more stairs up here somewhere. I was almost sure the first floor had another staircase on the far side of the main hall. It had to connect up here. *Oh, please let it connect up here.*

Shouts came from behind as we reached a landing. How many guards were after us? Maybe they'd called in the soldiers from outside. I ran faster, the heavy sack clinking in my arms. The hall sloped gently upward, but it was enough to make my thighs burn and slow me down. Soek wasn't faring much better. Tall windows lined the outside wall, and Geveg sprawled out before me, a tiny island on a vast lake. I tried not to think it might be the last time I saw either.

Another curve. More windows, then . . .

No!

My feet, heart, and breath all stopped at once. The hall ended in a circular sunroom with windows on all sides; one of the top spires. I skidded to a stop in the center of the room.

We had nowhere else to go.

FOURTEEN

"What do we do now?" Soek whispered, his gaze darting around the room.

Boot stomps echoed off the marbled halls, getting louder as the guards came closer. I studied the windows. Outside on the ledge, statues of Saints had their backs to me, as if disapproving of what I'd done. I hefted the pynvium sack. Even if it wouldn't flash, it was heavy enough to smash a window and let me get out onto the ledge and down the roof and— Wait, was that a latch?

"Over here." I darted closer to the window and unlocked it. The window swung smoothly outward.

The stomps were louder now, pounding up the last set of stairs to this part of the spire. Any second the guards would round the corner and find us. Tali would never forgive me if I got myself killed.

I climbed through the window to the ledge surrounding the dome. Soek followed and pulled the window shut. Wind slapped me, burning my eyes and flinging my beaded braids against my cheeks.

Don't fall, and for the love of Saint Saea, don't look down.

I kept my back pressed against the glass and inched along the ledge until I reached the statue of Saint Saea, looking down at Geveg with her outstretched hands full of bird crap. I crouched behind her skirts, afraid to breathe. Soek wedged in beside me, his face pale. He kept glancing at the sloped roof and the ground so very far below.

Shadows played across the roof, dodging shafts of light from the midmorning sun behind us. Light, dark, light, dark, alternating like the columns hiding me from the men who were now filling the room. More shadows danced as the guards moved between the light and dark areas.

Muffled anger sounded through the glass, but no windows opened. I smiled, imagining them standing there, scratching their heads and wondering where we'd gone. *Down another hall perhaps? How? They couldn't have doubled back. Maybe they vanished!*

A creak on my left turned my grin to a grimace. Was that the window? More shadows danced around the roof tiles like hands groping to snag me. Then they vanished, and the window thumped shut.

I exhaled.

Until another window creaked on my right.

"Found them!"

A guard leaned out, but he kept glancing nervously from the ledge below the window to me, then back. Guess he didn't like heights any more than Soek did.

"Go get them" came from inside. Soek grabbed my arm. I patted his fingers reassuringly, though I doubted how much comfort I could give.

"I'm not climbing out there."

"Go! That's an order."

The guard scoffed. "I was hired to watch doors, not run out on rooftops."

I grinned. You got what you paid for, and nobody paid well for labor these days.

Another guard stuck his head out the window, but this one didn't look afraid of heights. I reached into the sack and grabbed a pynvium chunk. If it had any pain in it, I couldn't tell. I angled for a clear toss. I gathered my anger and tried to duplicate how

I'd felt and what I'd done when I'd flashed a chunk at the guard.

I threw.

No flash.

It *did* hit him smack in the center of the forehead though. He yelped and yanked his head back inside.

Somewhat effective, but good aim and a sack of rocks wouldn't get us out of this. The League had more money than Geveg had beggars, and someone was sure as spit going to show up with a real pynvium weapon, one with a strong-enough flash to knock us right off the roof.

Another creak and the window swung open again. The same guard glared at me, a red welt on his forehead. Letting *him* catch me was a bad idea. I leaned forward a little and looked down the side. The roof sloped to the next set of domes, maybe forty feet below.

"Follow me," I whispered. I inched forward, holding my skirt tight under my knees. I had to angle it perfectly or I'd go sliding past and splatter what little brains I had all over the courtyard.

"Down there?" Soek asked

"Come on." My butt slid off the ledge, and gravity took over.

"She's getting away!"

And gaining speed. I slid along the tiles, knees close to my chin, feet grating against the slate in a long hiss. The lower dome and all its windows raced toward me, then not-so-toward me.

I was sliding off center!

I grabbed at the tiles with one hand. My direction didn't change. I tipped sideways, and a few pynvium chunks slipped out of the sack and clanked down the roof.

No! Without those chunks I'd never figure out how to make them flash again. I lunged for the sack, scraping my knuckles as I caught and closed the top. The escaped pieces rolled faster along the roof. They passed the dome and dropped off the edge.

So would I if I didn't stop my slide.

Soek cursed behind me. I continued sliding on my side, my shoulder and hipbones knocking painfully against the tiles. I cried out as I hit a bump in the roof, but it shifted me left, back toward the dome's tall windows. Soek cried out a second later, and we both picked up speed.

Bad plan, this was a bad plan. Grannyma was right. Fools act first and think later.

Smack!

I cringed as I crumpled against the dome's

window. The pynvium chunks trapped under my arms pierced my skin like snakebites. My sore muscles flared hot. Soek slammed into me from behind and the glass cracked. I sucked in a breath, but the window held.

"You're nuttier than pecan pudding," Soek wheezed into my ear.

The guards above yelled, but the wind tore the words away before I could make them out. I struggled to my knees. A good kick would be enough to break the window.

Guards ran into the sunroom on the other side of the glass. They gaped as if surprised to find us there. I certainly hadn't expected them to find *us* so quickly.

We needed a new plan. A real one this time, not the first thing that popped into my head. So far, none of the guards had wanted to chase us onto the roof. Staying out here might be dangerous, but it was probably a lot safer than trying to fight past the guards.

Below the sunroom, maybe eight feet down, was a half-circle ledge about two feet wide, with columns at both ends. Past that, the roof flattened out, but it was a much larger drop, a good fifteen feet at least. Two very risky drops, and a bad fall if we missed landing on the ledge.

Soek followed my gaze over the edge. "You can't be serious."

"Maybe this wasn't such a good idea."

Small pebbles skittered past me and I jerked my head up. I couldn't see over the roof's curve, but the guards from up top must be getting closer.

I inched along the edge. "Just don't look down."

"How am I supposed to land on the ledge if I don't?"

"Fine, then don't look *all* the way down."

I stopped at a spot with a good handhold, tied a knot in the sack, and tossed it down. Glass suddenly shattered on my left. I dropped flat on my stomach and scooted my legs around until they hung off the edge. I kept scooting until I dangled by my hands. Soek watched me, his hands clenching and unclenching at his sides. Despite my warning, he kept looking down.

"Come on, Soek."

"Stop right there," a guard yelled. Another dove forward as if trying to grab Soek.

With a quick prayer, I let go.

My sandals hit the window ledge, and I teetered backward over the drop.

No-no-no-no-no! Hug-the-wall-hug-the-wall!

I threw my weight forward—anything to force myself flat against the glass. My fingers hooked around the edges of the windows.

"Aahh!" Soek dropped next to me, his eyes wide as moons. He gripped the windows and didn't look down this time.

"Hurry, bring the rope!"

Rope! Now *that* was a good plan. Right now, I'd settle for a pair of wings. I clung to the grimy glass, trying to catch my breath. The wind threatened to sweep us off the building with the rest of the leaves.

Memories of Tali and me in our tree house hit me. Her on the roof, laughing while I climbed. The river delta and the ferryboats. All the fishermen hauling in their nets on the lake. Tali would cheer when I made it to the top. *I could never be that brave,* she'd say.

Down was never as easy as up. I swallowed. We could do this. Fifteen feet wasn't so far.

I took one last deep breath . . . *wait, not my last breath, don't think that. . . .*

A rope dropped down and thunked against the glass to my right.

"Nya, wait!" Soek called, reaching out and grabbing the rope. He yanked hard, and a startled cry came from above. The loose end of the rope rolled down, and Soek caught it.

"You're a genius," I said.

He grinned and tied the rope around one of the columns, then lowered himself over. Feet flat against the wall, he made walking down look easy.

"Your turn," he called when he reached the roof below.

I gulped but grabbed the rope, wrapping it around my arm as he had done. I crawled over the side and braced my feet. My right sandal slipped and I fell sideways. The other foot dropped, dragging my knees painfully across the wall. I clung to the rope, toes scrabbling at the wall. My hands started to slip, burning as the rope slid through them. I struggled to get my feet back on the wall.

Halfway down, my arms gave out and I fell. My feet hit the roof first, jarring my bones all the way up to my neck. Bright stars of pain twinkled around me. Above, the guards rappelled down another rope like pynvium scouters searching the cliffs for new veins.

Soek was at my side in a heartbeat. "You okay?"

"Yeah, I'm okay."

He helped me up. Fresh stings burned my raw knees where I'd ripped through Tali's underdress and scraped off quite a lot of skin underneath. If I made it off this vile roof alive, I'd spend a whole oppa on new clothes for both of us. Swear to the Saints I would.

Time to move. The long expanse of tile below had to be the general treatment ward. The roof peaked, but the downward slopes weren't too bad, and the edges looked good for hanging on to for the last drop we'd have to make to the ground. After that, it was just one long run to Tali and Danello.

"There they are!"

Still *more* guards appeared, tossing out an emergency ladder from the windows in the dome above me. Did they have the entire League after us?

I grabbed the sack of pynvium and walk-slid down to the roof edge. The gardens were on this side of the League, and landing in soft grass sounded a lot better than smacking onto cobblestones. Voices drifted up from below and I froze, holding out one hand to stop Soek.

I couldn't catch the words, but it didn't sound like idle conversation. I crouched low and peeked over. Two guards stood below. Young ones, around Soek's age.

Turning to Soek, I pointed at the guards below, then brought one hand down on top of the other. He stared for a second, then nodded.

The drop wasn't far, maybe seven or eight feet. I might not weigh a lot, but things dropped from above packed quite the wallop. Soek positioned himself next to me, right over the larger guard.

I gripped the sack of pynvium tight and jumped.

FIFTEEN

We hit the guards. I landed dead center on one while Soek smashed into the other. We collapsed in a heap of swears and screams; then both guards went quiet, knocked unconscious on the hard ground. Winded and bruised, I scrambled up and ran behind the bushes aesthetically arranged around the gardens. They might look pretty, but they didn't offer squat for cover if any more guards arrived. Soek settled in behind me, an odd combination of fear and excitement on his face.

"We got out! I can't believe we got out!"

"Shh—we're not off League property yet." No other guards had shown up, but with my luck, they'd catch us before we made it off the grounds.

"This way, and stay low."

"There they are! Behind the hibiscus!" a man cried from the roof's edge as we skirted the courtyard.

My muscles protested, but I pushed them harder, running toward the open gates and the safety of the crowd beyond. For once, the Saints were on my side and the usual bridge soldiers were gone, no doubt called inside to help search. We hit the streets as fast as our strained legs would carry us, Soek careening off a heavyset dockworker while I nearly slammed into a pair of girls carrying a basket of fruit.

"Hey! Watch it!"

I glanced back over my shoulder. The guards had slowed at the street, their heads swiveling back and forth. We kept running, threading between refugees, soldiers, and farmers until I no longer heard stomping boots or clanking swords behind me. A woman exited a shop ahead, and I dragged Soek inside before the door swung shut, hiding behind a rack of stone-inlaid boxes. The shopkeep glared at our torn and bloody uniforms and frowned.

"It's been a really bad day," I said.

"Get out or I'll make it worse."

Anger filled me like an overboiling pot. I reached into my pocket and grabbed some coins. "I have money," I said, waving the oppas in his face. "And I'll spend them somewhere else since you're so rude."

"You do that, 'Veg!'"

I stormed out, resisting the urge to slam the door. Loud noises might draw attention, and the shocked expression on the shopkeep's face was hardly worth getting caught over.

Soek chuckled and ran a hair through his disheveled curls. "Remind me never to get on your bad side."

"I'm not so terrible," I mumbled, my cheeks hot.

"Terrible? You're amazing. You just saved my life." He smiled at me, and I felt another blush coming.

"We need to get off the street until the guards go back inside."

We stayed in crowds best we could for a few blocks until I found a clump of bushes large enough for us to hide in. The soldiers couldn't have been told yet to watch for us, but who knew how fast that would change.

"Do you think your sister got out?" Soek whispered. Now that the excitement was wearing off, he looked as tired as I felt.

"I hope so." If we'd made it out with half the

League guards on our butts, Tali must have made it as well. But surely there'd be more League guards searching for her if she *had* gotten away.

I swallowed, my throat parched. There was never a bucket of water around when you needed one. Not that we'd get served anywhere. The rude shopkeep had reason to glare—not a *good* reason, but still legitimate. My borrowed apprentice uniform was speckled in grime, gravel, blood, and bird crap. All the ugliness you didn't notice about the League until you got real close.

"What should we—"

"Hang on," I shushed him as a familiar face appeared for a moment in the crowd. Danello? It *looked* like him, but he was wearing a long fisherman's overcoat. Buttoned too, even in this heat. I slipped out of the bushes for a better look, and Aylin and Tali popped into view.

"Tali!" I headed for her. She was startled for a moment, then ran to me, almost tackling me in a huge hug.

"You're alive!" I said, just as she cried, "You made it out!"

"I was so worried, I didn't think you'd ever leave, and then the Luminary came—and Saints, Tali, don't ever do that to me again."

"I won't, I promise."

Aylin threw her arms around both of us. "Don't you do it either, Nya. I almost died when Tali told me what you did."

We hugged and bounced and acted like fools while passersby stared at us like, well, fools.

"Better get off the street," said Danello. It really *was* him in that silly coat. He glanced at the soldiers and checked his buttons, then pulled us gently toward a cluttered alley.

"You're alive too!" I hugged him, accidentally shoving him against a pile of crates. "Are the twins okay?"

"They're fine. Tali fixed us all up." We stayed there together, not talking. Then his hug loosened and he stepped away, both cheeks red as berries. "Nya, we owe you our—" He frowned and looked at something behind me. "There's someone watching us."

I turned around and Soek stepped into the alley.

"Hi," he said.

"Who are you?" Danello asked, pulling open his coat. His hand darted at a rapier on his belt.

"What are you doing with a rapier?" I gaped at the gleaming steel. It looked well made and deadly, probably his mother's.

He didn't answer, just kept staring at Soek with a dangerous glint in his eyes.

"That's Soek," I explained. "One of the apprentices. We helped each other escape."

Soek chuckled and shook his head. "I didn't do much. Nya's the hero here. I owe her my life."

I blushed again, and the glint in Danello's eyes turned to worry. I put my hand on his arm. "Danello, it's okay."

He let me pull his hand away, and the coat slid back to cover the rapier. Wearing either was a big risk. Folks didn't usually wear those coats around the city, so it might draw just as much attention as the actual rapier.

"What are you doing out here with a weapon?"

"We were coming to rescue you."

"Danello planned it all out," Tali said. "We were going to go back in and save *you* this time."

"You were?" I wasn't sure whether to be touched or angry. After everything I'd done to get her out, she'd risk coming back and getting caught again?

"We couldn't just leave you there," she said.

"We were all so scared," said Aylin. "Tali told us you took her pain and her place. I can't believe you were that—"

"Stupid," Danello finished.

"Danello!" Aylin gasped.

With a quick glance at Soek, Danello reached out and took my hand, his jaw clenched and lots of worry in his eyes. "You shouldn't have gone back alone, Nya. You had the pynvium—you could have brought another Healer to us."

"Going back was the only way to get Tali out."

"No, it wasn't. It was the only way you thought of." He ran his hand over his lip and looked torn between hitting me and hugging me. "You helped *us*," he said. "What made you think I wouldn't help *you*?"

My mouth dropped open, but it was empty of answers. Why *hadn't* I thought he'd help me? Did I no longer expect folks to help each other out unless they were family?

No one but Tali and Aylin had cared about me in a long time, and no boy ever had. "Why would you? You have your own family to look after."

"You take care of family first, friends second, and neighbors when you can." He smiled sheepishly and rubbed a thumb over my knuckles. I noticed how scraped and dirty they were, but didn't want to pull away. "It's something my da says."

Aylin nodded. "My mother said that too. Gevegians stick together. Those greedy Baseeri would steal

252

the clothes off our backs without friends watching them for us."

"Um, hey, Nya," Soek said, tugging on my sleeve. "I hate to interrupt, but something's going on."

I looked up. The street was crowded, but that wasn't unusual these days. "I don't see anything."

"Don't look—listen." He walked to the front of the alley and cocked his head. After a second, Aylin followed.

"Nya, he's right," called Aylin, motioning us forward. "Everyone's talking about the League."

We left the safety of the cluttered alley and walked a few steps into the street.

". . . some kind of announcement . . ."

". . . about the ferry accident?"

". . . what will we do without . . ."

Dread settled into my stomach. People were running toward the League, worried looks on every face. Over the fearful voices, the faint toll of the gathering bell rang.

"We need to find out what's going on," I said.

"I'd rather not go back there," Soek said nervously.

"Do you have any family here?" I asked him. "Friends?"

"No one. It was just me in Verlatta, and I got out

right before the siege started. I knew it was about to get bad. I left, came here, joined the League. It hasn't been a good week."

"We'll be safe if we all stick together. Danello has his rapier. No one will spot us with so many people. We'll just go over there, hear what they have to say, and then we'll leave."

Soek still looked uncertain but nodded. "Okay, I trust you."

I trusted him too, though I couldn't say why. Maybe because we were both different, and we both risked a lot by going anywhere near the League.

Danello took my hand. "Come on, stay close in case there's trouble."

We merged with the crowd and flowed down to League Circle. The gathering bell rang loudly here, but after another minute it stopped, the sharp clang drifting away on the late-morning breeze. A small speaker's platform had been carried out, and the crowd hushed as Heal Master Ginkev stepped up onto it.

I swallowed and fought the urge to duck, but he couldn't possibly spot me in the crowd. I moved closer behind the safety of Danello's broad shoulders anyway.

"Good morning," Ginkev began, sounding

saddened and uncertain at the same time. "I have tragic news to announce, and I beg all of you to remain calm."

A nervous murmur ran through the crowd.

"Five days ago, several Healers fell ill with an unknown disease. They were quarantined immediately, but it's clear now that the rest of the apprentice and junior Healer population were exposed. Since many of those recently afflicted are Healers who were present at the tragic ferry accident two days ago, we surmise that their weakened conditions made them more susceptible to succumbing to this illness."

More nervous muttering. Folks around us looked scared. There'd been diseases during the war too, near the end when we didn't have enough people to clear the streets of all the bodies.

"Despite our best efforts, we have been unable to discern the nature of this disease, and therefore have been unable to heal it."

The crowd grew panicky, and Ginkev held up his hands.

"This is not cause for alarm. This disease is limited to Takers only, and you need direct contact with those infected for it to spread. The general population is perfectly safe." Ginkev paused. "I am sad to report that within the last hour, all of the afflicted have died."

Gasps and shocked cries raced through the crowd.

No! It couldn't be true! I'd just seen the apprentices. Surely it hadn't taken us over an hour to escape. I couldn't be certain though. It was all such a blur. I glanced at the sun directly overhead. Hadn't it been much lower before?

"Are there Healers left?"

"Who's going to take care of our injured?"

"How could you let this happen?"

"Rest assured the Luminary is saddened by this terrible loss, and is working with the Duke to rectify the situation. To ensure that no more Healers fall ill, the Luminary has instituted a full quarantine of the League. He asks that those needing healing contact the pain merchants, as the League will be working closely with them to maintain the care Geveg needs."

"You can't trust the pain merchants!"

The crowd started yelling and shoving forward. I'd have bruises on my bruises by morning. Danello moved closer, putting his arms protectively around me. Ginkev shouted over the crowd, words of reassurance, but no one was listening anymore.

Angry mutters were growing louder.

"Liar!"

"They're not really dead! The Duke stole them for his war, didn't he?"

A rock flew up and cracked Ginkev on the temple. He yelped and toppled off the speaker's platform. People surged forward, smashing between us and shoving us apart.

"Nya!" Danello called, reaching for me.

I lunged for his hand, but the surging crowd swept me away, hurtling me toward the League.

SIXTEEN

"**N**ya!"

"Over here!" I waved my arms but couldn't tell where the voice had come from or even who had yelled it. The mob kept shoving forward, banging me between them as they surged forward.

It felt like the first food riots at the end of the war, during the siege when all we had left was what we'd stored on the main island. When the Duke had control of our farming isles and the marsh farms, and trapped us so we'd turn on each other and stop fighting him. More riots had come in the early days of the occupation, when he'd kept us hungry, giving us food from our own farms and making us beg for it.

Memories flashed through my mind as anonymous feet squashed my toes and kicked my shins. Dozens of folks were trampled to death every riot, and *those* mobs had been desperate and weak from hunger. This one was angry and strong.

Danello's head popped above the crowd to my right.

"Danello!"

He found me and our eyes met. He called something I couldn't hear and struggled to get past the men trying to tear down the speaker's platform. Another surge, and I stumbled farther away. Danello vanished back into the mob. For a crazy moment, I felt as if I'd never see him again, but he had to still be there behind the crowd.

A man fell into me, and his elbow smacked my stomach. I gasped and doubled over, sucking in breath. Another person hit me from behind, and I staggered sideways. I bounced off the crowd and flailed for anything to grab and stop my fall. Images of trampled bodies flashed behind my eyes. I fell to one knee, and pain raced up my leg. My other foot slipped, and I was falling.

A hand shot out between broad backs and grabbed my arm. "Got you!"

"Aylin!" I sobbed as Aylin yanked me back to

my feet. Someone tripped on me and I fell forward again, but she caught and steadied me.

"I'm so glad to see you," I cried, fighting the crowd.

"Me too. I thought we lost you. Hold on, and follow me."

She held tight to my hand and headed against the surging mob, twisting and ducking, using her dancer's grace to get through. She kept one hand in front of her, pushing aside a shoulder or elbow and directing the surge of people around us. When one didn't turn, she found a soft spot and pinched.

I wanted to lift my head higher and search for Tali, but I was too afraid to break the smooth ribbon Aylin had somehow made of us.

"I got her," Aylin said, dragging me forward and pushing me against the outer League fence. Danello, Tali, and Soek stood clustered against it, protected from the crowd by the thick pillar and the gate.

Tali pulled me in and hugged me tight, her face streaked with dirt.

Aylin squeezed in near enough to yell over the mob. "My room is closest. Think we can get there?"

We all nodded. Aylin grabbed Danello's hand and wound her way back into the crowd that poured around the pillar. Danello grabbed my hand, I grabbed Tali's, and she took Soek's. We struggled through the crowd, but people kept surging forward, trying to get to the League. Rocks and other debris whizzed past us. Danello took an elbow to the eye, and someone shoved Aylin so hard she crashed into Danello and nearly knocked them both down.

The crowd had clogged up the more narrow entrance where the road led into the League.

"Get ready to shove forward, hard," Aylin called back, then a piercing scream split the air. People startled and froze, heads swiveling. Aylin screamed again and yanked us, darting into the small crack opened by the now-still crowd.

Was everyone in Geveg racing to the League to yell and fight? What could they hope to accomplish? Anger wouldn't bring the Healers back. It would only bring the Duke.

We crawled over a low wall and into someone's garden, clinging to each other as people rushed by.

"I can't believe they're dead," Tali whispered first, but we were all thinking it.

Soek nodded slowly. "We got out just in time."

"You were lucky," Danello added.

Were we? They'd lied about the disease, so what if they were lying again now? Not all the apprentices had been that close to death. Lanelle certainly wasn't, though it was possible she hadn't been counted as "one of the sick Healers."

"What if they killed them?" I said, not wanting to believe it.

Aylin hugged herself, rubbing her arms vigorously. "I believe they'd be that monstrous, but the logistics of it." She shook her head. "Wouldn't it be a lot easier for them to get more pynvium than murder that many people? Where would they even put the bodies?"

Soek nodded. "She's right—it would have to take longer than an hour to do all that. They couldn't have had time."

Danello nudged me and pointed at the street, past the crowd. "Soldiers are coming."

The Governor-General's soldiers shoved their way through, their blue uniforms cheery and bright on a day that wasn't. How many of them remembered the riots during the second year of occupation, when we'd tried to rebel, tried to regain our independence despite the soldiers lining our streets?

"It's going to get bad out here," Aylin said. The look on her face said she remembered those riots too, and the ships full of new soldiers the Duke had sent to stop them. "We'd better get to my place."

"Yeah, let's go."

I clung to Tali as we hurried, wondering how long it would be before the Duke sent his soldiers to crush us again. And if any of us would survive.

Aylin gave me the last of her dresses, and I went to the washroom and changed out of my filthy clothes. When I got back, Danello and Soek were sitting on opposite sides of the door, with Tali by the window. We barely had room to move with five of us in there.

"How's it look outside?" I asked Tali. She was watching at the window while Aylin rubbed a sweet-smelling salve on our cuts and bruises. Aylin acted embarrassed to own it with so many real Healers in the room, but no one seemed to care.

Tali turned to me. "Smoke's getting thicker near the League. I think one of the market squares is burning. People and soldiers are running past us, but no one is stopping." She pushed sweaty locks off her face. "I guess there's nothing here to loot."

"That'll change," muttered Soek.

"Can you see my neighborhood?" Danello asked from his spot on the floor. "Is there smoke?"

Tali leaned out for a few seconds, then drew back in. "No, I don't think so. It looks like it's all in the Baseeri neighborhoods so far. And around the League itself."

"I'm sure they're okay," I said to Danello, putting my hand on his shoulder. Jovan was a smart boy—he'd keep everyone safe until their father got home.

He nodded absently but still looked worried. I couldn't blame him. If Tali hadn't been with me, I'd be out there trying to get to her. But Danello was smart enough not to risk himself like that. He was older, and probably remembered the riots better than I did. The soldiers hadn't killed just those who were causing trouble.

"It's happening again, isn't it?" Aylin whispered.

"No, it's different this time," I said.

"Only the politics. We're angry again, and you know how this always ends. First the riots, then the denouncements of the Duke. People are already blaming him, and they'll turn on the Governor-General soon. All those soldiers are still in Verlatta. How soon before the Duke sends some here?"

"Maybe the Governor-General will calm everyone down." Even as I said it, I didn't believe it. Soldiers just made everything worse. Blue uniforms stirred up a lot of hatred in Geveg.

"I don't think so," Tali said, gesturing us over to the window. We squeezed in around her and stared out.

Six soldiers were herding people along the street, shoving and yelling at them. Several of the people had bloody heads. Those in the street yelled back, grabbing rocks and whatever smashed items were lying around and waving them threateningly. A man dashed forward and threw a broken chair at the soldiers. It hit one on the head and shoulders, and the others lunged over and clubbed the man who'd thrown it. He fell. They left him lying there, and blood slowly pooled beneath his head.

"This is how it started in Verlatta too," said Soek, pulling away from the window. He settled back on the floor near Aylin. "We even had a treaty with the Duke. Didn't matter."

"Maybe we'll win this time?" Tali asked. She didn't understand. She'd been too young to remember.

I shook my head. "We won't. We couldn't win when we had our own soldiers, and plenty of Healers and pynvium. How can we possibly fight without any of that?"

A knock banged on the door, and we all jumped. Aylin started to rise, but Danello waved her back down and went to the door. Soek stood opposite him, but out of sight and ready with a footstool in his other hand if anyone wanted trouble. Danello glanced his way and nodded as if he approved.

"Who is it?" Danello called through the door. He reached over and grabbed his rapier off Aylin's table, though there wasn't much space to use it if he needed to.

"I'm looking for Aylin." The voice sounded familiar.

"Open it," said Aylin, climbing over the bed.

Danello cracked open the door and peeked out. "Name?"

"Where's Aylin?"

"Kione?" Aylin said, shouldering past Danello and opening the door wider. Soek stepped back before it could thump him in the nose.

Kione took a step inside, but Danello didn't let him in any farther. "I need your friend, the crazy one who kept sneaking into the League."

"Why?" Danello said, moving forward as if he were trying to hide me and Tali. "Aylin, who is this guy?"

Kione took a step closer, and Danello flicked the rapier. I couldn't see much past his back, but I had a feeling the rapier was aimed at Kione's throat.

"Don't skewer him." I jumped up and tugged on Danello's arm until he lowered the weapon. Defending me was a sweet gesture, but Kione might know what had happened at the League. "He helped get Tali out. Kind of."

"Kione, what's going on?" Aylin asked.

"They're lying."

"We know—there's no disease; the pain killed them."

"No, they're lying about them being dead." Kione shoved inside until he was face-to-face with me. "Nya, the apprentices are alive."

SEVENTEEN

"They're alive?" I repeated, wanting to believe it, but afraid too.

"Most of them. A few died, and I think that's what gave the Luminary the idea to say they all did. Some of his men were seen taking bodies to the morgue."

Tali laughed, relief bright on her flushed cheeks. "That's wonderful! We can still save them then."

"What? No," I said. "If we go back, we're all dead."

"But we have to, Nya. We can't leave them there."

Kione nodded. "That's why I came to find you. They hurt Lanelle. I saw her in the spire room in

one of the beds. That Elder, the sick one who wants
to cut them up—"

"Vinnot."

"Yeah, Vinnot. He had me carry up some supplies, and I saw Lanelle *and* the others. I heard the
Luminary tell him they could finish in peace if the
Duke thought the Healers were dead. That they
could set sail long before he came to investigate."

"The Duke's coming *here?*"

"I'm not sure." He shrugged. "I couldn't quite
catch it all, but I got the impression that they
expected him to, and they wanted to leave before that
happened."

"Why would the Luminary lie?" asked Danello.
"Why would they *leave?*"

It didn't make sense. I glanced at the five scared
faces in the room. Though cruel, the Luminary
wasn't stupid. He had to know telling Geveg the
Healers were dead would upset folks, and when
Gevegians got upset, riots almost always followed.
He wouldn't do that unless—

I stiffened. "Could he have caused the riot on
purpose?"

Aylin hugged herself. "Why would anyone do
that?"

"I don't know." The Luminary had a plan, that

much was clear, but beyond that—what he was after was murky as marsh mud.

"Who knows what they're up to over there?" Kione said. "I just know that not long after I over-heard them, that announcement was made. Things are really bad now, Nya. You need to go back and save Lanelle."

I bristled at his tone. *I* needed to, not him. Not *us.*

I shook my head. "We'll never get back inside. The entire League is on alert. There are a thousand people clogging up the streets. Soldiers are all over the place."

"I know. But you got in before—you can do it again."

Saea be damned I would. "Lanelle helped them, Kione. You know that, don't you?"

"She had no choice! I helped them too, but I also helped *you.*"

I scoffed, and he glanced away.

"Okay, not a lot, but I could have said no."

"Nya," Aylin said, "if you're right and the riot is on purpose, then whatever the Luminary is doing is about more than just Lanelle—or the apprentices," she quickly added. "Look outside. Those people are angry because they *were told* the Healers are dead, not because they actually *are* dead. You heard them yelling—they think that's a lie, that the Duke stole them just like he did in the war."

"It *is* a lie," Danello said, his fists clenched at his sides. "Does it really matter which lie the Luminary tells?"

My guts said it did. The Luminary was telling a lie to make us angry when he could have just lied to the Duke. There was no *reason* to make us angry unless it somehow aided his plan. Maybe the Luminary thought the Duke wouldn't believe him unless Geveg did too? The Duke had to have spies here, and riots would support the Luminary's claim.

But why claim it? I sighed and ran my hands through my hair. The Luminary and Vinnot wanted to do something, and they didn't want the Duke knowing about it. So if the lie was *about* the Healers, then that something had to involve the Healers in some way. What value could Healers have to the Luminary that didn't include the Duke?

Lanelle had said Vinnot was doing "special research" for the Duke, so his creepy symptom list must fit in somewhere as well, though I couldn't see how. The only thing the Duke cared about was pynvium and getting more of it. No, it had to be something both he *and* the Luminary would want for themselves. Something valuable enough to risk a citywide riot over.

I jerked my head up and gasped. Of course!

"Unusual Takers!" I cried. No one listened. I climbed onto the bed and shouted it. "He's after the unusual Takers!"

Everyone gaped at me.

"The last few years," I began, "the Duke has cared about only two things—pynvium and unusual Takers. He's spent money and soldiers to get both. The Luminary and Vinnot have been searching for something among the injured apprentices at the Duke's request, something rare enough that they'd risk lying to him to keep it."

"Takers?" Soek said, puzzled.

"Takers like *us*. I think the Duke's figured out a way to force Taker abilities to manifest. Tali, you said apprentices were disappearing days before the ferry accident, right?"

"For almost a week."

"And Kione said there were two other rooms with Healers in them. Small rooms, so they were probably set up before the ferry accident as well. He was *already* testing for unusual Takers. The accident just gave him an opportunity to test everyone at once."

Aylin looked just as lost as Soek. "Test them how?"

"By giving them pain, and lots of it. It's just like the twins—I didn't sense anything about them until they were carrying pain, but then I did."

Danello paled and held a hand out. "Wait, what twins? My brothers? Jovan and Bahari?"

I bit my lip, sudden guilt quenching my excitement. "Oh, Danello, I'm so sorry. I should have told you before, but I was trying to protect them." I explained what I'd sensed when the twins had been linked and full of pain. How their talents had felt stronger. He paled even further.

Kione wiped a hand across his lip. "Lanelle did say she was ordered to watch several of the apprentices who'd exhibited specific symptoms. She had a whole list of them."

"She was paying a lot of attention to me when I first starting getting better," Soek added softly. "I started pretending I was more hurt than I was, and she stopped."

"But Vinnot works for the Duke," Danello said. "So does the Luminary."

Kione folded his arms across his chest. "Just because you work for someone doesn't mean you're loyal to them."

"Everyone knows what he'd do to them if he found out," Danello said. "So why risk lying to him?"

"Who cares? Are we going to go back for Lanelle or not?" Kione whined, his gaze darting to the window, the floor, the door, like he was—

"Distracted," I said, shivering at the thought. "It's all a distraction! *That's* why the Luminary caused the riots. Not only does it help support the lie that the Takers are dead, but who'd notice the Luminary and Vinnot escaping in all the chaos?" What heartless rats! Both had proper Baseeri travel seals, but the Takers they planned to kidnap wouldn't. They'd show up on the travel records the Duke received, proof that two men he'd trusted had *lied* to him. *Stolen* from him. They couldn't afford that. They had to bypass the checkpoints, distract everyone so they wouldn't see the escape.

Saints, they were actually planning to betray the Duke! I was all for turning against him, but not at the expense of Geveg.

Tali looked hopeful. "So if everyone hears that the Luminary lied to them and that this isn't the Duke trying to steal our Healers again, they'll stop fighting?"

"It's possible," I said, though it seemed like a lot to hope for. "It might make them angrier, but at least then the Governor-General could arrest him. That would calm folks down. But if the riots *don't* stop . . ." I didn't want to finish that sentence. The Duke might burn us out like he had Sorille.

"See?" said Kione. "You *do* have to go back to the League."

I wanted to, I really did. All those Takers were just as helpless as Tali had been, but they didn't have anyone to come save them. "We'd never get back inside. There has to be another way to prove the Luminary is lying."

"What if you flashed your way in?" Soek said. I winced as all eyes turned to him.

Tali looked at me. "What's he talking about?"

"It's how we escaped. She was incredible," Soek gushed. "She threw pynvium chunks at the guard and *flashed* them. I've never seen anyone do that before."

Tali's eyes got big as oppas. "You flashed? How?"

Soek and his big mouth. At least he hadn't mentioned what I'd done to Lanelle, and for that I was grateful. I pulled one of the chunks out of my pocket. "I don't know. I was angry, and hurt, and it . . . happened."

Tali got a funny look on her face and reached

for the chunk. "Let me see that." She held it in her palms, her odd look shifting to disbelief. "This is empty."

"It can't be empty—we used them all. I know we did."

"You . . . shifted it out, maybe?" She held the plum-sized chunk between her hands, brows pulled tight together. "I don't know what you did, but this is usable again."

Excited murmurs raced around the room. Soek mumbled something about me being incredible. Even Kione seemed to realize the importance of this and stayed quiet.

"That's not possible," I said. The only way to empty pynvium was to enchant it to flash, and after that, it would never hold pain again. No one had ever found a way to reuse pynvium, and the enchanters had tried for years.

"Possible or not, you did it anyway."

I sat there, staring at the impossible chunk. What if I really *could* empty pynvium? Forget testing for Takers; the Duke would send an army to bring me back if he found out. What a resource I would be for him! I shuddered.

"Can I see that?" Soek asked, reaching out his hand. Tali nodded and dropped the chunk into it.

His brows furrowed, and he nodded. "It *is* empty." A moment later he sighed and handed me the chunk. "Mostly empty now. Good to be rid of those aches." He handed it back to me. "Your turn."

I just stared at it. Danello looked torn, as if he wanted to spare me the embarrassment of explaining but didn't know if I wanted Soek to know I couldn't fill the pynvium chunk. Tali picked up the chunk and enclosed both our hands around it. My fingers tingled as she *drew* my pain away, into the chunk that should have been useless. She cupped the pynvium for a moment, then set it on the small table. Her fingers hovered over it, as if she was reluctant to let it go.

"So what about Lanelle?" Kione insisted again.

Soek shook his head. "After what she did to me? I'm never going back there."

"It wasn't her fault," Kione said.

"She got what she deserved."

Kione swore and stepped toward Soek as if he was going to hit him. Aylin grabbed his arm. "We don't have time for this. This isn't about one person. If the Luminary gets nervous enough, he might *really* kill them. We have to expose the Luminary before the Duke sends more soldiers here."

"And before people start taking their anger out on the Governor-General," I added. Once that happened, the Duke might decide merely occupying Geveg wasn't enough to control us. He might decide to obliterate us—just as he'd done to Sorille. I sighed. "You're right. We have to go back."

Heads nodded all around, except Soek's.

"I can't go back," he pleaded. "I want to help, really I do, but I've escaped both Verlatta's siege and that room, and I don't think I have another escape in me. My luck can't be that good."

No one said anything. Kione looked ready to join him, even though he was the one trying to get us to go.

"I'll stay here and guard Aylin's room," Soek said after the silence became uncomfortable. "I can make sure no one loots it. I know it's not much, but I don't . . . I just can't go back."

Aylin looked uncertain. "It's a nice gesture, and I don't mean to offend, but I have no idea who you are. I'm not just going to leave you in my room."

Soek didn't seem offended. "I'll stay in the hall then, or on the stairs."

She thought about it a moment, then nodded. "Well, okay, I guess that's good enough."

I stared at them: at Tali, the sister I loved, at Aylin, the friend I loved like a sister, at Danello— who was someone I probably *could* love if we survived long enough to spend any real time together and find out. They were all willing to risk their lives to save strangers. Just like Mama, like Papa, in the war. Should we do this? *Could* we? Grannyma's words nudged me. *Doing what's right is seldom easy.*

"We can't fight our way in. We're not trained soldiers, so even with the flashing it won't work," I said. I looked at the chunks just waiting to be emptied and filled again, and a plan started to form. "We'll have to sneak in, just like I did to get Tali, and then get back out."

Danello frowned and rubbed the back of his neck "How do we sneak out sixty injured apprentices?"

"We don't. We flash and use this pynvium to heal them and all escape together. We'll be able to refill the chunks inside, so we should be able to flash our way out as far as the courtyard. Once we get to League Circle, we can show everyone in Geveg the Luminary is a liar." And save who knew how many lives at the same time.

"Can we hold off the guards that long?" Aylin asked.

Danello shrugged. "Depends on how many the Luminary sends to stop us. But if we can get inside without alerting the guards, we might have a while before anyone checks on the apprentices. With the mob outside, they probably don't have many guards inside."

A big if. "The door to the spire room locks, doesn't it?" I asked.

Tali nodded.

"As you heal the apprentices, we could use their cots to barricade the door," said Danello.

It wasn't a great plan, but it was our only hope. I pulled out a handful of pynvium. "All we need to know now is if I can flash these things on purpose." If not, our rescue plan didn't stand a chance. I turned to Tali, staring at me with fear and excitement in her eyes. "Do you still have the chunks I gave you for Danello's pain?"

"Yes. I didn't know what else to do with them." She dug into her pockets and handed them to me.

"Everyone move back. I don't know how large the flash will be."

"I'll be in the hall," Kione muttered. Soek and Aylin nodded and followed him outside.

"I'm staying," Tali said.

"Me too." Danello leaned back against the wall and smiled.

I took a deep breath and tried to clean my churning mind. The pynvium felt cool and rough. How had *I* felt before? Hot and angry? I reached for that anger and threw.

Thud.

The pynvium bounced off the wall and rolled under the bed.

"It didn't work, right?" asked Tali.

"No. Trust me, you'll know it when it happens."

Anger wasn't right. I had been angry, but I'd been more scared of getting caught when it flashed. I took a deep breath and tried again.

Thud.

"Maybe if you—"

"Tali, I'm working on it."

"I'm just trying to help."

"Maybe you should wait outside."

"What if you—"

"Tali, will you just go . . ." *away.* I stared at the pynvium chunks in my hands while Papa's words whispered in my ears. *Enchanting a trigger feels like blowing dandelions in the wind.* I'd been six, maybe seven, sitting by the forge as Papa shaped and enchanted the pynvium bricks. *It's easy to set them, Nya-pie,* he'd said, cooling the brick in the water bucket at his feet. *You'll feel the pain gather in the metal, tickling under your fingers. Next, you think about what it needs to do, and you give it an order. Then you let it go. Just picture it drifting away like dandelions blowing in the wind.*

Dandelions.

"I have it. Stay back."

I took another breath and threw, picturing light and fluffy seeds bursting apart, flying away on a wind I couldn't see.

Whoomp!

The fine-sand tingle washed over me, same as it had when I'd flashed the guard. Tali and Danello yelped behind me.

"We're okay," Tali said as I spun around. "Just a sting." She picked up the flashed chunk and held it, her eyes closed. Then she looked at me with wonder and a little bit of pride. "You really *can* do it. And you thought you were useless."

My eyes watered, but she ran outside before I could figure out how to answer *that*. Maybe not useless, but was this how I wanted to be useful? I heard their excited voices in the hall. For good or bad, I *could* do this. There'd be no excuses to stay now.

Saints save us, we were going back to the League.

EIGHTEEN

Moving with the mob was a lot easier than fighting against it, and we made it to the League with less fuss than we'd left it. Most people were cramming themselves into the front court-yard and the main doors, so the side path around to the rear gardens was clear. We sank down behind the all-too-familiar hibiscus bushes by the side gate seldom used by anyone but apprentices and League staff. If I was going to keep this up, I might as well set up a cot here and move in. Guards patrolled the outer courtyard and stood by all the entrances, while the Governor-General's soldiers shoved angry people around League Circle. More than a few shoved back.

"So how do we get in?" Danello whispered into my ear.

Shiverflesh pimpled my arms. "We sneak."

"Is there a back way in?" Aylin asked, poking her head over his shoulder.

"Several, but all the public entrances so far have looked well guarded. Kione, think you can get us past one of them? Any friends working?"

"I know a few guys who work the south gate."

That gate opened onto the rear docks along the lakeside of the grounds. It probably wouldn't have crowds trying to shove their way in—not unless they came by pole boat. "Okay, so we pretend to be apprentices and Kione and Danello can pretend to be protecting us. They can say we were out on heal calls or something. We get inside, then make our way to the spire room."

"But we're not wearing uniforms," Tali pointed out. Those were too torn and stained to be of any use even if we had been wearing them.

"Kione is. Maybe he'll give us enough credibility. We both still have braids."

Her expression said she didn't believe that, but we didn't have much choice. If they didn't fall for it, we wouldn't get inside. Any fighting would draw not only more guards, but the Governor-

General's soldiers as well.

We crept through the gardens toward the south side. Two guards stood by the gate, neither of whom I recognized. But I did recognize the man next to them. Jeatar! What was he doing here? He was speaking to the guards, gesturing instructions I could guess by now. Keep an eye out, watch these areas.

Kione's colorful swear was exactly what my dry throat wouldn't let out. "Those aren't my friends," he whispered.

Nor mine, though who Jeatar really was I wasn't sure.

"Should we attack?" Danello edged closer. I put a hand on his arm and stopped him.

"I don't want to hurt them," Tali said. "The short one tells me a joke every time I see him."

Aylin waved a hand at me. "Nya, what if we go in the same way you got out?"

We all looked up.

"The roof?"

Kione shook his head. "You're as crazy as she is."

"What's wrong?" Tali actually smiled at him. "Lanelle not worth it?"

I never wanted to hug her more in my life.

"She is," he grumbled.

"Okay, new plan," I said. "We go around the garden wall and up on the roof. Hopefully, there won't be any guards there." And hopefully Jeatar wouldn't see us.

"And if there are?"

Had Mama and Papa been this scared the first time they faced the Duke's soldiers? "*Then* we fight them. Quietly."

We slipped away from the hedge's protection and crept around the vine-draped wall, staying in the trees and bushes as much as possible. For the first time, I was thankful the League charged so much for heals; otherwise, they'd never have had enough money to waste on so many gardens.

The area where Soek and I had tackled the guards was clear, but there was at least one patrol circling the grounds. Probably more by now, with the riots and the mob out front.

"Danello first," I said. Kione stepped forward and locked his fingers together. Danello stepped into his hands, and Kione boosted him up to the roof. He hung a few seconds, legs swaying, before he dragged himself up and over. His head popped back a heartbeat later, and he held out a hand.

"Tali next."

Danello hoisted her up easy, then hauled Aylin over the edge. Kione gestured for me to take my turn.

"I'll go last," he said, checking both ways for patrols. Or maybe just seeing if he could run once my back was turned. Despite his plea to save Lanelle, I wasn't sure he was willing to risk anything for her.

He boosted me up, and I grabbed Danello's hand with both of mine. My knee caught on my skirt, and I dangled like garlic in a window. Danello grunted but didn't let go. Kione gave me a boost, and Danello hauled me up and over the edge.

I grinned. "Step one com—"

"Shh!" He smooshed a hand over my mouth and pushed me flat against the roof. "Patrol."

"Kione," I mumbled under his hand.

"He's hiding."

Voices came from below. ". . . heard something. Like scratches."

"Wind's been gusting today. Probably just branches."

"Didn't sound like branches."

Footsteps tapped. I didn't dare breathe. The guards sounded right underneath us, and—Saints and sinners! A fold of my skirt hung over the edge

287

of the roof, dangling down like a banner that said "Here we are!"

I tipped my head toward it. Danello stared at me, confused, then looked in the right direction. His eyes widened.

"I think someone was over here." The voice was softer now, as if farther away from the building. Had they seen Kione?

Danello stretched a hand toward my skirt, drawing it back inch by inch with his fingers.

"The grass is trampled, and look—broken branches."

"Should we notify the Captain?"

The hem of my skirt flipped over the edge and out of sight.

"Yeah, we—did you see that?"

Danello gripped my leg, down near my knee. Both were inches from the roof's edge.

"See what?"

"Something flapped on the roof. Give me a hand."

Creaking wood, then grunting. Were they carrying the bench over? Danello rolled slowly away, farther up the roof. Tali backed up. A tile clicked. Gravel slid out from under her foot. I shifted my arm and stopped it before it rolled too far.

What had to be the bench thudded below, then more creaking. My gaze flew along the edge of the roof. Eyes suddenly met mine, less than a foot from my face.

"Hey—"

Danello leaned across me and slammed the hilt of his rapier against the guard's head. The guard grunted and fell back and, by the surprised yelp, landed right on top of his partner.

"Up! Up! Up!" I pushed at Danello's chest even as he was rolling off me. He grabbed my hand and yanked me to my feet beside him.

An unfamiliar cry from below, then Kione's head popped above the roof's edge.

"Grab him!"

"Not yet—I have to hide these guys or someone will find them." He jumped back down. After an agonizing few minutes, Kione appeared again.

"I tied them up and stashed them under some bushes on the far side. Let me move the bench back—then get ready to help me up there."

I nodded, my heartbeat racing. Hiding a knocked-out and tied-up fourth cord hadn't worked for me, but maybe Kione was better at it. He must have gotten *some* training as a guard.

Kione jumped, and Danello and I each grabbed

a hand and pulled him up.

Aylin stood. "Which way?" she asked, taking tentative steps along the roof.

"Over here." I snatched Tali's hand and scaled the tiles as fast as I could without slipping. The roof leveled out, and we reached a sunken corner with a wall on one side and a window on the other. Inside looked like a sitting room, possibly near one of the upper classroom wings by the look of it.

"Think your rapier can—"

Danello smacked the hilt against the window. Glass shattered and tinkled across the tiles like bells.

He grinned sheepishly. "That was a lot louder than I expected."

"Be ready in case more guards show up." I slid my hand through the jagged hole in the glass and unhooked the latch. The window ground open, scraping across the shards.

Danello tugged on my shoulder as I tried to go inside. "Me first." He jumped in, rapier drawn and ready. Kione followed. After several tense heartbeats, he leaned back out and said, "Clear."

I took his outstretched hand and slipped inside. "Tali, where are we?"

"Upper classrooms near the main ward."

"Can we reach the spires from here?"

"There should be stairs at the end of the hall."

Danello took the lead. "Stay behind me."

I followed him and Kione took the rear. The doors were all open along the hall, and the empty rooms and bare beds gave me shiverfeet. There should have been people in them, and Healers and apprentices hurrying about on rounds.

Tali pointed. "It's that way."

The hall ended at the interior atrium above the main entrance. An open-air walkway encircled the entire floor above the main antechamber, with stairs at the far end. The delicate railing was all that stood between us and the chamber below. When we were younger, Tali and I used to wait for Grannyma and watch the folks coming in and out of the League, sitting with our legs dangling around the bars and our faces pressed between them.

We followed Tali, keeping as close to the wall as possible. She skirted the room and headed for the opposite stairwell. I was pretty sure the private treatment rooms where I'd tied up the fourth cord were beyond it, so the stairs had to lead to the spire. We were almost there.

We sneaked the rest of the way up the stairs, slipped out of the alcove, and tiptoed the last few turns to the spire room. I peeked around a thick column bulging out from the wall. Two guards stood on either side of the doorway. One more than usual, but not as many as I'd feared.

"Think there are more inside?" Danello whispered.

"Has to be *someone* inside." I tried not to picture Vinnot, but he was probably there, checking off symptoms like items on a grocery list.

Kione moved closer. "Should we draw them over here?"

I cocked my head and listened for guards. Except for the shouting outside, all was quiet.

"Charge them?" Danello suggested. "Knock them out, drag them back, and start yelling? If there are others inside, it might get them to leave and we can deal with them out here."

Kione nodded. "I'll get the left one."

"Right."

I started to say *I'll just flash them*, but Danello took off like an angry crocodile. Kione raced behind him, pumping his arms and lowering his shoulder. The guards froze for a blessed moment, then reached for their swords. Danello slammed into the right one. Kione hit the left. Bones cracked, heads smacked, and both guards smashed into the wall behind them. Swords went flying, crashing to the floor loud enough to reverberate down the hall.

The spire room door opened, and two men dashed out. High cords, from the loops on their shoulders. They paused to stare at the fighting, then ran toward us, hands outstretched as if to tackle us. Aylin stepped forward and kicked one in the crotch. He gasped and doubled over, curling into a ball with both hands cupped between his legs. That left the other for us.

"Get him!" I cried to Tali, charging forward. She dove with me, and together we crashed into his chest. He wheezed and staggered, dropping to his knees and grabbing my arm as we fell. I tumbled down underneath him. I squirmed and kicked, my legs tangled up in my stupid skirt.

"Help!" I cried.

Tali beat her fists against his back, but he didn't seem to notice. Suddenly Danello appeared, grabbing the cord's shoulders and flinging him into the wall. A third guard ran out of the spire room.

"Behind you!" I yelled.

Danello turned and gasped. He staggered away, hands tight against his middle, while red stains spread outward from behind his fingers. The third guard stepped closer, his sword out and still smeared with blood.

Danello's blood.

NINETEEN

"Danello!" I dove forward as he collapsed, catching him before he smacked his head on the hard floor. I pushed up his shirt, searching for his wound. The guard drew back his sword, too far away for me to get a hand on him, but close enough to stab us both. Kione launched himself sideways, tackling the guard and knocking him to the floor right next to me.

With one hand tight against Danello's middle, I reached the other toward the guard's flesh. I *drew*, and Danello's pain filled me, burning around my middle like I'd run ten times around Geveg. I *pushed* it into the guard who'd stabbed him. I savored his scream, even as it sickened me. For once, I was glad there were no Healers left to heal. The guard fell to the floor and was still.

"Danello?" I cradled his head in my lap.

"Ny . . . uh . . ."

"Easy, don't try to speak yet." I stroked his hair. "I'm so sorry. I almost got you killed."

He patted my arm as if to say "It wasn't your fault."

"It *is* my fault."

"Nya."

"It is!"

"We have to get these guys inside before anyone sees us," Kione said, tugging at my shoulder.

Danello sat up, pale but no longer dying.

"Can you walk?" I asked, helping him up.

"I'm fine." He swayed to his feet and held on to me. "Thank you."

"You're welcome." I didn't look at him. We'd barely won this fight, and I didn't want to think about taking on more guards.

"You there! What are you doing in here?" shouted Elder Vinnot. He and several more guards stood at the top of the stairs.

I saw three before Danello shoved me forward toward the spire room. The others were already racing through the door. Slipping inside, I spun on my heel and grabbed the door as Danello barreled through, the guards right behind him.

"Shut it!"

Tali and I threw ourselves against the door. It slammed shut, but flew open again as the guards hit it, knocking me back onto my butt. Tali pushed against it again, but she didn't weigh enough to reclose it. Aylin jumped over me and added her weight.

Danello looked around wildly, patting down his hips. "Where's my rapier?"

One of the guards fought to wiggle through, pushing the door farther open. The hallway behind him was full of green uniforms.

"We can't hold it!" Aylin said, her face red.

Danello kicked the guard's leg. He cried out and pulled away from the door. Aylin and Tali shoved again, and the door thudded shut. Danello pushed a shoulder against it as I scrambled over and slid the latch, locking it. Banging rattled the door, then shouts and swears.

"I can't find Lanelle!" Kione said. He went from cot to cot, searching the apprentices as I had done earlier, looking for Tali.

Tali whimpered. "Oh, Nya, some are missing. Do you think they're dead?"

The first row of cots was empty, but the rest were still full. I shoved the pynvium sack at Tali. "Start handing them out, fast."

We'd need as many apprentices on their feet as soon as possible if the guards got in. They might be young, but Healers knew where the soft spots were on a body and where the vulnerable joints were. And that might be the only advantage we had.

"We have to block the door," I said, dragging over a cot. Aylin ran to help while Danello kept his back to the door, but the latch was already pulling free of the wood.

"I have to find Lanelle first," Kione said.

For a terrible moment, I hoped she had been in the row of empty cots. Shame twisted my guts, but if she was here, she'd tell them all what I'd done to her. "Later. We have to barricade the door."

"But she's hurt! I have to find her."

"She'll be dead if the Luminary's guards get through. Help us!"

Bang!

The door shook. Kione went pale and raced for the closest empty cot.

"That wasn't a fist or a foot," Aylin said, pressing against the door.

Sword hilts? One of the small statuettes from an

alcove? "They couldn't have found a battering ram so fast."

Kione heaved a cot into place. "Doesn't matter what it is, it'll break through."

We kept dragging cots and piling them in front of the door. Danello showed us how to interlock them to make it stronger. It wouldn't keep the cots from skidding along the floor when the door broke open, but they wouldn't be easy to shove aside.

Bang!

A spidery crack branched out above the latch.

Danello glanced around. "Is there anything heavier in here?"

"Some cabinets, but I don't think we can move those."

Tali ran up to me, her cheeks flushed pink. "I need more pynvium." She handed me the used chunks. They seemed so small, the room so large. I counted twenty-one heads in the dim lamplight. If they all held the same amount of pain as Tali had, I'd have to empty every pynvium chunk we had at least twice for each apprentice. Could we hold the guards off that long?

Kione wedged in a cot and looked hopefully at Tali. "Did you see Lanelle?"

"No, but I'll look for her and heal her next."

299

"She's last," I said without thinking. Fresh guilt hit me, along with everyone's shocked stares. "Heal the worst off first. Lanelle just got her pain, but the others are close to death. They don't have as much time. We have to heal them enough to get them mobile, then move on to the next."

More guards hit the door, and a sprinkling of dust showered down on us. Kione laughed nervously. "A lot of good getting them moving will do. They'll just die on their feet."

"Better than being slaughtered in your bed," Danello called as Kione raced back to look for Lanelle.

I grabbed the handful of pynvium. "Stand back." I didn't know if the pain would go through the door, but the guards might be close enough to get a sting or two. I threw the pynvium, concentrating on dandelions in the wind.

Whoomp. Whoomp, whoomp, whoomp.

Startled cries from the other side, then thuds and frightened swearing. Hope fluttered in my chest. Maybe we *could* pull this off.

"Aylin," I called as the empty pynvium clattered against the door and bounced down through the bed frames.

"Already going for them," she said, rushing past

me. She snatched up the chunks and ran back to the apprentices.

As Tali and Aylin brought the chunks back, I flashed them against the door. A few more yelps from the other side, but it looked like they'd learned to stay away for now. Soon other voices floated to me over the yelps and occasional tentative bang; apprentice voices, pained, scared, and angry.

"Help me, please. I need more."

"Elder Mancov made me heal. I didn't want to heal."

"Get us out of here!"

I will, I promise. We had more pain now, so maybe I could flash us past the guards and out of the League. Once we got everyone moving, we could heal and flash on the way.

"Here," Tali said, handing me another handful of pynvium. "We're going to need to do this a lot. There are a few that might only need one or two handfuls to be able to walk, but more need five or six."

"Maybe we should start giving one to everyone and reduce the pain all at once?"

"Not yet. I have a few still in too much pain for that."

"Okay, do what you think is best." She'd know

with a touch who needed it most. I focused on emptying the pynvium instead. I threw the chunks at the door again.

"Lanelle's not here!"

Instead of the low *whoomp*, the pynvium fell harmlessly to the floor around the barricade. Danello looked at me in surprise, then let go of the cots to gather them back up.

"You can do this," he said, smiling as if I needed encouragement.

Lanelle wasn't here? She couldn't be dead—she didn't get that much pain.

"Nya?"

I took the pynvium and nodded. Another throw, another handful of pynvium filled with pain. But instead of the prickling sting, all I felt was shame.

What if the Luminary had made an *example* out of her because of me?

The handful hit the floor, unflashed.

Danello gathered it again, this time more than surprise on his face. "Nya, what's wrong?"

"Nothing." Images of Lanelle crawling along the floor filled my mind. *Stay away from me!* she'd cried. Saints, I'd been so angry. But the Luminary would be a lot angrier. Maybe even angry enough to kill. It could have been her body people saw being carried to the morgue.

"We need pynvium over here," Aylin shouted. "Hurry up!"

I held out my hand. "Just give me the chunks."

"What's going on?" Danello asked warily. The pynvium fell like accusations into my palm.

The fight wouldn't stay out of my mind. The anger, the hatred that had washed over me as pain flashed over its victims. I concentrated on Papa and the dandelions and threw.

Whoomp.

"Get those to Tali."

Kione came over, twitching as if torn between leaving to hunt for Lanelle and staying where it was safe. "She was here before—I know she was. I saw her."

"Maybe they healed her."

"Then she'd be here, right? This was her post. She was taking care of them." He shook his head and pointed to the cots. "No, Vinnot and the Luminary were standing right there, and neither cared about her at all. If they'd wanted to heal her, they would have done it before I got there."

"Kione," I said, exasperated, "I don't know what happened to her."

He pouted and stalked over to the cots.

Aylin dashed up and handed me another handful of chunks. "We have four up and walking now." She said. "Their stories break your heart, but they're going to be okay."

"Good. How many more are close to death?"

"Just one."

I threw the pynvium at the door again. It flashed before it ever hit, leaving faint white speckles on the wood.

"Kione's pretty upset," she whispered, glancing over at him. He sat on one of the empty cots, head in his hands. "I think he actually wants to go look for her."

"If we get out of here, he can go look all he wants."

"That won't end well." Aylin took the empty chunks and dashed away.

Danello stayed quiet until Aylin was gone. "You think they killed her, don't you?" he asked from behind me, where it was safe from the flashing.

"I don't know. Maybe not. She helped them, so why kill her?" The white speckles stayed in the wood, not blowing away like the dust had.

"But did she help willingly?" He paused, and I fought the urge to turn around and check his expression. "From what Tali told us, a lot of people agreed to help because they had to."

"She knew what she was doing."

"Are you sure?"

I wasn't, but I wasn't going to say that.

Danello sighed. "You're acting strange. I know we don't know each other that well yet, but that just doesn't seem like you."

Didn't feel like me either. I was no better than Zertanik, trading one life for another.

Aylin arrived with another handful of pynvium. I flashed it, and she was off again.

"I don't know," he said. "You seem so different today, is all. You've been through a lot, and you might not be thinking clearly. I guess I'm just a little worried."

"What you should be worried about are those guards—" I stopped and stared at the door. "When did the banging stop?"

"What? I don't know." He crept forward and pressed his ear against the door, near the white speckles. It had to be my eyes playing tricks, but for a moment I thought the door bent out when he touched it.

"Do you hear anything?"

"No. Think they're unconscious? You've been flashing the door pretty hard."

More people for me to feel guilty over. But this was war, wasn't it? If they got inside, they'd kill us and the apprentices. I was just defending myself. Me shifting pain wasn't any different from Danello using his rapier.

It sure *felt* different though. I'd never wanted to be a weapon. All I'd wanted was to save Tali. I threw the pynvium again.

Whoomp.

No clattering, no thumps, no plinks of metals falling to the stone floor. I stared, shocked at the fine mist blowing back at me, and the soft hiss of coarse sand falling to the floor.

Saints and sinners! The pynvium chunks had disintegrated!

TWENTY

Had my anger poisoned the pynvium?

"What did you do?" Tali whispered, clutching my arm.

"Nothing. I did it the same way as before."

"But it's *gone,* Nya."

Not completely, but the sand wouldn't help us. Nothing would help us now.

Fearful twitters raced through the half-healed apprentices. "Gone?"

"There's no more pynvium?"

"Not again!"

Quiet sobs came next. I wanted to curl up on the floor and cry with them.

"I've never seen it do that before," Tali said.

"I don't know what happened." I couldn't have destroyed it. The Saints couldn't be that unfair. What good was a monster who shifted and destroyed the one thing that could help those she hurt?

I waved a hand at Aylin. "Bring me the rest. Maybe I tried to do too much at once."

She collected them off the floor and handed them over. I took them and threw one chunk against the door. It flashed like always. One of the apprentices even clapped, but the others hushed her.

"See? It worked! I don't know what happened before."

I threw a second. It flashed and turned to sand. Gasps and groans rippled through the room.

"I don't—it just—" I stared open-mouthed at the door. The pynvium was gone, but the white speckles now covered a band a foot high across the middle of the door.

I threw the rest, one chunk after another. All but two crumbled.

"Maybe pynvium can hold only so much pain?" said Danello. "Just like people?"

Bang!

We all screamed as the door cracked inward like a burst bubble. Right across the white speckled area.

Saints! Flashed pain hurt people; did it hurt *things* as well?

"They're breaking through," Danello said, pushing hard against the cots. "We need weapons. Kione, help us over here!"

I ran for more cots, dragging them over to fortify our barricade. I had to keep the guards out. Had to protect Tali and the apprentices. *Please, don't let me have hurt all those people for nothing.*

Aylin dashed to the cabinets and started searching for anything that could be used as a weapon, throwing rags and sheets over her shoulder as she dug through the shelves. The apprentices opened drawers along the back wall.

Bang!

Guards shoved at the cracked door, and a sword blade slipped through. An arm followed, creeping in and patting around as if looking for the lock. Danello slammed his fist against the hand, and it yanked back.

Nervous whimpers scurried through the room. The healed apprentices backed away and huddled together. I'd tried so hard to save them, but I'd only made things worse. The Luminary would kill all of us. We were nothing to him. Nothing but *pynvium*.

"Aylin," Danello called from the door. "Any luck on those weapons?"

"No!"

"Yes," I whispered, turning around. Maybe I wasn't a Healer, would never *be* a Healer, but right now we didn't need healing, we needed weapons—and *that* I could be. I had a whole room full of pain to shift. "I need an apprentice!"

Kione gasped. "You're going to use them on the barricade?"

"No, you henhead, I'm going to heal them *and* keep the guards out at the same time." Kione just stood there, but Danello raced to the nearest cot and picked up a first cord a few years older than me. Hurt, but aware, she gritted her teeth and held her hand out to me.

"Give those Baseeri scum all I've got."

I grabbed the first cord's hand as another arm snaked in. It stretched, exposing a thin band of wrist between cuff and glove. Aylin grabbed the hand, held it down for me. I reached for flesh and *pushed*.

The man screamed, and the arm's angle changed as if he'd collapsed.

"Bring others," I hissed, needle stabs fading along my legs. Crushed bones for sure.

From Danello's arms, another apprentice offered me a trembling hand and I took it, shifting quickly before the guards pulled another man away.

BANG!

The hole widened. Several cot frames snapped and fell to the floor. Wood screeched across stone, and the barricade moved a foot closer. A guard wiggled through the ragged hole in the door, kicking and shoving as he came, others right behind him, pushing him forward.

I turned. "I need more—" Words died. Behind me, the apprentices had formed a chain, hands clasped from cot to cot, the half-healed linking the rows and covering the gaps between those too weak to sit up.

Tali took the last hand and stretched her fingers to me, chin set, eyes hard. "Just like the twins, Nya, stronger when linked. We'll draw, you push."

It wouldn't be easy. Each Healer could heal the previous one in the chain, but the farther along the chain they healed, the worse it would get. By the time it got to Tali, she'd be unable to stop it—and neither would I. I'd have the pain from inside every last one of them. But unlike them, I could get rid of it without pynvium.

I wrapped my hand in Tali's, and Mama's face came to me. I suddenly knew how she'd felt that last day, facing Baseeri soldiers. She'd died to protect us. I wasn't going to let her—or Geveg—down now.

"Danello, grab him and pull back his sleeve," I said. I'd flashed pynvium, so maybe I could flash a *person*, channel the pain through them to the rest of the room. Skin touched skin, and my hand warmed against Tali's. It tingled and stung like I'd left it asleep for weeks.

We'd all done terrible things out of desperation. Things we'd never have considered before the Duke first invaded us, kicked us even harder when we tried to rebel. Danello wouldn't have asked me to shift into his family. Lanelle wouldn't have hurt her friends to keep her job. I wouldn't have hurt strangers to save friends. None of it was right, but stitch together enough wrongs, and it makes a blanket that almost keeps out the chill.

I was tired of shivering under the Duke's blankets.

I *drew* as Tali *drew*, as they all *drew*, reaching into one another, each healing the lower in the chain and dragging the pain up like a bucket from a canal. It rushed into me, boiling and hot. I opened a sluice-way as I'd done with the fisherman, the sisters, the parents, and families of those who came to Zertanik's for help.

Blinding pain sizzled between us. Two dozen voices merged in a single scream. It echoed in my ears long after the pain had left me, and it wasn't until Danello held me and smoothed my sweaty hair back that I realized the echoes were the guards' moans outside the door.

"Nya?" he said, sounding worried. "Can you hear me?"

"Danello?" My tongue felt thick and heavy in my mouth. My arms felt heavier, and I wasn't sure where my legs were. "Guards?"

"Unconscious, maybe worse. It looks like the pain went right through them all. As if it, I don't know, flashed from the man you had ahold of."

I sat forward and tried to move my limbs. Sharp tingling said my legs were indeed still there, though I wasn't sure I wanted them right now. "How . . . others?"

"They're okay. About the same as you, at least the ones at this end of the chain. The ones on the other side are better. They didn't have to heal as much as your side."

I managed to turn. Tali looked pale and sweaty, but was sitting up with a tired smile on her face. "Did it," she mumbled. The others smiled at me, at one another. They were all alive and moving.

"We have to get out of here." I struggled to stand. Danello helped me to my feet while Aylin helped

Tali. "More guards will come."

Across the room, apprentices stood, those at the far end helping those near the door. Excited whispers and grins raced along them, same as the pain had.

"What did we do?"

"Did Heal Master Ginkev ever say we could link like that?"

"Wonder what else we can do."

"Wonder what else *she* can do." Whispers ceased and eyes turned to me. My skin itched as if tiny spiders were running all over me.

I shook my arms. The last of the pain was fading and I felt like I had the morning after the ferry accident, but that muscle soreness would ease on its own.

I turned to the apprentices, the proof that the Luminary was lying, and the only people who could stop the riots and save Geveg.

"Come on—it's time to go."

TWENTY-ONE

Everyone raced forward and grabbed a cot, dragging them away from the door like trapped pynvium miners digging themselves out of a cave-in. Wood thunked and scraped across the floor, clattering into a growing pile where the pain-filled apprentices had once whimpered. Danello found a sword lying just inside the door and beyond the reach of a pale, still hand. The sword wasn't as thin as his rapier, but he looked like he knew how to use it well enough.

I looked away from the hand and searched for Tali. "Take the lead with Danello," I said. "Show him the way out. I'll follow behind."

She nodded. "Okay, but stay close."

The apprentices filed out behind them. Some knelt down and grabbed the fallen swords littering the hall outside the spire room. I stepped around the guard I'd shifted into, lying in the doorway between the spire room and the hall. Though some of the other guards groaned and twitched, he didn't move. Part of me wanted to check and see if he was alive, but I was too scared to learn the answer.

A dozen more guards were in the hall, so the Luminary had probably sent most of the inside guards after us. I didn't want to look at them either, but I had to know if Elder Vinnot was among the unconscious and the—

No, I wouldn't say it. They were all just unconscious. I found Vinnot groaning at the top of the stairs. I smiled. Let him put *that* in his notebook. I resisted the urge to kick him as I passed, and started down after the others.

I followed the apprentices as they trailed after Danello and Tali. I scanned every hall, every intersection, every room we passed. No guards so far, but that couldn't last long.

As we turned onto the second floor, nervous whispers raced back through the apprentices.

"Guards!"

"What are we gonna do?"

316

"Shhh, they'll hear you."

"Hold it," one guard called, though I couldn't see him or how many were with him over the herd of apprentices. "What are you doing here?"

"Leaving," said Danello. I could picture the dangerously determined set to his chin, raised high like his sword probably was.

"Who are you?" Another voice, younger than the first guard.

"Dead apprentices," said Tali. "Only we're not dead, and we're getting out of here."

No answer from the guards. I stood on tiptoe but wasn't tall enough to see over the heads.

"You can't be apprentices. . . ." Hesitant voices echoed his words. Several guards were up there at least. I looked around the intersection for anything I could stand on for a better view and found—

"Lanelle," I gasped, face-to-face with her as she rounded the corner.

Eyes wide, Lanelle backed away, not limping at all. So she *had* been healed!

"Mestov, it's me, Dima," an apprentice called. "You have to let us go. Please."

"Dima? Saints, they said you were dead!"

Now the guards were yelling questions, not just muttering them. It was clear they'd had no idea what

317

had been going on upstairs.

"Stay away from me!" Lanelle said, not loud enough to rise above the guards, but loud enough to get Kione's attention. He turned.

"You're alive!" he gasped, looking just as shocked as I'd been.

Lanelle turned and ran down the hall, right toward—

Saints and sinners! This hall led to the Luminary's wing! She was probably headed right for an Elder to save her job and betray us again.

I chased after her. Kione called her name and started following us.

"Lanelle!" he whisper-yelled. "Where are you going? We have to get out of here."

He still didn't realize what she must have done. I pictured her lying in her cot, the Luminary hovering over her, shaking her, demanding answers. I doubted she even hesitated to give them. Saints, I bet she'd even *offered* information about Tali and me to get herself healed.

"Why isn't she stopping?" Kione asked.

I kept running, passing the windows overlooking the city. Smoke rose off the burning market square. I couldn't make out any uniforms in the mob below, but League green and Baseeri blue were likely hacking their way through the crowd, just as they had at every riot before.

Kione pulled ahead of me, and I followed him and Lanelle into a rectangular room that was almost Sanctuary quiet, with thick green carpets. Double doors were set in the middle of the far wall. On either side of the doors, padded benches sat between statues. Kione was halfway down the hall, but Lanelle was nearing the doors at the end of it.

My steps halted. I knew this hall, though it had been years since I was last here. We were outside the Luminary's office.

Suddenly a guard stepped out from a side nook and grabbed Lanelle. She screamed and yanked back.

"Let go of her!" Kione hollered, charging at the guard. Before he reached him, another guard appeared and shoved Kione down.

"Let her go! I work here," Kione said, trying unsuccessfully to yank himself free.

"Not in this wing you don't."

I turned to run before the guards saw me, but a wall of green slammed into me. Or maybe I slammed into it. Either way, I fell back and landed on my butt.

"Busy day today," said the guard looming over me.

"It'll calm down," said the other. "Always does."

The guard hauled me to my feet as easily as picking up a sleeping chicken. I kicked him in the shins, then stumbled forward in pain.

"Ow!" I cried, my toes stinging.

He chuckled.

Eyes watering, I lifted my foot and rubbed my bruised toes. Only then did I notice the silver greaves strapped around his shins. Shifting bruised toes into him probably wouldn't even get his attention, much less distract him long enough for me to escape.

At least they'd caught Lanelle too.

Lanelle was slapping ineffectually at the guard holding fast to her arm. "I have to see the Luminary," she said.

One side of the double doors opened, and a man dressed in a mountain of silk stepped out. All the strength left my knees, and only the guard's grip on my arm kept me standing.

"What's all the noise out here?" Zertanik said with a frown. That changed to a smile when he looked up and saw me. "Well, Merlaina, how nice to see you again."

"Sir, sir!" Lanelle waved a hand at Zertanik.

"This is the girl I told Elder Vinnot about. Tell the guards to let me go."

Kione stopped struggling. "Lanelle, what are you doing?"

"I saw the apprentices in the main corridor. They're getting away!"

A muffled voice came from inside the room.

"What's that?" Zertanik said, leaning back into the office. He popped out a moment later and gestured at the guards. "Bring the girls in," he said, stepping aside.

"What about him?" the guard holding Kione asked. Kione kept staring at Lanelle, a tortured look on his face.

"Holding room for now." Zertanik grinned. "He might be useful later."

"What's going on?" I said, knowing it sounded stupid.

"One does have to admire your tenacity, dear. Please, come inside."

They dragged me in behind Lanelle. I couldn't take my eyes off Zertanik.

"This is the shifter?" asked the Luminary. You needed to hear a croc speak only once to know its voice forever.

I turned to that voice and blinked in the bright

light from the room's tall windows. Everything glittered as if painted with jewels—furniture, paintings, trinkets on the desk and tables—even the curtains sparkled. The Luminary had added a lot of art, like he'd robbed a museum.

"Yes," Lanelle said. "And a lot more, I think."

The Luminary stared at me. "You're the girl from the spire room. The one with the seizures. You're looking much better than the last time I saw you."

"I heal fast."

"So I hear." He waved a hand at Lanelle. At the guard's insistence, she sat on an overstuffed chair near a green-draped padded bench. "She told Vinnot a lot of interesting things."

"Traitor," I said before I could stop it. She glared at me and folded her arms across her chest.

Zertanik laughed. "Didn't I say she was spirited? Now, Merlaina dear, please sit. We have business to discuss." He settled himself onto a wide sofa, then extended a hand toward a carved chair with green tassels. The guard shoved me into it. A few seconds later, the door opened and shut, leaving me with the last three people I wanted to be alone with.

The Luminary turned to Lanelle and she straightened in her chair. "She does more than just shift, you say?" he asked. I glanced at him. Something in his tone sounded off, like he was nervous. "Vinnot didn't mention that."

"Um, well," she stammered, sneaking looks at me as if reluctant to be the rat I knew she was. "Maybe he—"

"What did you tell him?" the Luminary snapped.

Lanelle jumped and grabbed the arms of her chair. "She threw raw pynvium chunks at us, and they flashed pain."

"Twenty-one pieces, if I remember right," said Zertanik. He actually seemed to be enjoying himself.

Lanelle glanced at him, confused, then back to the Luminary. "I guess so. I think that's when she emptied them."

"Emptied them?" This time the Luminary sat up straight in his chair. I wished I could melt into mine and disappear. "What did she do—exactly? Don't skip any details."

Lanelle reached into her pocket and pulled out an all-too-familiar pynvium chunk. "She flashed this at me, and after she ran away with that boy, I sensed it right next to me. I was able to put enough pain into it again to call for help. I *know* it was full before she did that."

Zertanik laughed and applauded me. "You are a delight, my dear. I had no idea you had such talents. What luck! She could be of tremendous value to us," he said to the Luminary.

He didn't seem so sure but appeared even more agitated. "If she can really do it."

"She did! I saw her," insisted Lanelle.

The Luminary snorted. Lanelle snapped her mouth shut. She obviously wanted to say something but was too scared to speak.

So was I.

"Your guards' hazy recollections confirm it as well," Zertanik said. "Think of what this means. We'll never find another like her."

The Luminary pursed his lips and stared at me, tapping a long finger slowly against the arm of his chair. Finally he turned to Lanelle.

"Thank you—that will be all," he said.

"Sir?" She didn't move. "What about my promotion?"

"Talk to Vinnot," he sneered. I had a feeling Vinnot wouldn't be sailing away with them when the Luminary and Zertanik made their escape. "You're his problem, not mine."

Lanelle jumped to her feet, her cheeks flushed. "But I worked in that awful room for days! She almost killed me! Vinnot promised me my fourth cord for information about her!"

I seethed, but I couldn't do anything but glare at her. How could she? Any last bits of guilt I had over hurting her vanished. The traitor.

"Anything you *think* you deserve is between you and Vinnot." He pointed to the door. "Now go. Or do I need to call the guard and have you removed from the League?"

Even Lanelle couldn't miss the threat. She shot me one last hateful look, then stormed out of the room.

"Now then, Merlaina," the Luminary said, turning his sharp blue eyes on me. "Let's talk about emptying pynvium."

TWENTY-TWO

I gripped the arms of my chair. They couldn't prove I'd done it. Lanelle wasn't credible; I could say she lied about the pynvium. Better yet, I didn't even *have* to answer. "You know the apprentices got out. Everyone in Geveg knows you lied to them by now."

"No, they don't," said Zertanik, getting up and pouring himself something from a blue crystal decanter. "As soon as the guards spotted you on the roof, I sent Jeatar to watch the exits. He's no doubt corralled your wayward apprentices."

That fiend. That liar. Jeatar had actually seemed nice, and now he had Tali and the others. My hot anger chilled.

"You can't just hide Takers away in a tower and think no one will notice."

"We have been doing so, dear, and no one has." Zertanik lifted the bottle toward the Luminary. "Drink?"

The Luminary shook his head.

No one offered me anything, not even bad excuses. "People *do* know. Did you think I was dumb enough to come in here without telling people about this?" I clenched my fists, wishing I hadn't been dumb enough to do *just* that.

He chuckled. "Dumb, no. Shortsighted, yes, oh truly, yes."

It was all for nothing. I'd done such horrible things, and none of it had mattered. Tears started, and much as I wanted to, I couldn't hold them back.

"Don't be so hard on yourself, dear." Zertanik paused and picked through a plate of fruit and pastries, acting as if this was his office. Did he think he owned everything and could buy anyone, just like he'd bought me? The Luminary didn't even seem to care that Zertanik was taking charge of— I sniffled. What *was* going on here? Healers *never* got along with pain merchants. They thought pain merchants were beneath them, and from everything I knew, they were right.

So why was *this* Luminary taking orders from a pain merchant?

The Luminary sat in silence, watching me. One hand kept tapping on the arm of his chair, but the other was clenching it. He was *definitely* nervous, and I'd bet it was about more than just Vinnot not telling him what Lanelle had said.

"Why am I here?" I asked. And what in Saea's name was going on?

Apparently unsatisfied with the food choices, Zertanik returned to his chair with just his drink. He wasn't nervous at all. "We have a business proposition for you."

My mouth went dry, and the echo of the fisherman's screams rang in my memory's ear. I'd had enough of his business propositions. "Forget it."

"*We* haven't decided anything," the Luminary spat. For a moment, his forced calm slipped even further. What was he afraid of? Not me, surely. Zertanik? Had the Luminary also made a deal he was now regretting? "This doesn't change the plan, Zertanik."

"Of course it does." Zertanik flapped a dismissive hand at him. "Merlaina dear, it's all very simple really. If you prove you really can do this, I'd like to hire you to empty pynvium. I'll pay you well for it."

That was all? They didn't want me to empty it over an advancing army or anything? There had to be more to his request. No one paid ten oppas for a single hen. "Why?"

"So I can sell it."

The Luminary huffed. "So *we* can sell it."

"Back on my side again, are you?" He laughed, then smiled at me again. "Imagine what Verlatta would pay for pynvium right about now."

Everything they had. Just like we would have when the Duke had us surrounded and we couldn't get supplies.

"You'd be *helping* them, dear. Providing desperately needed items at a time when they need them most."

Trading on misery, on pain. Like offering a fisherman to a rich couple with a dying child.

"What about the apprentices?" I asked. I didn't mention Tali and the others by name, just in case he didn't know how much he had that was mine.

"A simple exchange. Your services for the lives of the apprentices. All of them, not just those you tried to sneak away when no one was looking."

He had to be lying. Once the apprentices started

talking, Geveg would tear the League apart to get to the Luminary. He'd never agree to let them go.

"I don't believe you," I said. "The Luminary hurt the apprentices for a reason. He's not going to just walk away after all that effort."

The Luminary jumped up and went right for the blue crystal decanter. "You stupid, ignorant 'Veg," he mumbled. He took a deep breath and turned to face me. "The apprentices were *Vinnot's* pet project, not mine. You can ask *him* why the Duke is so interested in stuffing Takers full of pain. I couldn't care less."

"I don't understand."

"Obviously." He turned to Zertanik. "This is pointless, and we're wasting time. We have enough— let's just leave now."

"Don't be hasty."

"We don't need her."

"But I want her."

The Luminary slammed his glass down and went to the door. He opened it and spoke to the guards outside, but I couldn't hear anything they said. I could, however, see the angry looks he cast my way. Preparing to leave anyway, or planning his next move if I said no?

Zertanik cleared his throat. "Dear, we have no interest in the apprentices. Just you."

I shivered. I'd heard *that* before, but Zertanik made it sound a lot creepier than Jeatar had.

"Ideally, you'll leave with us," Zertanik continued. "And once we're all safely away and you've done as we requested, the apprentices will be released. We simply require assurances."

"Assurances for what?"

"That you won't agree to our terms, then renege on the deal." He smiled. "You *do* have a reputation for that."

I frowned. "I hardly consider refusing to shift into a bound and gagged man *reneging*."

Zertanik shrugged and sipped his drink. "We'll need you for only a few months; then you're free to go. You'll be well paid. I really don't understand why you're resisting this offer. By winter, you'll be back with enough money to buy a villa on the aristocrats' isles. You'll never worry about food again. You and your sister will never worry about *anything* again."

Saints help me, it was tempting. Even if he was an opportunistic slug, Zertanik *had* done what he'd promised with the pynvium chunks. I doubted he wanted me to empty pynvium for the good of anyone but himself, but more pynvium right now was a good thing, and if he could get it to those who needed it . . .

"What would I have to empty?"

Zertanik beamed and jumped out of his chair. He went to the green-draped bench in the back and yanked off the fabric like a peddler at the fair. "We'll melt *this* down into smaller, portable bricks and sell them throughout the region."

My breath stopped. The *Slab*. Bigger than the rumored hay bale, and so rich and dark blue, it looked like a giant sapphire. My eyes widened as the real implication hit me. They weren't stealing Takers, they were stealing the *Slab*. The Duke counted on pain-filled Slabs to forge into weapons. He'd *never* allow them to take it.

My guts twisted, and I looked at the room again, all the furniture, the paintings, the crystal and gold. The kinds of things you stole once you took someone's home, killed their family. They were both just looters and thieves. I looked at the Luminary. *We have enough.* . . . I'd bet Geveg didn't have any pynvium because Zertanik and the Luminary were also stealing *that*.

Zertanik tossed the drape over a chair and smiled at me. "This would be the first one, but we can travel from city to city, offering your services for a, well, not a very reasonable price, but one people will pay. And it will still be less than what new pynvium would cost."

"I see." They were insane. They had no idea how flashing worked. Saints, even *I* wasn't sure exactly how it worked, but flashing something that huge would probably kill me. Even if I *could* find a way to flash it and survive, you didn't steal from the Duke and get away with it. You didn't cause riots and force him to pull troops away from a fight he'd rather have just to cover your tracks when you fled. Didn't they know how stupid a plan this was?

"The Duke will know you took it. He'll come after you."

"Oh no, he won't," said Zertanik. "You see, there'll be a terrible accident and we'll both be killed in the riots. Simply tragic. The looters will overpower the guards and come right inside. Bodies burned beyond recognition. Only a few notable pieces of jewelry and League rank insignias to identify us."

The Duke would blame Geveg for their deaths. He'd send soldiers. He'd lock down the city, lock up its people, interrogate everyone who might know something about the stolen pynvium and the deaths. When no one talked, he'd get mad, take his anger out on us.

I stood and walked slowly toward the Slab.

Zertanik continued to smile, and the Luminary watched me, as untrusting of me as I was of him. I reached out and put both palms flat against the cool metal. That was all I felt. No call and draw, no special tingle asking for pain. Nothing like real Healers felt when they touched pure pynvium.

A hard, cold lump sat in my stomach. I was just as much a weapon as this Slab would be. But I still had a choice about what *I'd* be molded into.

I looked up, and familiar brown eyes stared back at me from a painting on the wall. Grannyma, the last Gevegian Luminary, who was taken from us when the Duke's soldiers took the League. I could hear her advice even now.

Better to take the lash than whip the horse.

I chuckled, my eyes tearing. Grannyma was always right, always fighting. Even on that final day when we surrendered, and the Duke's men dragged her from the Healers' League and took her away. They never even sent back her body, like they had Mama's. Saints, I missed them both.

"You'll let the apprentices go if I do this?" I said. My voice trembled, but my hands were still.

"Of course, of course." Zertanik was on his feet again, practically dancing, and waiting for my answer. The Luminary didn't move.

The fisherman's voice drifted back. *My family has a year to get back on their feet. We could sure use that right now.* How long did a Slab last? Thousands of heals? This one was full, but if I emptied it, could I give Geveg a year? Give them time to demand a Luminary like Grannyma had been, who would protect them rather than use them?

Maybe, but I was tired of maybes.

I wasn't a Healer, but I *could* trade my life for theirs, and do it without hurting anyone who didn't deserve it. I looked at the painting again. I knew what Grannyma would do. What Mama and Papa *had* done. I had to save the ones I loved.

I'm sorry, Tali. I didn't want to leave her, but if they had me, they had no reason to hurt her. And if they were gone, there'd be no one to hurt the rest. I was only sorry Vinnot wasn't here.

"I accept your offer," I said, smiling at Zertanik. "I'd be delighted to flash this for you."

He beamed and actually rubbed his palms together.

I closed my eyes, pressed my hands against the Slab, and pictured three dandelions blowing in the wind.

TWENTY-THREE

Pain exploded from the Slab, slamming me back against a bookcase. Fine sand stung my eyes, my skin, ripped my hair back like a gale. Zertanik and the Luminary screamed, then fell silent, their anguished wails swept away by the roar. Wood creaked, then cracked, and splinters showered me seconds before the gale lessened and I dropped face-first to the ground.

I lay for hours . . . days . . . seconds . . . I had no idea. My head thumped almost as fast and hard as my heart. My fingers were cold in a way I'd never felt before. The rest of me was just numb.

Why wasn't I dead?

Something cool and sharp covered my eyes, and

I brushed it away, wincing as flecks scratched the tender skin. I brushed more gently, flicking away bits that felt like cold salt. I opened my eyes and blinked at the white crystals melting on my fingers.

Ice? Grannyma had told us about ice. From the stories *her* grannyma told her when they were mountain folk. It fell from the sky like rain when it was cold. Tali had laughed, not believing her. It never got that cold in Geveg.

It was cold now though. Shiverflesh rippled down my body and I shivered. I rubbed my arms. They were coated with ice, same as my eyes had been. I reached to pull my collar tighter, and shredded cloth slipped between my fingers. A tickle of icy water ran down my scalp, my back, my—

Saints! Where were my clothes?

Cold and shock pushed the last of the fuzziness out of my head. Aylin's dress was gone, nothing but frayed tatters around the cuffs and collar. My sandals were still there, but the top straps were snapped. And that blue thing next to me was . . .

The Slab.

I reached out and touched it. Warm, like skin, despite the chill all around it. More warmth against my back. I glanced over my shoulder. Late-afternoon sun poured in through shattered windows, and dust and bits of fabric floated around the room. Broken glass littered the floor. The carpets were threadbare under the Slab, long scraped areas radiating outward like paint sanded off a hull. Ice covered everything in a white sheen.

"He-hello?" I squeaked, my voice unrecognizable. I didn't see Zertanik or the Luminary, but the room was in pieces, same as my clothes. Everything had been shoved away from the Slab with the same force that had thrown me against the bookcase. Furniture was crushed along the walls, paintings hung in strips over shattered tables and chairs. Even Grannyma's portrait was gone.

A warm breeze blew. The curtains were missing. Part of the roof too, and chipped stones lay gathered with the rest of the debris. A fine red mist coated the far wall and, underneath, torn silk in bright colors. Stuck to a cracked brick, a chunk of frost-covered hair shone black in the sun.

Zertanik's.

There was nothing else left of him. He'd disintegrated, same as the pynvium chunks I'd flashed one too many times. I didn't want to look for the Luminary, but my gaze went to everything green just the same. Not far from what was left of Zertanik, a single braided gold bar poked out from between a desk and a broken statue. The same red mist coated the wall behind it.

Oh, Saints! That was *blood*.

I gagged, forced myself to breathe. Pressed my hands against my face until the world stopping spinning.

Why wasn't *I* dead too?

I had to get out of there. I crawled to my knees and scanned the wreckage for the double doors, suddenly so far away. The way out was there, under all the death.

"Nya!"

A man's voice, outside somewhere. Familiar, but not Danello. Not Soek. I tried to call back, but all that came out was a raspy squeak. Everything swirled around me, silvery flecks dancing, tunneling down just like they had that day on the bridge, after I'd shifted into the fisherman. I stumbled, fell. Glass bit into my knees.

A loud thump, and a wall of debris on the right moved. The remains of the sofa Zertanik had sat on toppled to the floor. Another thump, and a strip of light shone through.

"Is anyone there?"

"Here," I wheezed.

Hard thumps and cracks sounded, and the strip widened to a shaft, then to a door. Blue and gold suddenly filled it, bright spots on the silver dancing around my vision.

"Nya?" A man. In the doorway. "Saints, Nya, what happened?"

I tried to answer, but the words wouldn't come. I knew this face, this man, but the name wouldn't come either.

He took off his shirt and pulled it over my head, threading my arms through like I'd done to Tali when she was little. He held my face, searched me with worried eyes. His chest was bare. He had a lot of scars. "Can you hear me?"

I nodded. Then the swirling silver took over and washed me away.

I woke in sunshine. It shone through tall windows all around me; and outside the windows, the lake sparkled like nothing bad had happened today. The need to have that be true almost outweighed my fear of where I was. Of who I'd killed—and how.

Of how I'd survived it.

Aches and pains pinched me all over as I sat up. I was in a sunroom, on a soft chaise next to a table with a vase of bright pink violets. Blue silk soothed my bruises, and I tugged at a shirt too large for me. When had I last worn silk?

"Good, you're finally awake."

I screamed and pressed back against the chaise. Jeatar stood in the doorway.

"Stay away from me!"

He held up his hands, palms out. "Nya, you're safe. I'm not going to hurt you."

I had no weapons except the small vase that probably wouldn't hurt all that much if I threw it. Maybe I could grab a chair, but they were wrought iron, and looked heavier than I was.

"Where am I?" I asked. I'd have to talk my way out of this, though that had never worked with Jeatar before.

"Zertanik's home. It was empty and close."

It all came back to me. His offer, his threats, the Slab. The fine red mist and bits of hair. The room shifted sideways.

"Easy now, take deep breaths." Jeatar was suddenly there, holding me up.

"I killed them."

"You did." He looked as perplexed as I felt. "I don't know what happened. The Luminary's office wing just . . . fell apart. The whole League shook." He eased me back onto the chaise, then went and poured a glass of water. "What did you do?" he asked cautiously as he handed me the glass.

I didn't want to answer that. I didn't even want to *think* about it, though the truth kept screaming in my head. I drank, realizing he also wore a shirt too large for him. He had given me his. Dressed me. Saints and sinners! He'd seen me naked! I couldn't look at him, my cheeks hot as the sunbeams coming through the windows. "What did you do with the apprentices? With Tali and the others?"

"I let them go. The mob was a bit distracted by parts of the League suddenly exploding, but once they saw the apprentices and heard their story, they got right back to trying to burn things down. The Governor-General's soldiers finally got the mob under control, but it's tense out there. It's going to be a rough night for everyone."

"You were going to kill them. The apprentices."

He shook his head. "No. I just needed Zertanik and the Luminary to think so."

"Why?"

He sighed. "So I could catch them doing what I was pretty sure they were going to do."

"Steal the Slab."

He seemed surprised. "Yes."

"Who are you?"

"I work for the Duke's—"

I jumped up, swayed, and nearly fell. "Let me out of here, right now!"

"Nya, listen, please. I work for the Duke, but that doesn't mean I follow him. I'm an investigator for the Pynvium Consortium."

The Pynvium Consortium? They controlled the pynvium mines, employed the enchanters. They held so much power even the Duke wouldn't risk defying them. "I don't understand."

"Pynvium has been disappearing all over Baseeri territory. Shipments coming up short, or getting lost. The shortage is real, but I don't think it's natural. Someone is stealing it."

"Zertanik and the Luminary."

"That's what we suspected, but we couldn't prove it. The last Healers' League the Luminary was posted to also had a mysterious shortage. It was blamed on a clerical error, but the Duke was sure he was up to something. When Zertanik closed up shop and followed the Luminary here, I came too. I got a job working for Zertanik so I could find out what they were up to."

I set the glass down. "What about me?"

"You were"—he paused—"unexpected. And you almost ruined the whole thing."

"You kidnapped me."

"I'm sorry. I tried to talk Zertanik out of that, but after the ferry accident, he found out about you and the shifting from his spies at the League. He saw a way to make more money and an easy way to get out of Geveg."

"The Mustovos' boat."

Now he *really* looked surprised. "How did you know that?"

"He wanted me to heal their son. I refused, and the father said something about a boat. Kione overheard the Luminary say they planned to sail away." I shrugged. "It all fits."

"Zertanik said you were a lot smarter than you looked."

I wasn't sure how to take that. "So what did *you* find out?" I asked. My knees were shaking so hard Jeatar probably noticed. Wasn't like I had anything to cover them up with.

"Probably the same things you did. Vinnot was testing apprentices by overloading them with pain. It doesn't have anything to do with the pynvium, but it does have something to do with the Duke."

"He's trying to find unusual Takers."

Jeatar paled, looking downright shocked. "He's what? Why?"

"I honestly don't know." Whatever it was, he didn't seem to want the Luminary to know about it either. That suggested the Duke's plan was bigger than what I'd thought. "I need to go," I said, though it was hard to stand.

"Nya, what did you do up there?"

"Do you think there's anything in the closets that would fit me?"

"Nya."

"I'm sure Tali is worried sick right now. She might even think I'm dead. I'm going to go find my sister." Saints, how often had I said those words this week?

"I sent someone to bring her here—it's just taking longer than expected."

"I don't care. I have to go find her."

"I know, but I can't let you leave here. It's not safe."

"Nowhere is safe for me anymore."

He sighed and pushed both hands through his hair. "Lanelle told people you could flash," he said sharply. "There's even a rumor you can empty pynvium. She was babbling to everyone at the League who would listen."

My knees gave out, and I dropped onto the chaise.

"I grabbed her and scared her enough to keep her quiet for a while, but she won't stay quiet for long. Your secret is out there now, Nya. If the Duke hears this, even if it's not true, he'll send his best trackers after you."

"I know."

"I'm not sure what the Consortium would do either."

"But you work for them."

He shrugged. "I take the jobs I can find."

I pressed my hands against my face. I didn't know what to do. I hadn't expected to have to *do* anything ever again.

"Nya," he said softly. "What did you do in the Luminary's office?"

What had I done? Killed two men. Flashed enough pynvium to destroy a whole wing. And survived it. Saints! I'd *survived* it! "I can't tell you. You know I can't."

He stared at me a moment, then nodded. "Yeah, I guess you're right," he said wryly. "But I *really* want to know for sure."

There were so many things I wanted to know too. I lifted my head. This wasn't over yet, much as I wished it was. "Do you know who I shifted to before? All those people? The fisherman?"

He gaped, obviously caught off guard, then nod-ded. "There are records."

"Does Zertanik have any of that stolen pynvium here?"

"Yes. I found some when you were asleep."

"I need it. Plus the names and addresses of those I shifted into. I want to leave as soon as Tali gets here."

To his credit, he didn't even hesitate. "I'll get it. And I'll see if I can find anything for you to wear."

"Thanks." I shouldn't trust him, but I wanted to. I needed to. He'd had no reason to keep my name a secret before, but he had. He could have taken me right to the Governor-General when I was unconscious, but he'd hidden me away.

He brought me clothes and showed me to a washroom to change. Zertanik's home was just as opulent as his office. How much of it had been stolen? Or was it all just purchased with stolen wealth?

As I was combing out the last of my fake Healer's braid, voices drifted in through the door. Very demanding voices. I left the washroom and headed for the sunroom.

". . . to know where my sister is!" Tali was yelling

as I walked in. Aylin and Danello were with her, but I didn't see Soek.

"Nya!" Tali raced to me, and once again, we were all hugging and laughing and crying. Jeatar didn't stare, just watched with a sad smile on his face. He lifted a hand and scratched the back of his neck, and his too-large sleeve slid back, revealing a long scar on his inner forearm.

Just like his chest.

I chilled at the memory and tried not to look at him. *I work for the Duke, but that doesn't mean I follow him.* How had he earned those scars? Had he faced Baseeri blue and lost, just like we had?

"Where's Soek?" I asked. "Looters didn't hurt him, did they?"

"He's fine," said Aylin. "He guarded my room just like he said he would. The Governor-General wants to question all the apprentices, so he went with some soldiers. Soek's telling him what the Luminary did." She held out her hands as I started to speak. "And no, he's not going to say one word about you. He promised."

"What happened, Nya?" Tali said. "You vanished just as we were about to escape. Then Jeatar shows up and we think we're under arrest, but he hides us and then there was a huge noise and stuff started falling from the ceiling. They're saying the Luminary is dead!"

I winced. "There's no time to explain. We have people we need to heal."

"What people?"

I pulled Tali toward the door. Jeatar had dropped a sack next to it.

"Danello, grab that sack, please. It's full of pynvium."

"Pynvium?" He looked puzzled but picked it up as asked.

Jeatar handed me a list. "The fisherman's name is at the top."

"Thanks." I dragged Tali out of the room and headed for the front entrance. Danello and Aylin followed, both asking questions I wished I could ignore.

"Is the Luminary really dead?" Tali whispered.

I shoved open the door and blinked in the late-afternoon sun. How long had I'd been asleep? Hours at least. "He is."

"How?"

I didn't want to tell them, shouldn't tell them. They were safer not knowing, but I'd kept so many secrets, told so many lies, and I didn't want to do it anymore.

"They told me if I didn't help them steal the Slab, they'd kill you and all the apprentices."

Gasps all around. Not about killing the apprentices—that wasn't new—but stealing the Slab was. A Slab full of pain was worth almost as much as an empty one.

I glanced at the League's spires in the distance, hazy behind the smoke. It was faint now, which hopefully meant the fires were almost out. I could barely see the League above the rooftops, but one section did look broken away, as if something with lots of teeth had taken a large bite out of it.

"Nya?" Danello said. "What *happened*?"

"Hmm? Oh, they wanted me to empty it, and they planned to melt it into smaller bricks to sell."

"I don't understand," said Aylin. "What does this have to do with hurting the apprentices?"

"Nothing."

"Nya," Tali said, yanking her hand from mine. She stopped and shoved both fists on her hips. "For the love of Saint Saea, what is going on? I'm not moving an inch until you explain."

I bit my lip. I didn't like it, but I guessed it was time to tell them everything. How I'd gotten the pynvium. What I had done to Zertanik and the

Luminary. And most of all, the truth I didn't want to face.

I was immune to flashed pain.

"Well, Nya?" Tali asked.

I turned around. This was *not* going to be easy.

TWENTY-FOUR

"**S**o I told him I'd be delighted to empty it for him, and I flashed it." I finished, then held my breath. There were few people in the street outside Zertanik's, and no one even bothered to glance at us as they passed. I guess the rich folks were staying locked up tight until the riots were over.

"Wow," Danello said, too softly for me to tell how he felt about the whole mess. "It didn't kill you?"

"No."

"So you're . . . ?"

"Yeah."

"Wow."

Aylin wasn't so impressed. "You *helped* a pain

merchant hurt people?"

"I didn't. I healed them—"

"You gave their pain to people when you *knew* it would kill them." She glared at me, and I felt sick all over again. "You *knew*, and you did it anyway."

Her shock hurt, but she was right. After seeing what it had done to Danello, I *had* known, and I'd done it anyway. I guess this *was* different. It was so hard to tell anymore.

"You wanted to die?" Tali said incredulously. "You were going to leave me all alone?"

I shook my head. "No! I just—I don't know—I didn't see any other way to stop them." I could have done as they asked and gotten rich from it. Part of me had wanted to say yes. *Really* wanted to, and live again as we once had. It hurt to admit that, but I couldn't ignore it any longer.

"It's what Grannyma would have done," I said.

Tali pursed her lips, thinking it over the same way Mama always had, and nodded. "She would have."

"I think she's a hero," said Danello as if daring Aylin to disagree. He looked a lot like his little brother had while demanding I give him his da's pain. "She was willing to sacrifice her life to save us all, just like our parents did."

"Danello," said Aylin, "those people were inno-cent."

"They would have done it even if they'd known."

Aylin folder her arms and scoffed. "You don't know that."

"Yes I do, because *I* would have done it. I had her give me pain before she shifted to save my da. I knew what I was diving into, and it wouldn't have mattered if it would have killed me. I'd still have taken the risk to save my da."

Aylin didn't answer, but her angry scowl softened and she looked away.

Danello continued, softer as well. "And now you're trying to save them, aren't you, Nya?"

"I am, honest. I always planned to, I just didn't have enough time or pynvium to save everyone who needed saving."

"See?" he said to Aylin.

"You had a choice—they didn't," she mumbled, but she looked even more unsure. "It's not the same."

"It is," Tali said before I could reply. "Those people made a choice to go to Nya. Grannyma always said, she who has a choice has trouble. Sometimes your choices aren't good ones, but you have to choose

354

something. None of us was there. We didn't have to choose between our family's lives and a bunch of Baseeri aristocrats. We didn't have to face *any* of the choices Nya faced, and Danello's the only one who faced what those folks she shifted to did. It's not fair to judge her for choices we didn't have to make."

"I'm not judging her," Aylin said quickly.

"Aren't you?" Danello said.

Aylin opened her mouth, then closed it. Her cheeks flushed and she sighed. "I'm sorry, Nya." She took a deep breath and pushed her hair out of her eyes. "You're right, I wasn't there. And even when I saw you were really upset, I didn't do too much to help. Maybe if I had pushed harder, you wouldn't have had to shift into anyone."

"Thank you," I whispered. Maybe things *would* be okay. Maybe I hadn't dropped as far as I'd feared.

"I'm sorry I doubted you."

Danello took my hand. "Didn't you say we had lives to save?"

We hurried to a small boardinghouse near the fishing docks. The hall was cramped with the four of us standing there, but no one wanted to wait outside alone. I knocked, and a boy about twelve answered, his eyes red and puffy. My throat caught, and I couldn't speak. Danello leaned forward.

"We're here to heal your father."

The boy choked back a sob and shook his head. "You're too late. He died this morning, right after the sun come up."

I sank to my knees and cried.

TWENTY-FIVE

Danello carried me out. No matter how hard I tried, my legs wouldn't listen. Nor would my eyes. They kept spilling tears, kept seeing the fisherman.

"It's okay, Nya." Danello rubbed my back in small circles. "We tried. There's nothing else we could have done."

Aylin was right. I should have said no. I should have refused to shift into him.

Murmurs of sympathy washed over me, nothing more than empty phrases of encouragement. They all knew I'd killed him. He'd still be alive if I'd told Zertanik no.

Tali knelt and held my face in her hands. No

words yet from her. She probably hated me, never wanted to see me again for trading his life for hers.

"Nya, sitting here bawling isn't going to help anyone."

I blinked at her matter-of-fact tone, unable to answer.

"There are other people we have to heal," she continued. "People who gave those they loved a chance to survive. How many would have died if you *hadn't* shifted to the fisherman?"

I sniffled. "I dunno. Lots."

"Then get up off your butt and don't make his sacrifice be for nothing. What's done is done. . . ." She let it trail away. It was up to me to finish it. Finish everything.

"And I can't change it none."

"Just like Grannyma said."

Danello helped me to my feet. "Don't give up now, Nya."

I almost started crying again. "Let's go. I don't want to lose another one."

It was like that night in Zertanik's, only in reverse. The Jonalis, with four uncles holding the pain of two broken legs. Kestra Novaik, holding her son's crushed shoulder. An anonymous young lady who

358

took pain from the brothers Fontuno. Her name was Silena, and we barely made it in time. Danello had to kick in the door, and we found her alone, her blood so thick, I was shocked it flowed through her veins at all.

I watched Tali heal them. Pull their pain away and fill the pynvium. Do what I couldn't do. I kept picturing the fisherman with his hat in his hands, begging me to help save his family. Zertanik tricking me into helping him. Jeatar warning me to keep quiet. After a while, it all tumbled together into one voice. *Please, miss. The Duke doesn't have a weapon like you in his arsenal.*

How long would it be before the Duke found out I existed? I wouldn't shift or flash for him. I couldn't hurt anyone like that again. Three had died, and my soul couldn't bear any more. I'd run if I had to, leave Geveg and travel south beyond the Three Territories and out of the Duke's control. Go across the mountains and see if I could find the mountain folk Grannyma always told us about.

Leaving Geveg would hurt, but it was better than being the Duke's secret weapon. Saea willing, it wouldn't come to that. Lanelle might be talking, but she didn't know my real name, and in all the confusion, the stories were bound to sound far-fetched.

Someone who was immune to flashed pain? It was crazy. Maybe no one would even believe them.

No. I was done with maybes. Someone *would* take it seriously, and eventually the Duke or the Consortium would come looking for me. I had to prepare for it. Cut my hair, dye it. Tali would have to disguise herself as well. She'd always wanted red hair like Aylin's, so it wouldn't be too hard to convince her.

We'd be okay until everyone forgot about the shifter, and she turned back into a myth the wards and apprentices told one another after class. Then Tali and I could get our lives back. Better lives even. Well, better for me. Tali had had a future as a Healer, and probably a good one, but no more. I'd saved her life, but had I sacrificed that future? What would happen to the League now? To us? Had I sentenced her to a life of hiding?

The last rays of sunset wrapped the city in dark gold as we walked to the final house. More soldiers were on the streets now, squashing the last of the trouble the Luminary's lies had caused. People were still angry, still fighting, but many had gone home after the apprentices started talking. Though after everything that had happened over the last two days, it was impossible to quell the rumors. "No pynvium" was on everyone's lips, followed by gossip about an attack on the League.

I knocked on the door to a small farmhouse on a tiny farming isle. Neat fields of sweet potato vines spread out behind it.

A woman answered, neat as her fields. "Yes?" Caution in her eyes, but she didn't look scared or grieving.

"We're here to heal your daughters."

Her fingers went to her mouth, covering a grateful cry. "Oh my, they're this way, Saints praise you and keep you safe, thank you so much!" She turned and dashed inside, calling out names. She left the door wide open.

"I guess we go in?" Aylin said, poking her head inside.

"Hard to heal from out here." Tali entered and followed the woman into the back. With a shrug, I went inside as well.

A simple house welcomed us. Old furniture, though well cared for, polished to a deep shine. Full cushions, none faded except those under the windows. Clean curtains and rugs, both thin, but doing their jobs.

"Nice house," said Danello, a wistful look in his eyes. Aylin had it too.

Seven hooks with matching dustcoats hung by the door. Seven chairs at the table. Only three bedrooms, so they must share. Family farmers, working their small patch of island and making enough to keep this inviting house. No, not house. *Home*.

I remembered them well, the last two women I'd shifted into before I'd run from Zertanik's. Three sons and their father had gone to help at the ferry accident and gotten hurt themselves, caught up in some wreckage and battered against the docks. Four men who couldn't work to help keep the family farm with harvest a week away. Four men with sisters and daughters willing to take the pain to keep the family afloat.

My shifting hadn't saved their lives, since none of them had been in danger of dying. But it had saved their livelihood, their home. It let them stay together and be a family. Geveg had so few of those left, and we needed them to remind us and give us hope.

Danello wandered around the room, smiling. "See what you saved?"

A family. A *Geveg* family. I'd done harm, but I'd also done some good.

I wasn't just a weapon. I was just the one who had to make the tough choices. Like Mama. Like Grannyma.

My chest grew tight, and it was suddenly hard to

breathe. "I'll be outside," I mumbled, heading for the door. I plopped down on a vegetable crate.

Danello came out and sat next to me. "You know," he began, rubbing the back of his neck, "I feel like this is all my fault."

"How could any of this be your fault?"

"If I hadn't asked you to heal my da, you might not have been talked into healing the others. I feel like maybe I pushed you down that slope."

I didn't know what to say to that, so I just stared at him for a while. The bruises he'd gotten in the riot were turning green now. They'd be purple by morning. He was still cute, even without the moonlight. "It's not your fault," I said at last. "Your da would have died. And Tali and the apprentices too. We only knew about them because of Tali. If I hadn't done the shifts, everyone would have died and Zertanik and the Luminary would have made off with our Slab. We'd probably have the Duke's soldiers on our borders right now, ready to burn us out."

"Yeah, you're probably right, but . . ." He sighed.

I sighed too, tired to the bone. Guilt and fear really took a lot out of a girl. "It isn't anyone's fault. All you can do is pluck the chickens in front of you and worry about the geese later."

Danello laughed, and I gave him a small grin. "Grannyma?" he asked.

"Yeah. I miss her." Mama and Papa too, plus a whole lot of other things I'd never get back. But I could start new.

"Well," he said, "it feels like *someone* should be punished for all this."

I knew how he felt. Wanting to blame someone, but not knowing who. Though, honestly . . . the rioters were right, this *was* the Duke's fault. He was the one who stole our pynvium, our livelihoods, our lives. The Luminary wouldn't have stuffed people full of pain if the Duke hadn't told Vinnot to hurt people to find unusual Takers.

Saints! If he told Vinnot that, he sure as sugar told other Elders. How many Healers' Leagues had someone like Vinnot testing apprentices on the Duke's behalf?

"What are you going to do?" he asked.

"Stop him," I blurted. Like so many choices in my life, it was made before I had a chance to think it over.

Danello paused, his mouth hanging open a few heartbeats before he snapped it shut. "Stop who?"

"The Duke. He's probably hurting apprentices

all over the Territories, trying to force new Taker abilities to surface. But he isn't using unusual Takers in his armies, or we would have heard the rumors. So what is he using them for?"

"Nothing good, I bet."

"I have to find out. I have to stop him." Even if that meant going to Baseer itself.

"Nya, taking on the Duke isn't like taking on the League. The Duke has entire armies with pynvium-enchanted weapons."

"They can flash me all they want. Won't stop me."

"A rapier in the gut will." He winced and rubbed his stomach. "So would six soldiers with subduing nets. They'd tie you up and carry you to Baseer."

"He'll do that anyway if he finds me."

Aylin stepped outside before Danello could argue further. "What's going on?"

"Nya's declaring war on the Duke," he said.

"I thought we already did that."

"She thinks she can find out what he's doing with unusual Takers and stop him." He looked smug, like he knew Aylin would agree and back him up.

"Why can't she?"

Danello gaped again. If he kept this up, he'd

start attracting flies. "One person can't take on an entire army."

"She isn't taking on his army, she's taking on him."

"You're insane. It can't be done."

Aylin leaned against the house. "You underestimate Nya. Kione told her she was insane for taking on the League, and look what happened."

I winced. I was trying very hard *not* to look at the crumbling remains of what had happened.

"That was different," he said. "She wasn't trying to fight him—she was only trying to rescue people from him."

"But the Luminary didn't want them, so she was *really* rescuing them from the Duke all along." Aylin harrumphed and squeezed herself onto the crate next to me, shoving me against Danello. "She just got to them first."

He argued with her, but their words flowed over me like excited bubbles. I *had* gotten there first, so why not keep doing it? Tali knew who the apprentices were. Aylin knew just about everyone else. We could find them, hide them until we knew what the Duke was up to and how to stop him.

Grannyma always said the Saints hide your fate in their pockets. What if my fate wasn't to heal, but to protect? To speak up when others were silent? To do what everyone said couldn't be done?

Like shift pain. Survive flashing. Empty pynvium.

Take on the Duke.

"That's what I'm going to do," I said, standing. "I'm going to find them first. I'm going to protect any Taker who wants protection."

Danello stared at me as if I'd just grown gills, but Aylin beamed.

"You mean we," she said, standing beside me.

"What? No, I don't want to risk anyone else."

"You can't do it alone. You needed our help to stop the Luminary, and you'll need our help to stop the Duke."

I wanted to say no, keep her safe, but she was right. I *had* needed them, and even though I didn't ask, they'd come anyway. I hugged her.

"Thank you."

Danello closed his eyes for a moment. "This is crazy."

I grinned at Aylin, and she grinned back. We both crossed our arms at the same time. "We know."

"Lanelle is bound to tell one of the Duke's spies about you. He'll come after you," he said.

"I know, but he'll have a hard time finding me.

And if he does, it would sure be handy to have someone around who knew how to use a rapier."

Danello sighed and stubbed his boot in the dirt.
"I'm not agreeing to anything, but what would you
do? You're not going to storm Baseer or anything,
right?"

"Don't be silly. We'll look for Takers. Tali and
Soek can probably tell us who Lanelle was focusing
on in the spire room, so we'll start with them."

"The Governor-General will be looking for you
too," Danello said. "Plenty of League guards know
you were there when—" He glanced away. "You
know, the Luminary . . ." He waved a hand.

I gulped and refused to look at the League. "I'll
hide, and disguise myself when I go outside."

Danello still looked dubious. "How are you going
to eat? You won't be able to work if you're hiding
from soldiers and searching for Takers."

Aylin pulled a small silk pouch out of a pocket
and dangled it in front of me. "I think I have that
covered."

"What's that?"

She dropped it into my hand. I looked inside,
and my mouth fell open. "Aylin! Where did you get
these?" I spilled two emerald rings, a ruby necklace,
and three sapphire pins into my palm.

"On the front table at Zertanik's. I figured he owed you."

I grinned wide as the lake at sunset. "This will buy a lot of dinners."

Aylin nodded. "And you and Tali can stay with me for now, until we find a bigger room. The show house pays well, so between that and these, we should be okay for a while."

Selling them would be the hardest part, but I knew a boy who knew a girl who "found" things for Baseeri aristocrats—for a price. She could find us a buyer.

"So," I asked Danello, "will you help us?"

He stared at the jewels, then gazed across the lake to a smoldering Geveg. He watched the smoke curl over the city so long, I was worried he was about to tell us no, we were on our own. I'd always been used to that, but now that I'd seen how much easier things were with help, I wanted his.

"Even when they stop the riots, the anger won't go away, will it?" he said unexpectedly. "People will stay mad, and they'll start talking about independence again."

"May—" Aylin began.

"Probably," I finished. No more maybes.

"So sooner or later, I'll have to fight anyway," he

said. "We all will. Just like our parents did."

"Probably."

He sighed and thought it over some more, tossing a rock back and forth between his hands. "Okay, I'm in. The Duke can send only so many soldiers at once, right?"

"It's a small island," said Aylin. Danello chuckled.

"Yeah, but it's *our* island."

I shook my head, feeling strangely better about the future, dangerous as it was bound to be. "No, it's our *home*."

And we were going to fight for it.

ACKNOWLEDGMENTS

There are tons of folks to thank for helping this dream-come-true book thing actually *come* true. Let's do the mushy stuff first: Thanks to my hubby, Tom, who put up with me and didn't mind that I was too scared to let him read a single word until I sold it. To my family, who listened to me ramble endlessly about plots and conflicts and other writerly things that bore nonwriters to the brink of coma. My best bud, Juliette, who had the crazy idea to run off to Surrey for the writers' conference that made "so *that's* how you do it!" lightbulbs go off like crazy. Who also spent hours on the phone with me talking about the story, as well as reading it with her razor-sharp brown pen. Thanks to Bonnie, whose critique comments were as hysterically funny as they were helpful; to Ann, who never let me slack off saying what something looked like; and to Birgitte, who stealth-crit on the sly. The not-so-mushy thanks go to Glo, Melody, and the rest of the gang at FYN, who read and ripped apart the first draft with great gusto and insight. Thanks also go to the Bloodies—Dario, Traci, Aliette, and Keyan—for their keen eyes and dead-on advice that helped my "I thought it was polished, honest" draft really shine. Much screaming-with-joy thanks goes to my agent, Kristin, and my editor, Donna, who are both way too fabulous for mere words to describe. They really taught me what a red pencil is for, and the book is astonishingly better because of them. I'd be remiss if I didn't give a quick thanks to Sara and Ruta, the assistants who did all the important behind-the-scenes work they probably thought no one noticed. And finally, I'd be beaten to death (lovingly so) if I didn't mention my niece, Elise, who is a constant source of inspiration and delight.

Thanks all—you're the best.

ABOUT THE AUTHOR

A longtime fantasy reader, JANICE HARDY has always wondered about the darker side of healing. She tapped into her own dark side to create a world where healing could be dangerous, and those with the best intentions often made the worst choices. She lives in Georgia with her husband, four cats, and one nervous freshwater eel.